DAYSPRING

HARRY SYLVESTER

Dayspring

with a
Foreword by Philip Jenkins

IGNATIUS PRESS   SAN FRANCISCO

Cover art:
Top image: © Craig Aurness / Corbis
Bottom image: © Julio Munoz / epa / Corbis

Cover design by: Riz Boncan Marsella

TO
RITA
with love

FOREWORD

Literary reputations are delicate things. An author who today is touted as the next Faulkner or Dickens can be completely forgotten in only a few years, while others rise from utter obscurity. Harry Sylvester, unfortunately, followed the first of these trajectories. He was hugely popular in the 1940s, when knowledgeable critics compared him to other great Catholic writers of the era, to Thomas Merton, J. F. Powers, and Dorothy Day. Today, though, he is all but forgotten, and until recently even his best-known works were hard to find.

That eclipse is a tragedy. Not only was Harry Sylvester a powerful novelist in his own right, but *Dayspring* belongs in the very select list of American spiritual classics, of its great Christian novels. If the book had been written in Europe—if the book you have before you had been translated from French, say, or from Russian or Danish—then we would now regard it as a cherished religious text, a mainstay of college literature courses. We would know it as the kind of book that changes lives. Any literate person would be ashamed not to have read it. As it is, the book suffered from being just too accessible, and then it vanished without trace. Ignatius Press deserves our highest thanks for bringing it back to a general readership.

Born in 1908, Harry Sylvester seemed destined to be known as one of America's great Catholic writers. After graduating from Notre Dame (where he played football for Knute Rockne), he enjoyed a solid reputation as a prolific journalist

and short-story writer. As he wrote so much about boxing, sports, hunting, and bullfighting, it was natural to call
him the "Catholic Hemingway". By the 1940s, Sylvester
was one of the most frequent contributors to magazines
like *Collier's* and *Scribner's*, and he also wrote for *America*
and *Commonweal*. At the end of the 1940s, though, an "intellectual dis-conversion" pushed Sylvester away from the
Church, and that transformation cut him off from his natural readership. He effectively dropped off the Catholic map,
and none of his later writings had anything like the same
appeal for a mainstream secular audience. By the time of
his death in 1993, he was largely forgotten in the literary
world.

Forgotten writers often deserve their oblivion. Either they
were not all that good in the first place, or their work made
sense only in the context of a particular era. Neither applies
to Harry Sylvester, and especially to his three finest novels,
Dearly Beloved (1942), *Dayspring* (1945), and *Moon Gaffney*
(1947). In the mid-1940s, a generation ahead of their time,
his novels were already exploring such enduring themes as
Catholic social activism, corruption and secrecy within the
Church hierarchy, and Church involvement in civil rights
and racial reconciliation. *Dearly Beloved* denounced the
Church's failure to confront segregation and racial discrim-
ination. *Moon Gaffney*, meanwhile, presented a daring and
sometimes anticlerical portrait of New York Irish-American
life, exploring the cynical involvement of some clergy in
political and financial wrongdoing. Neither book makes any
boast of calm objectivity, and we could easily dispute their
historical accuracy, yet both remain eminently worth reading, and not just for the rich and unexpected picture they
offer of mid-century Catholic attitudes. Each in its way rep-
resents the agonized response of a devout Christian to the

compromises that a powerful institution makes to live in the world. The questions Sylvester raises are timeless.

Dayspring, though, is timeless in another sense, in that it deals with an ordinary man suddenly and shockingly exposed to eternal realities far beyond his experience or comprehension. Spencer Bain, who is wholly a man of his time, must confront the primal spiritual facts, of sin and damnation, redemption and revelation, and this encounter forces him to re-evaluate everything he thinks he knows about his life and the world around him. *Dayspring* is above all a novel of conversion, of how the rising sun of faith begins to "enlighten those who sit in darkness and in the shadow of death". And although the transforming spirituality Bain comes to know is passionately Catholic and Christian, it is a Catholicism utterly different from what he has come to expect in the sophisticated technological society of twentieth century America.

Like many artists of the time, Harry Sylvester spent lengthy periods in New Mexico, which had become wildly fashionable because of the primitivist vogue for Native American cultures. In the late 1930s, moreover, Anglo visitors turned their attention to the Penitentes, who used different forms of self-torment to subdue their sinful bodies. But while many Americans saw in Hispanic religion merely another tourist attraction, Sylvester found here an intoxicating and radically different version of Catholic Christianity, and one apparently free of the clericalism, bureaucracy, and compromise he so detested. This culture forms the backdrop for *Dayspring*.

Sylvester's profound admiration for southwestern religious culture goes far to explaining the novel's poor reception among critics, who could not believe they were seriously expected to admire the ridiculous savagery of the Penitentes.

In the *New York Times*, literary oracle Orville Prescott reacted coldly to what he described as "only a religious tract spiced with plenty of sex", while to his eyes, the Penitentes were "not masochistic; only barbarously fanatic". No reviewer found time to admire Sylvester's superb descriptions of mystical experience or the visionary encounters that transform the puzzled Bain, trampling all his previous experience and expectations.

Nor could the critics understand how the absolute religious vision of the Penitentes—their medieval obsession with sin and salvation—might have the slightest relevance to Bain's own Anglo community, which was so firmly rooted in the secular modern world. Initially, Bain himself is a dispassionate observer of the Hispanic world, and only gradually does he come to see through their eyes. When he does, though, he is appalled by the ways and customs of his own people, especially among the sexually liberated progressive colony centered on the horrendous Marsha Senton. (The colony is a barely disguised version of Taos, and Marsha is just as clearly meant to be Mabel Dodge Luhan.)

Bain comes to realize that his own Anglo people are at least as deeply imbued in sin as the "primitive" Hispanics, at least as pagan and bloodthirsty, although they lack any awareness of the need to change. Who are the real barbarians, he asks? Who are the true fanatics? Adding a powerful contemporary theme to the novel, his wife's plans for a second abortion serve to focus Bain's growing awareness of sin and personal responsibility.

Dayspring is a thoroughly modern book in the questions it asks about the nature of Catholic Christianity and the tremendous spiritual appeal of the forms of faith found outside the European mainstream. Sylvester was after all writing during the 1940s, at a time when other Westerners were seeking enlightenment in the religious mysticism of India, Japan, or Tibet. In contrast, he was among the few who grasped the power of Hispanic Christian spirituality and the astonishing depth of the Christian mystical tradition. Sylvester's openness to hearing those other voices is all the more relevant at a time when Catholic numbers are growing so rapidly in the global South, and when churches across the United States are being transformed by the Latino presence. Christians worldwide are again exploring the power of charismatic faith and visionary experience.

Perhaps Americans forgot *Dayspring* because the book's vision meshed so poorly with the religious commonplaces of the 1950s. In the early twenty-first century, though, it seems more relevant than ever.

> Philip Jenkins
> Professor of Humanities
> Pennsylvania State University
> March 2009

I

HE SLEPT AWKWARDLY, in the attitude of complete exhaustion, his cheek pressing through the thin mattress against the wooden sidepiece of the antique Spanish bed, his body turned downward and out toward the edge, so that his rather long arm depended from the bed straight down, the fingers half-closed where they touched the floor. A dirty sheet covered all his naked body but the shoulders, and the quality of the body showed clear: lean, rather strong, but now quite thin. His dream of the moment was an old one, undisturbing and without point. Even his friends, the psychiatrists back east at the University, gave little or no meaning to it: he was in the classroom, lecturing soundlessly and wordlessly to a class in anthropology. They were attentive, but he had a sense of guilt, possibly from advancing one of his own theories that had not been proven. There was a knocking—as sometimes in this dream—and he knew it was Schapper, the head of the department, who had been listening at the keyhole and found him teaching a subtle heresy.

The knocking grew louder and, about this time, Bain crossed the—now to him frequently—vague border between sleep and waking, and he knew it was not Schapper knocking in the dream, but Mirabal at the door of the house. So that now Bain was awake, but his body remained in the position of exhaustion and of sleep, his eyes as yet unopen, his lips unopen as though glued to his teeth. From the white-flaked adobe wall, at the bed's head, there looked down Santiago, Saint James, in one of the crude religious paintings on wood, the *santos* of New Mexico. The saint seemed cheerful and pleased on his small horse: dressed like an old Spanish grandee, he carried his sword as though it were a bouquet and without evil. His beard was pointed and his eyes merry.

From wakefulness Bain drifted back to the edge of sleep. The dream of the classroom did not return, but it seemed to him that he was back in the dim bedroom at Peñasco by night with the sounds, stylized, of the next-door bar in his ears. And only now, near sleep, did he know clearly that he had taken the room, so located, to be near the bar should one of the town's periodic killings occur. The three nights were one to him now, the last night, and the girl, she too restless in the arms quickly grown indifferent, and saying, half giggling, in bad English, "Say, Meestor Bain, what you doing in town here, anyways? Prospectings, maybe?"

"Sort of", he had said.

But only now, knowing he had waited in that town three nights for a killing to happen, where ordinarily he would have stayed but one. And the fornication on the third night. But not that, either. Adultery. Yet the terminology was not his, either. He moved uneasily and heard the knocking again.

It was not loud, but it persisted, so that Bain, still unstirring, wondered what Mirabal wanted at this time of day. Bain had disciplined himself over a long period of time not to show annoyance with people he was observing, so that now he rose slowly, using all his strength and the counterweights of his feet swinging downward to the floor to pivot on his hip upward to a sitting position. "All right, Joe", he called, his eyes still shut. "For God's sake, stop banging."

The noise stopped and Spencer Bain remained for a little while seated upright on the edge of his bed. He was exhausted, he told himself again: an occupational disease of the work. Rubbing his eyes, he glanced downward. Not that exhausted, though: you hardly ever became that exhausted. He thought resentfully of his wife in Los Angeles and how he wouldn't see her until Christmas.

"Hey, Spance," Mirabal called, "you fall asleep again?"

"No. What's your hurry?" He resented petty things now, such as Mirabal making the *e* in his name into an *a*. But it is the Spanish value of the letter, he told himself. By stressing the obvious to himself, he frequently dulled his annoyance with the natives. He stood up, his weakness making him sway, and reached for a pair of crumpled shorts. He found his glasses, put them on, and went into the next room to unlock the door leading outside.

In the white sunlight of the place, Mirabal certainly did not look like a sorcerer, much less a diabolist. It was a thought Bain often had at this time of day, both a joke and an annoyance. There were no diabolists, he knew, and yet the name Mirabal had as one was a help to himself in the work. Bain said, now in English: "You certainly get up early. Come in."

"Well," Mirabal said, ducking his head slightly to one side, "you say I should wake you when I get ideas that would help." His voice was slow, slurring a little. "Also, you say you don't like to sleep late, but you will if no one wake you. When you get back?"

"Late last night", Bain said quietly. "Have breakfast yet?"

"Long time ago." Mirabal sat down in what could be called the living room, with its scattering of creaky chairs and low tables, *santos* leaning against the wall, half-empty gallons of wine, and good Indian rugs. He watched Bain, now fully awake, dress quickly in rough clothes, finish one cigarette while dressing and light another with the butt of the first as he turned on the current in an electric plate and put a percolator on it.

Bain sat down and asked Mirabal if he wanted a drink.

"Too early", the Spaniard said. "You take your pills yet, Spance?"

"No", Bain said. "You think of everything."

"Well," Mirabal said in his slow English, "that's what you say I should do when I work for you."

Bain reached for the bottle. When he thought of it, he took a whole day's dosage with each meal. He sat down again and said: "What's on your mind, Joe?"

Mirabal contemplated him and smoked a cigarette. His face was a curious one and puzzled Bain more than the anthropologist knew. It was flat, with flaring nostrils and a full upper lip. The hollowed cheeks were lined and marked with a scattered and uneasy red under the pale, rheumy eyes. The quality of the face came principally from the eyes; they looked through one in an unfocused sort of way and could easily be mistaken by the credulous or superstitious for those of a diabolist. Mirabal knew the eyes were an asset, one of the many things by which he supported his family, and rather unconsciously he had cultivated this pale, mild glare.

"I been thinking about that thing again, Spance," he said, "and like I tell you before there's only one thing for you to do."

Bain was slowly and without emotion shaking his head before Mirabal had finished. "That's crazy."

"All right", Mirabal said, with exaggerated resignation. "You find out. If it was hard, it would be something. But it's easy. Father Nunes is always glad to make a convert." He smiled as he put the cigarette to his mouth. "You say in your work you do anything to find out things. Well—" He shrugged.

"Look, José," Bain said, rubbing out his cigarette, "that's right. But there's no use making more complications than we can help. And I think I can find out all I have to know about los Hermanos de Luz without pretending to become a Catholic. Why, every lady tourist that happens to be here around Easter time gets to be an expert on Penitentes. If they find out as much as they do, even if most of it is wrong, I ought to be able to do better." He wondered why his words sounded lame.

Mirabal shook his head and drew in his lower lip. The other man's conscience could amaze Mirabal, with its balking at seeming trivialities, the more so since Bain had no religion. His own people had the right kind of conscience, Mirabal knew. What concerned the Spaniards was the important verities: God and the Devil; hunger and food; killing and adultery; not such petty things as a little dissembling. He said: "You say you want to really know about these people. They're a Catholic people. So you become a Catholic."

"Like hell", Bain said. He got up to pour the coffee.

"All right", Mirabal said, in resignation. "You think you know all you want to know?"

Bain didn't speak. Mirabal had deliberately struck where it hurt. "No", Bain said. "I haven't been here a year yet, and I've got over a year to go." He poured coffee for both of them.

"You ought to eat something", Mirabal said.

"I can't eat in the morning."

They smoked and drank the black coffee without speaking. Behind his glasses, even in the rough clothes, Bain looked as a scholar is popularly supposed to look. It had once been an old joke with him that he wore the glasses to appear intelligent. Mirabal gave no sign, but he knew with satisfaction what Bain was thinking. He said, presently: "What you going to do today, Spance?"

"I thought I'd have you maybe check some of my new notes with me", Bain said. "I'm kind of pooped and I don't feel like going outside."

Mirabal nodded, smiling his thin smile for pride. "And tonight you going to play poker over in Ranchos with Father Nunes."

"Why, yes, I guess so", Bain said with some annoyance. It had little to do with the work and was outside Mirabal's province.

"The reason I ask you, Spance," the Spaniard said, "Guadalupe is going to be there. She's taking her instructions, you know, catechism, and I thought maybe you could bring her back with you from Ranchos."

"I might be pretty late for her, eleven or twelve o'clock."

Mirabal shrugged. "It's better than make her walk six miles by dark."

Bain almost smiled. Even diabolists, he thought, worried about their daughters having to walk in the night. He said: "How is it she's going to be baptized? She's how old— fifteen? That makes her conspicuous to be baptized in these parts, doesn't it? Wouldn't that be bad for business, José?"

Mirabal didn't like the kidding. He said, too elaborately: "I don't mind. She just said she felt bad in school with all the other Spanish children Catholics. And then Father Nunes he got talking to her."

Noticing Mirabal's annoyance, Bain didn't ask questions that could have followed. At times he almost believed Mirabal was a diabolist. "I know", he said. "I want to read you some stuff." He reached for a notebook, an elaborate loose-leaf one, and paged through it to his most recent entries. "You hear this story repeated all over the mountains without much variation. I got this version of it in Rio Arriba County. It's an allegory on the relationship of Spaniard and

Anglo here. You know what an allegory is, all right, don't you, Joe?"

"Sure", Mirabal said. He didn't know, but he was a translator, too, by reputation. After Bain read the story, Mirabal might know.

"There was once a grasshopper", Bain began in a curiously flat voice. He always read field notes in that tone, believing it helped in appraising the material objectively. "The grasshopper lived in a hole and was happy. One day a toad came along in the rain and asked if he might come in out of the rain. 'Why, yes', the grasshopper said politely. 'You are welcome to.' So the toad came in out of the rain. The rain stopped but the toad stayed on in the grasshopper's hole. After a while the toad began to puff up and swell so that the grasshopper was crowded against the wall of his hole. 'It is certainly getting crowded in here', the grasshopper said. 'Well,' said the toad, 'those that don't like it in here can get out.' "

Bain looked up. The Spaniard had a twisted and embarrassed grin on his face. Bain wondered if Mirabal knew he had just listened to the history of his people for a hundred years. "You hear that story around here", Mirabal said. "I was going to tell you it some day."

"I picked it up in Vadito, too, a couple weeks ago", Bain said. "I'd heard the story before then, though."

"Nice girls there, all right", Mirabal said. "Near there, anyhow, around Peñasco. I go over there selling once or twice a year. When were you in Peñasco?"

Bain shook his head, drawing hard on his cigarette and looking at his notes. By "nice girls" Mirabal meant anyone under fifty who would sleep with him. Bain said: "As far as you know, the morada at Trampas is the only one actually attached to a church? That is, in the same building as an official church?"

Mirabal shrugged easily. "Why, sure. Don't the book say so, too? I—"

"You know I'm not interested in what that tourist-bait book says. There's a lot of stuff in it, too, about the relationship of Penitente practices to Indian ones."

In spite of the rebuke, Mirabal almost smiled. It was easy to see what was troubling Bain. Sooner or later, Mirabal knew, Bain would do as he had suggested, and Bain would continue to think well of him and continue to pay the five dollars a week. There was also the matter of prestige. Mirabal was a lot of things: an interpreter for the courts; a patent-medicine salesman; a professional diabolist; and now the native assistant to an anthropologist. His own influence in the region was waning, Mirabal knew, so it was important he continue as Bain's helper.

They went on throughout the morning, Bain checking, and rechecking—to the point of ennui and even a kind of nausea—the culture and customs of a people reduced to overcareful notes in a loose-leaf book. He wondered how many of his notes he would throw away or modify at the end of a year. His anger, oddly enough, was more than academic when he thought of the many inaccurate books, mostly the work of women excited by the altitude and by the promise of easy and unlimited copulation that formed part of the legend of the place.

Closing the notebook, he placed his hands over his eyes. It was noon and he was again very tired. Some business, he thought, and began to think of his wife. Mirabal said: "It's like I told you, Spance, there's only one thing for you to do."

"No", Bain said. In the silence he thought of a lot of things. You could dislike the Church, as he had always disliked it, but out here you could not ignore it. Where the others before him had made their mistake was in ignoring the Church, or everything about it except its almost heretical offshoot, the Penitente Brotherhood, and they had misunderstood and twisted that as the dictates of their own sick sex had prompted.

He remembered his first talk with Father Nunes about the Brotherhood and how he had asked the priest why the Hermanos de Luz were permitted to use the church in Ranchos when they were supposedly heretics. "They aren't necessarily heretics", Nunes had said. "And I always ask them what they think of when they punish themselves. They know they should be thinking of Our Lord's Passion and of penance for their own sins. It isn't often that their penance becomes gross. I don't know, myself, of any time that it actually has."

Of course, the priest had a naïve streak, Bain knew, strange in a man who had been an archbishop's secretary. It was, at times, as though Nunes refused to see evil where it indubitably was. He must ask Nunes sometime why he had given up that kind of job to come back to the mountains. One could be very blunt and direct with Nunes. Although not a Jew, he had the great, the almost embarrassing respect of the Jew for learning. It was how Bain had got the priest's respect and confidence.

Mirabal said: "What about this afternoon?"

"I don't know." Bain opened his eyes. "I'm pretty tired. I might try to sleep. Playing poker with a couple of priests isn't my idea of fun."

Mirabal grinned. "Who's the other one?"

"Some Irishman just come here. He's the new chaplain at the hospital, or supposed to be, but I think he's a kind of a troubleshooter to take care of Mrs. Senton."

"Take care of Mrs. Senton", Mirabal repeated in the slurred voice of his often terrible mirth. "How's *he* going to do that? Only one way to take care of Mrs. Senton."

Bain laughed because Mirabal wanted him to. "You ought to know Mrs. Senton better", Mirabal said. "She likes to help people like you."

"Oh, sure," Bain said, "she likes fine to help them. For six weeks. Then she gives them the heave-ho." He wondered what it would be like to have to go to bed with Mrs. Senton so that you could get up the next day and be sure of eating so that you could keep on writing or painting or studying. Some writing or painting, Bain thought, some studying.

"I guess I better go home", Mirabal said. "Got to get the kids' lunch." He stood up.

"Have a drink before you go", Bain said. "You ought to remarry, if only to get someone to take care of the kids."

"All right, I'll take a drink", Mirabal said. He poured and drank in a gulp the cheap, white port that was almost the standard drink of the Spaniards here. "Soon's I find a woman with a little money, I'll marry her, don't worry. You want me here again today?" He stood before Bain, hat in hand.

"I don't think so, José. I have to get out a routine report to my boss back at school. See you tomorrow, huh?"

"Sure", Mirabal said. "And you bring Guadalupe back with you tonight from Ranchos, huh?"

"That's right." Bain leaned back and, as the Spaniard left the room, closed his eyes. He was near exhaustion again. Of course, he knew and told himself once more, it went in a kind of cycle, and when he felt better again in a week or so, he would go back up into the mountains. He wondered how far he should go on food habits? Or whether he should let all the food-habit study wait on the coming of Mardaña, the Mexican from the University of Chicago, who would succeed him here. That was Mardaña's specialty. . . .

Bain slept; and again from overhead Santiago looked down upon him from his miniature horse.

2

THE RURAL-ROUTE CARRIER'S HORN WOKE BAIN at about two o'clock and he went outside for the first time that day. There were air-mail letters, from the two most important people in life, his wife and Schapper. Like a child Bain saved the best for the last and read Schapper's letter first. Schapper had done some perhaps great work in the field, particularly among South American Indians. He was tough and affected to be tougher, the constant implication of everything he said and did being that anyone who had not done things as completely and as hardily as he had done them was not much of an anthropologist and indeed not much of a man. His letter to Bain was not untypical. There was a patronizing tone in it. Some advice. An attempt at humor about Bain's trying to justify the few corrupt priests.

Bain released his breath. He was not impressed, he told himself. Schapper's manner was always unfortunate, as though only Schapper were the teacher and everyone else a student. But he had learned to discount the manner, Bain told himself; what he didn't like now was for an anthropologist, and especially Schapper, not to know that patterns changed in any society. There were only a few French priests left out here and they were all old and some of them even retired as monsignors doing petty things around the chancellery in Santa Fe. The Spanish-Americans were tolerant toward them. After all, Pedro Teran had told Bain, probably very few people, even priests, would come here all the way from France unless they expected also to make a little money. It was curious, Bain considered, that the Spaniards were tolerant of the corrupt priests, while the Indians were not. Of course, the few remaining Frenchmen were almost all in Indian parishes. But he felt exhilarated. Schapper, in general, seemed pleased with the work.

Hunger for food came suddenly to him, not unlike a blow. He should eat more often and more regularly, he told himself, or he was going to get ulcers. He supposed he should eat the cold beans and tortillas—native food—that were in the electric icebox, but he felt that he needed a good meal. He put his wife's letter in his pocket, fingering it as he did so. Taking a felt hat and a corduroy jacket from a peg, he went outside to where the expensive coupé stood in the mud road. Two of Mirabal's younger children played in the dirt across the road in front of their home. "'Allo, Spance", they said. Their brown faces were very dirty.

"Hello, kids", he said, absently. But he was aware of them staring quietly at him, with awe and even respect; and something that was nearest to sorrow—of anything with a name—moved in him, so softly he hardly knew it, turning away from the children.

The car started with difficulty. It was about time he had smaller jets put in for the altitude, he told himself. He needed a valet or someone to attend to such things, he thought with irony. An existence more dual than he already led. The children still watching him, he turned the car in the road and drove off toward town.

The village of Terra-Luz, or Earth-Light, got its name from the same phenomenon that gave the Sangre de Cristo mountains their name. The late sun struck the mountains and turned them into a luminous and unearthly red, so that their substance often seemed to glow and change. More practical or less sentimental people thought the name a Spanish corruption of the Indian name of Tarale. And already the Anglos, or those neither Indian nor Spanish, were corrupting the name to Terralut.

The town lay at the foot of those mountains the Spaniards, perhaps as much in fear over their sins as for any other reason, had named for the Blood of Christ. It was a county seat, had a library, an art gallery, and was much visited by those tourists who talk most about the Southwest.

Bain drove between a row of adobe gas stations and tourist courts, coming suddenly into the small plaza at the heart of the village. Cars were parked diagonally all about the little square, the dusty and expensive cars from New York and Kansas, Ohio and California. Together, they were as numerous as those with the red and gold New Mexico plates. Bain drove twice around the plaza before finding a parking space. Too late he discovered that he was parked next to Mrs. Senton's long, dove-gray Cadillac, and that Mrs. Senton was in the car.

Getting out of his own car, Bain pretended he did not see her, but she rapped on the steering wheel with a heavy, silver-and-turquoise ring, and when Bain still did not look around, called to him.

He turned to her, moving slowly back toward the open window of her car. Leaning across the seat of maroon leather, she smiled in fond impatience. The inside of the car smelled of expensive scent. Her head inclined or lolled to one side as she scolded him gently: "Where have you been, Mr. Bain? I've seen practically nothing of you since your advent here."

Bain's shoulders moved in the gesture he had taken from the Spaniards. "The work", he said, truthfully, "is practically a twenty-four-hour job", puzzled that now he should finally state the truth as an excuse.

Mrs. Senton shook her head, smiling but unconvinced. "I should imagine you needed some relaxation?"

Bain looked away, nodding involuntarily. "To some extent, I get it when I go out to the fiestas in the mountain villages."

"Oh, how nice!" Mrs. Senton said.

Bain lit a cigarette, cupping his hands elaborately around the flame although little wind blew. Mrs. Senton went on, almost desperately it seemed to Bain: "I thought you might like to come to my party the night after tomorrow? Those movie people, you know, that are on location between here and Santa Fe?"

Bain said, "I'll try—and thanks", starting to leave; "I haven't eaten all day." He walked backwards, turning away, seeing the smile fade with the turning. Now turned fully away, he heard her car start with a sudden, heavy roar. Her heavy scent stayed with him, and going toward the native restaurant he fingered again his wife's letter, not quite smiling or pleased as he thought again of the frequently ridiculous things he wanted to do with her new letters when he was separated from her. He wondered about his continuing diffidence with Mrs. Senton. Other scientists, visiting here, sought her out.

He sat down, the only customer in the restaurant at this time of day, and took the letter out of his pocket. Seeing the printed return address in the corner, he smiled unpleasantly, thinking how almost everything carried within itself the seeds of its own destruction: the letter its own anaphrodisiac: her name written in full over the return address: Dr. Elva Bailie Bain, University of California at Los Angeles, Los Angeles, California. Some name for a university, all right.

He fingered the unopened letter again but now without pleasure. It read:

DEAREST:
I hope the work has been going well. Your last letter sounded irritable, displeased with yourself and the whole

world. I was sorry about this, because everything is going well with me. I've only to teach six hours this semester instead of nine, so that I can finish the book. But it looks as though I won't get to that either for a while. Of all things, I'm going to be working for the movies!

Now, don't get worried. I'm not going to be an actress or anything like that. At thirty I guess I'm a bit too old to start *that*. What I'm going to be is a "word consultant". That is, I'm going to see to it that this new super-super picture about "Life in America" uses the proper speech rhythms as well as the simplest possible language. I don't know how long I'll be at it, but the initial contract is for thirteen weeks at 250 a week, so that will be a nice little nest egg for us. And I can do the book as soon as the movie job is over.

That's about all for the moment. I have to go to a luncheon date and I'll write a longer letter soon. Try not to be irritable and don't forget to take your vitamins. I wish it were Christmas so we could be together.

Much love,
ELVA

And who, he wondered, would be her boyfriend on that job? Even at thirty she was good-looking, although with all those twenty-year-old tootsies around what would anyone want Elva for? He recognized almost instantaneously the change in his own thought pattern. Since their separations began a few years back, he had thought of Elva favoring younger men: bright students of the classes she taught. And now some fat-bellied Hollywood pig. At the left of the letter the little printed line read: Department of Philology. Even Elva bore the seeds of her own destruction. He put the thought aside hastily, even angrily: it was forcing things into a pattern and besides, if Elva was going to sleep with someone else, she did not have to be seduced through being a professor of philology in Hollywood.

He looked up. Maria Sanchez, the waitress, was standing near him, looking uncomfortable in the too-bright apron, the handkerchief tied over her hair. "I guess you'll be glad to get that trick stuff off when the tourists go, Maria?"

"You bet, Mr. Bain", she said. "What you going to eat?"

"What's good?"

"It's kind of between meals but we got the Spanish plate or most anything, chicken or tamale pie, anything."

"I guess you better give me a steak", Bain said. "Medium rare."

"French fries?"

"All right. And give me an enchilada on the side. All right?" Must eat the native food, he told himself, the irony conscious.

"Okay", Maria said. "Coffee after?"

He nodded. "What's the matter, why don't you talk Spanish to me?"

"Get in the habit of talking English in the summer with the tourists", she said. She turned away and as she approached the kitchen door, Bain heard her starting to give his order to the cook in Spanish.

When the food came, he made himself eat it slowly, feeling or seeming to feel the strength come back into him with almost the same speed with which he ingested the food. He remembered the pills in the middle of the meal and reached into his coat pocket for the bottle he always carried with him. It was empty. It had been empty for three days, he remembered.

Maria felt sorry for Bain, and went over to stand near his table. She said, in Spanish: "You going to be at that dance in Ranchos Saturday night?"

"I don't know." He had either not known about it or forgotten. It would be a big dance as these dances went, and he would probably not go. What happened at the large dances near town was all carefully filed in his notes; he was interested now in the small dances at remote mountain villages.

"It ought to be good", Maria said.

Bain nodded, eating. "I guess so. They go there instead of Billy Gruber's on Saturday nights, now, huh?"

"That killer!" Maria said. Her voice had gone suddenly vicious, but in Spanish, Bain noted, the word did not sound melodramatic. He said: "I don't blame them. You think they'll hang him?"

"Never", Maria said. "He's got too good a lawyer, and he's out on only ten thousand bail. He could walk away if he wanted, only his business here is too good."

"I thought it was hurt because the Spanish people don't go to his place anymore."

"He gets by in the winter on the Anglo trade, then cleans up summers on the tourists. He did good this summer."

"Sure", Bain said, with enough heat to surprise himself. "They get a kick out of going into a place owned by a man that killed another man. When does he go on trial? Next session of court, I suppose, in the spring."

Maria nodded, walking away to where two tourists, a man and a woman, had entered and were sitting at the counter. Bain looked at them, the man fiftyish with soft, double chin and drooping mouth under his white linen cap; the woman painted badly and marcelled, but with a good figure for forty-five. Bain wondered again why they came to this country, what it was they rationalized into a fondness for mountains or paintings.

"En-chi-lay-das", the man said, painfully. "What are those, girlie?" to Maria.

"Just by the name I know I don't like them", the woman said. "You got any ham and eggs?"

Bain stopped listening. For some time he had found himself hating these people and now he wondered why. Nothing so romantic as a liking for the country and its people, he was sure. He stood up and leaned over to sign the check. The dime he put down rolled onto the floor and he bent to pick it up. The woman at the counter stared arrogantly at him until he had passed her on his way to the door.

It was not yet four o'clock but shade was deep in the plaza. Bain walked through the thin crowd on the sidewalks in front of the stores and hotels which formed the plaza's four walls, feeling the chill of the shadows as he moved through their bars across the light. There were several hours to kill and the last of the afternoon was a good time to talk to the natives. They came into town then for late shopping or a drink to end the day. It improved his Spanish and his knowledge of them; although standing now under the arcade which ran along one side of the plaza, the shade cold around his body, the sunlight at his feet, he thought that he had about milked the life of the town, the plaza, dry: gregarious, he had always liked the city.

Pedro Teran moved toward Bain in the idling stream of men and black-shawled women, not seeing him until Bain spoke, then stopping with a dry smile as he answered.

"How are things in the mountains?" Bain said in Spanish.

"Well", Teran said. "And your work?"

"Well, also," Bain said, "though not finished. There remains much to be done concerning the knowledge of your Brotherhood."

Teran's smile was only a widening of the lips. "We have no secrets", he said. "It is a question of privacy only. Even Anglos have seen us in the morada at times. They have even written about us", he added with almost unconscious irony.

"But not well", Bain said. "Of all, only one book is accurate. And I would like to check that more than I've been able to."

Teran shrugged vaguely, looking away. The cause of his uneasiness was apparent: it was not a good thing for Teran to be seen by the Hermanos talking too long to Bain. They were passing now in the crowd, most of them unknown to Bain. Teran said: "You could come next Easter to our services if you wish. I think the Hermanos would respect your intention. It is the tourists and the people like those of Santa Fe that we wish to avoid."

"Good," Bain said, "and many thanks. I shall remember that. If I were a Catholic I would become one of the Hermanos." When Teran looked at him curiously, Bain said: "There is no rule against an Anglo becoming one of the Hermanos?"

"No", Teran said, slowly. "I have heard of one farther north who came into the Brotherhood. In Colorado. But I could not vouch for this."

"Many thanks", Bain said, noticing the increase of Teran's unease. "Bring your wife and come to visit me soon. My own wife will be here Christmas."

Teran nodded, turning away, but not before Bain had seen the surprise on his face. Many things surprised and puzzled them, Bain knew, which Anglos never thought about. He himself would never be one of the Brotherhood. He could hardly know that Teran's surprise was over Bain's reference to his wife and to Christmas, still a long way off. Going without women was not common here; nor was adultery. The mouthings of a man removed from his wife and unwillingly continent, sounded strange in this country.

The Indian whose Spanish name was Joe Concha, a cheap pink-and-white mail-order blanket wrapped around his head and upper body, stopped near Bain and said, "Hello, how things going?"

"All right", Bain said. "How are things out at the Pueblo?"

The Indian hadn't expected the question and didn't like it. It showed in the lined and shapeless face before he said: "All right. You got a quarter?"

"I don't know", Bain said. He reached in his pocket. He had a dime, a nickel, and some pennies. "That's all I've got now." He dropped them in the cupped hand.

"Okay", the Indian said. "Give it back you when I sell some necklace." He walked away toward the Tarale Bar and Grill.

Bain stood in the now quick-coming dusk, alone and unmoving against the concrete shell that covered the adobe wall and simulated it. The crowd had scattered to their homes and only a few people passed. A few more, Bain and an Indian or two, stood in the shadows that came now from the lights of the plaza. Nostalgia for things he did not try to identify, self-pity came up in Bain. He swore aimlessly and under his breath; then, like the Indian, moved toward the Tarale Bar and Grill. Two high school girls hurried past him, late for supper. Their dark, clear features seemed very beautiful to him. He went into the brightly lighted bar, again swearing, but now over the soft swell of their breasts where the wind of their passing had blown the open coats away.

Inside there was no wind, and Bain hesitated by the door before going toward where only the Indian, one old and drunken Spaniard, and the barkeep, white-aproned, stood without speaking beside the slop-wet and polished wood of the bar.

3

DRIVING ALONG THE ROAD TO RANCHOS about an hour later, Bain felt the liquor working in him—he could consider things that had eluded him before: Mrs. Senton, once a lion hunter in Boston, now almost unable to contain herself because a movie company on location was coming to her home; the Indian's terrible boredom, which he assumed everyone else knew and recognized because he no longer thanked them for money; his own almost complete loneliness. The loneliness he had anticipated, although its manifestations could still surprise and dismay him. He had not yielded to any of the aberrations other anthropologists sometimes had when living with savage tribes. Perhaps it was because he was not working among savages. . . . He wondered how often these others had rationalized the sickness of their own character into a scientific desire to live as their subjects did.

The houses of Ranchos came up darkly in the clear night, the dim lights without radiance. The bulk of the square, buttressed church was solid and stone-like in the night, as though bedded forever in the earth. He turned off the road and past the church into the plaza in front of it. The priest's house was south of the church and Bain parked there, next to two other cars, one of them with a New York license. That would be the hospital's new chaplain, Father Gannon, Bain knew. He knocked on the door of Nunes' house and it was opened almost immediately by one of the acolytes from the church, a boy of about fifteen, wearing thick glasses. Bain had seen him before, but had forgotten his name.

In the tasteless room—its Grand Rapids furniture against the *terra blanca* on the adobe wall—the two sitting priests rose from the supper table the housekeeper was clearing, and Nunes greeted Bain pleasantly. He was a man in his late forties, of medium height and size and with a somewhat finer type of the round head often seen among Spanish peasants. Nunes said: "Father Gannon, this is Mr. Bain, also from the east."

The other priest was a plumpish man with a flushed and cheerful face. He seized Bain's hand in a brief and powerful grip. "Oh, I know the name all right. You taught at Columbia for a while, didn't you?"

"Why, yes", Bain said, surprised. "That was some years ago, though. I didn't think anyone remembered."

"Oh, I'm up on these things", Father Gannon said. "I've got a good memory, too. That was before I went to Burma."

"You were a missionary there, I suppose?" Bain said.

The priest nodded, giving Bain a sidelong glance as he turned to his chair, as though he and Bain shared a secret. There was a second acolyte in the room, Bain noticed, and in a corner, so good-looking he was startled, Guadalupe Mirabal. She smiled at him shyly and with a kind of meek pride—her father's friend and so well thought of by the padres—so that he felt desire quicken in him with unreasonable swiftness. He had forgotten he was to take her home or that she would be here. He said, "Hello, Lupe", and turned back to the priests. He heard her husky voice say, "H'lo, Spance" to his back. Her face, or rather the memory of beauty and actual innocence, remained with him clearly as he faced the priests at the table.

Father Nunes said: "How is the work going, Spence?" and Father Gannon leaned to listen attentively. Bain felt diffidence grow in him. "All right", he said. "I've still got a long way to go. It's like proving something new in medicine. You've got to have a relatively large number of examples of the things you claim are so. Otherwise your stuff is called just an interesting observation or something equally damning."

Gannon said: "I thought you usually worked in more primitive surroundings. I mean the culture here is old and not primitive. It's—"

"We don't necessarily work always among savages", Bain said.

The door opened and Estevan Maes, the sexton, came in. An old man, he greeted them all respectfully in Spanish, bowing separately to the two priests.

"I guess we can start the game now", Nunes said. They moved their chairs around the table. The priests, Bain, Maes, and the older acolyte, whom Bain now remembered as the waitress's brother, Alfredo Sanchez, were to play. The housekeeper, Natalia Lujan, placed worn cards and frayed, cardboard chips on the table. Father Nunes said: "First jack deals. Regular penny ante all right with all of you?" Gannon raised his eyebrows, but said: "It's all right with me if it is with the rest of you."

"That's our regular game", Nunes said. "I guess you play a faster one in the east."

"We usually play a quarter limit", Gannon said. "I suppose a quarter there doesn't go much further than a nickel here."

"In some ways that's right", Bain said. He wondered for a moment why he was here. The first jack fell in front of him and he picked up the worn and dirty cards, shuffling them with difficulty. In the warm room he started to feel the drink again. The housekeeper said good night and went home. In the close air, with the children watching, they played without much talking. Bain and Father Gannon won consistently. Maes ran out of chips and Father Nunes slipped him a small stack of his own.

Bored, Gannon said: "I suppose, having to work in this country, you learn a good deal about the Church whether you want to or not?"

"I not only want to," Bain said, "I have to. Believe it or not, I studied the Baltimore Catechism as a preparation for coming out here."

Father Gannon laughed, too loudly. Nunes grinned and the other Spanish-Americans smiled uncertainly. "He's always inquiring about the Church", Nunes said. "That's how I came to meet him. I bet two cents."

Gannon said, archly: "You want to watch out. First thing you know, you'll be in the Church."

"I guess worse things could happen to me", Bain said. Something like chill or shock went over him, briefer than a woman's shadow passing in the sun. "Two cents more." Keep your mouth shut, you drunk.

"I'm out", Gannon said, dropping two high pairs face down. "I guess you've heard of Fulton Sheen in the east, Mr. Bain. He sort of specializes in converting intellectuals."

"No," Bain said, "I never heard of him. I see you, Father."

"Anyone else in?" Father Nunes said.

The acolyte, Alfredo, dropped his cards face down and yawned. Nunes laid down a pair of aces.

"Beats queens", Bain said.

"I think you'd better go home, Alfredo", Nunes said. "You look tired."

"No school tomorrow, Father."

"I know. But you'd still better go. And take your cousin with you." He indicated the other acolyte, half-asleep in his corner. "I don't want either of you late for Mass Sunday, remember."

"No, Father", Alfredo said. His cousin grinned stupidly and followed Alfredo through the door.

"I'd better get Lupe home, too", Bain said.

"Couldn't I take her home?" Gannon said.

"She lives just across the road from me", Bain said. There was a little silence which Lupe finally broke by saying: "I'm not sleepy. Honest, Father Nunes."

Gannon, perhaps sensing the little tension he had created, said: "I suppose you know I'm to be stationed at the hospital?"

"I'd heard so", Bain said. "I guess you'll be battling with Mrs. Senton as your predecessor did."

"But not in the same way, I hope", Gannon said, with so much urbanity that Bain was sure he had prepared in advance for the question. "I hear he used to yell at her in the halls of the hospital, calling her an adulteress."

The men laughed and Nunes said: "That's the trouble with being a monsignor. They are always so sure of themselves."

Bain said: "Why, I thought you'd be a monsignor yourself in time, Father? Particularly if you'd stayed as the archbishop's secretary?"

"I know", Nunes said, shrugging. "He asked me why I wanted to come up here, when I requested the assignment to this parish. So I told him the truth. I said: 'First thing I know, if I stay here at the chancellery, I will be made a monsignor. And you know, Bishop, that when a priest is made a monsignor, it is the beginning of the end.' "

They laughed and Gannon said: "How did he take it?"

"Oh, not bad; not bad at all", Nunes said. "Why don't you two have a drink before you go? It's cold tonight."

In the warm room they were silent and unreasonably pleased, although neither Bain nor Gannon liked the mixture of bourbon and sweet white soda that Nunes poured for them. Nunes said: "How much longer do you think you'll be in these parts, Spence?"

"Another year. Maybe a little less. I don't know. Depends on how the work goes."

"This will interest you, Father", Nunes said, turning to Gannon. "Spence, here, just in the course of his work, has learned and knows more about the Church and its theology than most Catholics do in the course of their lives. And he isn't a Catholic."

Gannon nodded with a kind of humorous and assumed sagacity. It was as though he meant to indicate a secret existing between himself and Bain alone. Bain resented it. Gannon said: "As I said, you'll slip and fall into the Church, Spence." He laughed silently.

Bain had listened with his head down, the chair pushed back from the table, and his body bent over his spread legs. The weariness had come back strongly again, and it was the weariness, the heat, and the liquor—releasing a shapeless and terrible despair—that spoke in him. He resented something in Gannon that he could not name, and the slyness of his own words would later frighten him. He said: "I guess maybe you're right", and drank quickly from his glass.

The silence was impressive, so that the beginning of fear was already in Bain before anyone else spoke. Even Nunes said, gently: "That's fine, Spence. I hope it's something you will think about."

Bain shivered: from the liquor, he was sure; there was the strong, quick desire to throw the glass against the wall. The priests saw and misunderstood his emotion. Nunes spoke again. "You know, for someone like yourself to come into the Church—well, he must come in on, you know, his own intellectual level. And must stay in it on that level. Cold, like. With you, it must be intellectual, I am trying to say. It cannot be merely emotional as with simple people." Nunes' own voice had emotion in it, Bain perceived, because it was accented as Nunes' English rarely was.

"I know", Bain said. He stood up. "I guess you want to get home, Lupe?"

"Whatever you say, Spance", the girl said. "I'm not tired, though."

"Lupe's a good girl", Nunes said, mildly. "She'll be confirmed the next time the Archbishop comes here."

They stood for a moment without moving in the room's silence and dis-ease. Gannon was bothered again. But if Gannon, why not Nunes? Bain wondered.

"We'll have another game, maybe next week", Nunes said.

"That'll be fine, Father", Bain said. "See you soon." He followed Lupe out into the cold air, hearing Gannon saying in the room: "I'll probably be able to give the mission you asked me to, Father. I think I'll have time", and Nunes' murmur as the door closed. It opened again as Bain and Lupe got into his car, and Bain saw Gannon, with hat and coat on, come out. Bain started his car with the choke pulled all the way out so that it wouldn't stall in the cold, and drove quickly off.

"It sure is cold", the girl said.

"What do you think of Father Gannon?" Bain said.

"He's all right. I never saw him before."

They were halfway home before Bain spoke again. "I didn't know you were so far along with your instructions. What does your father say about your coming into the Church?"

"He doesn't say much about it", the girl said. "Father Nunes says I was never really out of it."

That was pretty sentimental for Nunes, Bain thought, but maybe that was the way you had to be with children. He said: "What does your father say about my coming into the Church?"

"He never said anything", the girl said. She might have given a little start: Bain was not sure. "I don't talk to him much; he's away so often."

"What do your boyfriends say about it?"

"I guess they don't mind", Lupe said. "Most of them are Catholics, too."

Bain knew it wasn't why he had asked the question. These days, his lusts were sudden and unpremeditated, more devious than he ever remembered their being. His mouth had gone dry. After all, he knew, Lupe had a great respect for him and her father was obligated to him. Bain drove the car and, to himself, seemed literally to sway. He wondered why he didn't stop the car on the lightless road. Even to touch, he thought, desperately.

But he drove on, puzzled and angry, and it was not until they were almost home that he noticed the lights of a car following him. He stopped in front of his house and as Lupe got out, the other car stopped, too, directly behind Bain's own. He knew whose it was before he could see the license or Gannon stepping out of it after turning on his parking lights.

Lupe said good night, slipping across the darkness of the road before the priest spoke. Gannon said: "After you left, I thought you might like to sit up and talk a while. If you don't mind—"

Standing there in the night Bain felt his anger depart as the girl left them. "Not at all", he said. His voice croaked.

Coming closer, the priest said: "After all, our work is similar. And I have to know something about this place. In a way, your viewpoint would be more like my own than would Father Nunes'. Not that—"

"I know", Bain said. "Come in. I think there's something to drink, although the house will be cold." The anger was almost gone. It was just possible the priest was frank, if stupid, and not merely following him to prevent a seduction. But while they were entering the house and while he stood piñon wood in the dirty fireplace, Bain could not look at the other man.

The fire caught, flared up as the draft whipped along the seasoned wood. Bain stood, facing finally the sitting priest in the cold room. "I'll keep my overcoat on," Gannon said, "if you don't mind. I won't stay long, anyhow."

"I've got some wine", Bain said. "Sweet and not very good. We—"

"Never mind", the priest said. "When I drink, it's brandy. I can take it or leave it, so I drink only what I like, except for politeness as at Father Nunes' tonight."

"Sure", Bain said. The anger gone, he looked at the priest, considering him coldly as he would one of his subjects in the work. In the chill and untidyness they sat and looked at each other for a few seconds before speaking. The priest's face was quizzical, as though he regretted his own brashness and hoped Bain would excuse it; yet some purpose continued to show through.

"Have you met Mrs. Senton yet?" Bain said.

"No", Gannon said, his eyebrows lifting. "I haven't met her, although I've received an invitation to some sort of party she's having tomorrow night. I wanted to ask you about her. That's one reason I came here tonight."

"Almost everything you hear about her is true."

The priest nodded. "I know she's interested in many charities and generally tries to help people. And yet she has a very bad name."

"Her intention", Bain said, "is always good. Or she alleges it is. I find it a paradox when I'm able to consider her coldly. But much of the time I dislike her."

Gannon nodded, smiling his superior and annoying smile. Bain felt the anger begin again even before the priest said: "When you come into the Church you'll accept a belief in the Devil. Although you probably know about that, by now?"

"I work with a diabolist", Bain said. "My native assistant is one."

The change in Gannon's smile—incredulous, impressed, and frozen, not quite sure but that he was being baited—was very satisfying to Bain. Gannon said: "Of course, I didn't mean anything as direct as that. The Devil is very devious and incredibly subtle. I didn't mean that Mrs. Senton was anything as obvious or evil as all that. Who is your native assistant, by the way? I suppose they resemble the catechists we missionaries use, in a way."

"José Mirabal", Bain said. "The father of the girl we just brought home."

Gannon's face became even more torn. "You wouldn't be kidding?—"

Bain shrugged like a Spaniard, savoring the moment and revealing his effort not to smile. "Not unless I'm being kidded, too, which is entirely possible. Almost all anthropologists are occasionally spoofed by the people they work among. It's one of the many variable factors in the work, and it's one reason we try to be careful in picking our native assistants."

"So you picked a diabolist?"

Bain flushed. More than the remark itself, its coming from Gannon struck him. He had not thought the priest that quick. "I didn't know he was that when I picked him", Bain said. "I chose him because he knew the back country around here from selling patent medicines and fruit trees to the mountain people. And because he has a kind of native intelligence."

"How do you know he's a diabolist?"

"He has that name—in the back country, anyhow, the mountains. And he admitted he was one when I asked him."

"But you've never seen him—well, in action?"

"No", Bain said. "He does—whatever it is, only for money, that is, when someone wants something tangible accomplished."

"As for example?"

"Well," Bain said, realizing the awkwardness of his position, "he's done it only once since I've been here. Finding some water for people on a farm. I couldn't go along that particular time. Something or other had come up. And what he did then could have been an accident as easily as not. But he has, by reputation, saved the lives of sick people when a doctor or priest couldn't get to them or had even failed to cure them."

"Of course," Gannon said, as in an aside, "priests aren't supposed to 'cure' people. Nothing so sentimental."

"I know", Bain said. He felt the weariness coming again.

In the little silence, Gannon said: "I don't believe any real and obvious diabolism exists here. Mirabal seems to be something of a charlatan. I mean, he's a salesman and so on. Although I would imagine that working with even a fake diabolist would be distasteful to you, your attitude toward the Church being what is?"

Bain shrugged once more. "He's a good assistant and in this work, we have to be completely ruthless." He flushed, wishing he hadn't said it, but Gannon seemed to have missed any possible connection. Mawkishly, it seemed to Bain, Gannon went on: "Of course, if you come into the Church, it may make for a slight change of method in your work. Not that the Church restricts scientific research, but I mean the business about 'the occasion of sin', and ends and means, and so on."

Again the coldness in Bain as for that instant at Nunes'. Something in him cold and now quite hard. He heard himself say: "I'm aware of that and don't think it will hurt my work", knowing exactly and coldly the precise degree of his acquiescence, seeing even with pleasure the pleased grin come to the priest's face.

"That's fine", Gannon said. "I like your attitude."

Bain's lower jaw trembled. He had locked it to keep from talking, so probably the trembling was from that. But he heard himself say, with the lower lip stiff, "I'm going to have a drink."

"I didn't hear you", the priest said.

Bain spoke again, more clearly.

"Go ahead", Gannon said. "Don't mind me."

The sweet, white port slopped over the side of the glass. Bain sat down, the wet glass in his wet hand. He looked at the glass, drinking slowly, sipping it, or trying to. Gannon looked steadily at Bain and finally said: "You know, you could be baptized at almost any time. I mean, as Father Nunes said, you know more about the Church now than most Catholics. A brief period of formal instruction would suffice."

Bain nodded, still not looking at Gannon, sipping the wine as though it were broth or a medicine and himself ill. He still did not look at Gannon as he said: "Almost any time will do."

The priest's grin broke through. "That's fine. That's really good. You don't know how much pleasure that gives me and Father Nunes. We'll tell him tomorrow. I guess he's suspected, though, and, of course, he'll have to be the one to baptize you?"

"Why don't you?" Bain said, one hand almost concealing his mouth. The fatuous, he thought, always made the most satisfactory cuckolds.

"Oh, no", the priest said. "I appreciate your wanting me to, but Father Nunes should do it. Or the pastor here in Tarale, Father Lanigan."

"I don't know Lanigan except to say hello to", Bain said. "I know Father Nunes because he's a native, and Ranchos is a more typically native village than Tarale."

"Of course", Gannon said, nodding. "It's Father Nunes that's done the—I mean, you know him best and—"

"But it really doesn't matter who", Bain said. He finished the wine, not having tasted its thick sweetness. He had begun to sweat and, sitting in the now warmer room and in his heavy clothes, he felt harassed and wished that the priest would go. "It's a very complicated thing", he said. In his tiredness, he had, without premeditation, spoken the truth. Tension built swiftly in him. He wanted his wife again. It was—the whole thing composite now in him and she only part of it—like a series of light shocks or starts through most of his body.

Watching Bain, the priest felt sorry for him, although he did not know what moved in the lean and now slightly stooped body. He stood up. "I have to go. It's been very fine meeting you, even apart from its coinciding with such a momentous thing as your coming into the Church."

"I'm glad to have seen you, too", Bain said, getting to his feet. They moved the little distance to the door, and Bain opened it. The priest put out his hand. Bain took it; he had forgotten his own hand was still wet. "See you soon", Gannon said.

"Sure. Good night." Bain closed the door and leaned against it, unconsciously dramatizing himself. "The bastards", he said, but suddenly did not know whom he meant, because he thought strangely of Schapper again, seeing the man clearly: the expensive clothes worn with elaborate carelessness, the slight disarray of the hair, the lined face, alert and marble-like eyes; the protruding lips, the seemingly careful patches of gray at the temples; the pride, so terrible it was almost nameless.

But principally and like a river running through him, Bain thought of Elva, his wife. The river running was a groan although he did not know it. Half-stumbling toward the room he had just left, he switched off the light and fell face down on the leather couch. To even wrap the letter around, he thought: the river still running. The dying fire's light touched his long body, fully clothed, lying there, and over it Santiago smiling with quiet cheer from his ridiculous horse. The river stopped running; the fire broke and died. In the darkness, Santiago's small sword was raised against more terrible dragons yet to come.

4

MRS. SENTON STOOD at the main door of her large adobe house and greeted the arriving guests. From her blank and powdered face the eyes stared darkly although they themselves were not dark. Her gown, of a purplish, watered silk, flared delicately from the thickened waist, but a dark, rich shawl was gathered chastely about her bare shoulders. In the always dim lights of the place her hands moved whitely in small, sharp arcs of greeting, in what she was aware might be taken for symbolic gestures. Behind her, on low couches and leather chairs, her regulars, a few men and women of the sort vaguely known as artistic, formed a languid and slowly smiling background for her. Other friends came through the doorway and with them, in their own small and separate groups, the movie people, most of them in riding clothes, bored, indifferent, consciously stupid, most careful to let others, particularly their hostess, know it.

Bottles of Scotch stood open on various small tables in the dim rooms of the place. The rooms themselves opened one on another with their doorways frequently in line, the floors at random levels, *santos* on the walls, so that it was a place of curious vistas. Women servants, some Indian, some Spanish, moved quietly or stood in bright aprons and white or yellow blouses. The largest room was the lowest, and in it Indians had gathered, the dancers in spangled and feathered ceremonial costumes, the music makers in their ordinary blankets. The Indians talked and ate cookies from plates near them. There was no liquor in this room. The Indian faces were fixed, grave or dignified, a faint, sardonic humor

in some. Three children were with them, boys to do the
hoop dance. In the dull light, the faces of the children were
smooth, anxious, and quietly fierce.

Bain came alone, from a day of work on his notes. His
mouth was sour and dry from almost continual smoking.
He had taken off his glasses as he frequently did in a group
of strangers, so that the deep-set eyes now gave his tight-
skinned face a not unascetic appearance. When he arrived
the doorway was partly blocked by a weaving line of people. Looking past them into the house, Bain saw Mrs. Senton and the white hands moving in arcs. The more people,
the more did she seem to withdraw in manner from them,
the smile fixed now and fleeting. So that it was startling
and to Bain somehow a little frightening when she actually
came to greet him, the smile no longer fixed, one hand
extended in what could not be mistaken for any mystic
gesture. "So glad you could come, Mr. Bain", she said, her
voice raised. "I know how important the work is and how
difficult it must be to get away."

Bain stood before her, amazed, his mouth gone slack.
The movie people—those nearest—stared at him curiously
and with the beginning of hostility. The starlet in jodhpurs
looked at him. Her blonde hair fluffed out from a face so
hard that Bain, just glimpsing it as he turned to Mrs. Senton, was startled. He knew why Mrs. Senton's manner had
changed for him: she was rebuking the movie people through
him: the scientist and the playboys: her own infallible per-
ception of values.

"This is Mr. Bain", Mrs. Senton said. "And you know
of Sandra Hunt, of course, Mr. Bain? Mr. Bain is an anthropologist working out here. You—"

"Gee, that's swell", the girl said. "I've always been interested in birds, myself." Seeing their faces change, she said:

"You ought to come out on location tomorrow. My husband is here and—"

People came through the door, crowding. Mrs. Senton moved her hands again, turning toward a greeting. The hands shifted back and forth, so that one always moved while the other held the chastening shawl. "There is someone here I very specially want you to meet, Mr. Bain", she said over her shoulder. "She's in another room. I'll see you a little later."

Bain, too, now turned to where Sandra Hunt had been. The girl was moving away. A sense of unease came strongly to him: he thought of a dream whose actions were stylized. He had become part of a line of four or five men which trailed the girl. Bain stopped walking. His mind, quick to obscenities these days, went back to the time of his puberty and dogs following a bitch in heat. What had disturbed him then was the number of them. He supposed he was lucky that was the only thing that had disturbed him. Something had intervened, something the Church called Grace, that came sometimes to a man without apparent merit, without reason. What Gannon and Nunes thought had come to him. He tried to smile but couldn't.

Now, it was also the number of them that disturbed him. . . . Was it something innate, he wondered, or was the desire for monogamy a thought pattern imposed from without? The hell with it, he thought. He filled his belly with that stuff all day long. Moving toward the nearest bottle of whiskey, he saw that two of the movie people, men, were there before him. One of them was tall, thin-faced, his gray hair pushed back in a flattish pompadour; he stared briefly at Bain in a kind of cadaverous and mocking grin. The other man was shorter, and in his twenties, his body muscular, his face stained, dark, unhealthy, and foreign. Bain

disliked both of them until the younger one held out the
bottle and a glass to him. "Go ahead, you first."

"Why, thanks", Bain said. "I need one."

"I guess we all do", the younger man said. "I heard my
wife say you were interested in birds. I—"

"Not birds; people", Bain said. "I'm an anthropologist."

The older man, still amused, looked at Bain and moved
away.

"What's bothering your friend?" he said.

"Oh, that's just the way he is", the younger man said.

"What is he?"

"A kind of assistant producer. He has his eye on Sandra.
That's the only reason he'd come out here in the mountains."

Bain felt his stomach start to turn. "Why don't you kick
his tail for him?" he said.

The other man shrugged, his face pained at the lack of
understanding. "Well, you see, I work for them, too. And
he's really relatively harmless. I mean, in the ordinary sense.
He only—"

"Jesus Christ", Bain said. In the lowest room, the sound
of the Indian drums had begun. Bain moved toward them,
the glass in his hand cold and reassuring. He passed through
bands of heat and cold, for piñon fires burned in some rooms;
through bands of expensive scent, tobacco smoke or whiskey fume. All his perceptions seemed heightened, his head
clear, his body light and brittle, erect though not strong.
He remembered that he had not eaten all day.

People filled the room, the short stairs leading down into
it. By squatting, he could see under the doorway, over the
crowd on the stairs, hear the clash of the bells edging the
dancers' clothing and see the dull and undulating flash of
their feathers, but could not see the drummers. Each man
danced according to his age, faster or slower, the bodies

moving more than the legs or feet moved, but all of them concatenating in a marvelous wholeness of rhythm. On the edge of the group the children moved in imitation of the men, but when the music broke, all but one drum silent now, the men retired to the far side of the room and the children, carrying hoops, advanced to the center, still dancing. With grave and eager faces, with a formal and yet vigorous grace, they began their subtle and complicated dance. Feet crossing and recrossing over and through the wooden hoops their hands manipulated, backward and forward they moved, the young bodies bent almost to meet the high-flung knees, the painted faces grave and concentrated, the beaded buckskin legs flashing through the hoops, at times almost too fast for the eye to follow. They moved so for some minutes, their slight bodies controlled meticulously, their grace so joyful to watch that joy was close to sorrow. There was regret, too, in what the watchers, not knowing, felt. For the children's bodies would thicken and coarsen as their own had. The dancing ceased on a note not apparently different from other notes, and the clapping filled the room like surf. Bain's legs hurt and he stood up.

Mrs. Senton hurried past him, a thin woman with dullish brown hair trailing after her. "How is the dancing going?" Mrs. Senton said, still moving.

"Oh, very well", Bain said.

Mrs. Senton stopped moving. "I almost forgot. You're the two I wanted to meet. This is Spencer Bain, Ruth. Mrs. Trevelyan, Mr. Bain. Yes?"

"Hello", Bain said.

"I'm so happy to meet you", Mrs. Trevelyan said, one thin hand touching the almost imperceptible hollow between her breasts. She managed to convey the impression that, like Mrs. Senton, she was merely pausing in flight. Her face was unattractive. The large brown eyes were over what is called a pert nose. Her cheeks were so high that over the receding chin they helped the whole face to look not unlike an apple. Her hair was vaguely curled and reached almost to her shoulders. Bain was not attracted to her but, tired, thought it might be pity he felt for her.

Mrs. Senton said: "I must go down there with the dancers a moment, but don't let *me* take you away, dear Ruth. I have so wanted you and Mr. Bain to meet. I go—but I shall return." She turned from them, the shawl still drawn about her shoulders.

Mrs. Trevelyan smiled knowingly up at Bain, who had the feeling that she waited passively, in that room of noise, light, and people, for him to woo her. He said: "You're new in Tarale, aren't you?"

"Why yes, but I expect to be here quite a while. I think it's marvelous here. Marsha is so kind to have me out, so I can go ahead with my work."

"What do you do?" Bain said.

"Oh, I write." She waited, coy and expectant, her small teeth bared to smile.

"There are a lot of writers out here", Bain mumbled. He wanted to get another drink and he was also feeling the sharpness of his hunger. He had noticed the Indians eating from their large plate of cookies on the other side of the dancers' room, and he wondered if he could make his way through the crowd to the plate. There was no other food in sight.

Mrs. Trevelyan said: "You know so much about the people here, I'll probably be running to you to check on my novel."

"Oh, you've been here before, then?" Bain said.

"Well, just for a week or so. I—"

"Then you mustn't be going to start the book for a while?"

"Well, pretty soon", she said. "You see, I've been writing some time. Since I was in college. For the women's magazines and so on. But Marsha said there wasn't much point in doing that. That I should do my *real* work. Give up the commercial stuff and live here with her while I did some *good* work. She—"

"I know." He found that he was nodding his head.

"Of course," Mrs. Trevelyan went on, "I guess I will have to be out here a *while* before I'll get to know *them*." She had begun to move, uneasily, like an awkward and embarrassed child, her head and shoulders turning back and forth slightly, her eyes refusing to meet Bain's. He thought of the Spanish girl near Las Vegas he had slept with one night, and how sure she had been of herself, although her English had been bad, and how firm her body.

"Yes", he said, nodding, wanting to get away.

She tapped a cigarette and he lit it for her. Leaning back from the waist, she took on assurance like a garment. "But I *will* stay", she said. "My little girl is in Santa Fe at school and I'm not going to take her out."

"How old is she?" Bain said aimlessly.

"Three and a half. But very precocious. You'd adore her."

He nodded, distracted by his hunger. "I wonder if there's going to be anything to eat?"

"I imagine so." She had rested one arm on the other and, tapping the ashes from her cigarette, was now more assured than Bain. In the room behind them, the dancing had begun again. It reminded Bain of the cookies. "If you'll excuse me," he said, "I have to get down there. There's something in this dance I want to see."

He turned hastily and went down the steps. The room was less crowded than it had been. The heads of the dancers nodded in rhythm, exaggerated by the sardonic faces into the mockery of wisdom. People were annoyed with Bain as he passed among them. He did not notice it, and when he was near the table, took a handful of cookies and began to munch them, watching the dancers. An Indian he knew, one of the drummers, winked at him.

The children were more active now in the dance of the whole group. They seemed to have borrowed confidence from their elders and turned it into something stronger and more certain than the others possessed. The knees and chests moved toward each other, then away, the bend of the back careful, the bent neck and head coming up graceful and sure.

Beyond and over the dancers, Bain saw Father Gannon standing in the high doorway above the stairs. He had forgotten about the priest's being invited here. In something only partly admiration, Bain saw Gannon had managed to make himself and his garb inconspicuous. The well-tailored coat of his traveling suit hid most of the Roman collar and all but a small V of the silk clerical vest. The priest moved his head in recognition of Bain.

The drums died again and the dancing, the applause now a patter. People stirred, many of them going toward the stairs. Bain followed them. The priest was waiting to one side of the doorway in the higher room. "I didn't expect to see you here", he said.

"Nor I, you", Bain replied.

"With me, it's business", Gannon said. "Although I haven't seen our hostess yet. And no one sufficiently distinguished looking to be she."

"She doesn't look any way", Bain said. "It's surprising. How about a drink?"

"All right. I don't imagine anyone here takes scandal easily."

"They enjoy taking scandal", Bain said. With the side of his eyes, he noticed the priest looking at him.

People moved and turned in the rose umber lighting of the rooms. Bain stretched, seeing how unbeautiful most of the women were, remembering his wife. "Let's see if there's anything to eat", he said to the priest.

"Don't worry about me", Gannon said.

They went up another short set of stairs to a larger room, almost as big as that of the dancers. Most of the people in it were strangers to Bain, but he recognized Charles Atwood, one of the doctors from the hospital. As lean as Bain, but shorter and with wide-set, pale eyes, Atwood was new from the east, the only surgeon in the northern counties of the state.

Sandra Hunt went by, her tail wobbling over cowboy boots, through expensive jodhpurs. Three men trailed her now, and Bain shook his head to clear away the ready obscenity: the line being reduced to three. Across the procession, Atwood grinned at Bain and made a repeated motion like a dog sniffing. Bain stifled his own laughter, embarrassed for Gannon. He wondered if the doctor knew Gannon was a priest, remembering Atwood's dislike of anything religious. It was really quite a set-up Gannon was moving into, Bain thought.

"That's Dr. Atwood across the room", he said to Gannon. "He's the surgeon at the hospital."

"I know", Gannon said.

Atwood moved toward them, vaguely insolent. As Bain introduced the men, the priest seemed curious and faintly hurt. Atwood said: "I heard you were due at the hospital. Expect to stay long?"

"It depends", Gannon said. He evaded Atwood's stare.

"The old lady can certainly be a tough old bitch when she wants", Atwood said. "She gave the hospital, so she thinks she can run it."

"So I understand", Gannon said. "Although I must say I haven't met her yet."

"You will", Atwood said. He looked away, mollified. "When my wife got pregnant last spring, the old lady said she didn't think I should be saddled with a child just now, and told me to perform an abortion. On my wife, mind you. Now, an abortion is an abortion to me, and I make no never-minds about it when it's necessary. But it wasn't necessary, we wanted the baby, and I told her so. She didn't seem to realize either thing, or that it was unhealthy to abort, and she kept saying I was a medievalist, and that the nuns at the hospital had corrupted me. And a lot of crap about the child dividing my wife's affection. Imagine, that old witch that's divided more people's affection than rum has."

Gannon moved uneasily, moistening his lips. In the conversations of the groups around them there was a broken but general hush as a few of Atwood's words came clear. The hush broke as Atwood stopped talking. Gannon nodded in something vaguer than approval.

They were both smug, Bain thought, the doctor and the priest. He ought to get out of here. For a moment he was distracted, staring at the groups of people in dim lights. Mrs. Senton's regulars he recognized by their affected gestures and slight sense of proprietorship: a portrait painter and his third wife, an owl-eyed young man named Barston, short and poorly dressed, who was writing what Mrs. Senton proclaimed was the "first non-introspective novel". Barston had been there a long time, six months. Any day, Bain thought, Barston would get the heave-ho.

Gannon's words broke through Bain's distraction, "—and that's the Church's position. Not dissimilar to that of science, I think."

"A mere coincidence", Atwood said. "I'm against the Church. All churches. Nothing personal, of course."

"I understand", Gannon said. "By the way, it might interest you to know that Mr. Bain, here, is coming into the Church."

Bain choked. He had forgotten. Happening to another person it would have seemed ridiculously funny to Bain. But Atwood looked both terrified and scornful.

"Don't you believe him, Father", Atwood said, managing to smile. "He's kidding."

"What the hell. Why shouldn't I go in the Church?" Bain said.

Atwood's face grew fixed, the drawn mouth more prominent, the emotion in the eyes complicated fantastically. Bain felt as he had before a fight in grammar school. He was grateful that Mrs. Senton came sweeping across the floor, followed by Mrs. Trevelyan.

"*There* you are", Mrs. Senton said to Bain while she was still a little distance away. To others, in other groups on her way, she nodded with a faint, mechanical smile. Before Gannon she halted, the smile muted amazingly into a respect that managed to be at once itself and its own mockery. Bain started introductions again, but already Mrs. Senton was making her own, one pale hand unfolding from the dark shawl. Mrs. Trevelyan looked pained and stupid, conveying with amazing and intended clarity her stupefaction at finding a priest in this otherwise pleasant and intelligent company.

"It is certainly good that you were able to come tonight, Father", Mrs. Senton said.

"Why, thanks", Gannon said. "It's certainly a pleasant gathering."

In the pause that followed his words, Gannon became obviously embarrassed. His pleasantry was so untrue that the others, even, were aware of it now that a priest had said it. The drums had begun again but none of them noticed. Although it could not be given a name, the tension and the conflict were there, half-blown, among them. Perhaps from the whiskey, Bain felt distant from and above the others, an impartial observer, a spectator and hence the true intellectual. . . . He saw with sudden and disturbing clarity how they were separately arrayed against Gannon; saw Gannon's wonder and dismay; sensed Gannon's inability to cope with hate; and felt a quick sorrow for the priest.

Mrs. Trevelyan said: "Don't you think it's wonderful the way people gather from the four corners of the earth to come to Marsha's? I mean, there's the Hollywood people, and Mr. Bain from the east, and myself, from Cape Cod. Why, it's marvelous. All coming to this remote mountain village. I mean—"

"Oh, they still come", Mrs. Senton said. She smiled with her mouth. "Don't you think that women are less reserved than they used to be, Father?"

"I hadn't thought much about it", Gannon said.

"I mean", Mrs. Senton said, the shawl drawn more tightly about her, "that they should emphasize their purity and aloofness by wearing shawls over bare shoulders. I mean, they—" She stopped talking.

Mostly, of that moment, Bain would remember Charles Atwood's glassy and incredulous stare, himself thinking of the four husbands, the other men in many places. Atwood said, his stare now affected: "Being sort of an amateur on the subject, I've always thought that the more clothes on a woman, the more sex appeal. Those women, thirty, forty years ago with half a dozen petticoats on, were miracles of sex appeal."

Mrs. Senton drew her shawl closer, smiling with satisfaction. Bain started to say something about his wife, without knowing what it was, but Mrs. Senton said: "I don't know about that."

Laughing almost unpleasantly now, Atwood said: "Have you heard the latest, Marsha? Spence, here, is going into the Catholic Church."

That's it, Bain thought, talking behind the old lady's back and now calling her Marsha. Mrs. Senton looked at Bain with distaste. Mrs. Trevelyan seemed ill. But Gannon was not displeased. Atwood continued to laugh.

"Well, that is a surprise, Mr. Bain", Mrs. Senton said. "When did you reach such a momentous decision?"

"Oh, I've been in touch a lot with the Church out here", Bain said. "In connection with the work. The Church is about all that keeps what's left of country society together in this state." That much at least was true. He found that he was sweating.

"Oh, I'm not so sure about that", Mrs Senton said.

Barston had crept up on them unaware, owlish through his heavy glasses and grinning. "That's correct", he said in something like an English accent. "That's perfectly correct, Marsha. The Church has *not* held society together. Rather, tears down."

"I mean here, sport, in New Mexico", Bain said.

Gannon said: "Let's not discuss it now. I'm sure Mrs. Senton has other things to do."

"Not necessarily", Mrs. Senton said; but Sandra Hunt came over to say good night. Not less than six men trailed her, including her husband and the assistant producer. No one bothered with introductions now. Gannon was quiet, his face blank and faintly smiling. The girl said: "It was terrific, Mrs. Senton. And yet very nice, too."

Mrs. Senton smiled coldly. "I'm so glad you liked it."

"I'd like to stay longer, but—that is, I have to get to bed. You know, on location and so on."

Bain turned away. His imagination was out of control, but through its images he thought bitterly of Elva and the thousand miles between them. He went to the nearest bottle of Scotch and drained the heel of it into his glass. When he looked up he was not surprised to find Gannon near him. What surprised him was his own feeling of kinship with the priest. He wondered if priests experienced the same almost constant state of desire he did when separated from his wife. He must ask Gannon about it some time. Now Bain said: "What do you think of the old lady? She can be an insulting old witch."

Gannon smiled almost sheepishly. "I'll pray for her at Mass in the morning."

Bain choked on his drink. When he could speak, he said: "Why, she hates you!"

"I know," Gannon said, "but I'm not permitted to hate her."

Bain looked at his glass. He saw clearly that it was not the idea that had shaken him, but its coming from Gannon. If it had come from Nunes, it would have been natural and not surprising. He thought of an unpleasant answer, but said: "I see what you mean."

Gannon said: "I'm tired. And I'm settling down to work, too. I'm going to be chaplain at the pueblo as well as the hospital. So I think I'll get some sleep. See you soon, though", he added, with clumsy significance, as he left.

Mrs. Senton was coming toward Bain once more. "I'm glad you're not gone yet", she said. "Ruth and a few *intimate* friends are staying after the others go. I'd like you to stay, too." She spoke firmly and not altogether pleasantly. Her fingers touched but did not hold his arm. To hell with her, he thought, but it was way in the back of his mind. He heard himself say: "All right, for a while, anyway. I've got to get to work", thinking, any port in a storm, and how in the dark, if there was a dark, Mrs. Trevelyan could be Sandra Hunt. Thinking how, for only slightly different circumstances the Church had its own name, fashioned laboriously by moral theologians mouthing Latin because it was a dead language and its meanings did not change with time and custom. *Mental adultery*, they had called it, their mouths weary. And what would they call *this*, Bain thought, consciously sardonic, if *this* should ever happen? He was not yet in the Church, but already a sin without a name had occurred to him. Ordinarily, the thought might give him pleasure. He remembered Nunes saying that a man must come into the Church on his own intellectual level. And in a horror, remote but clear, saw that the more intelligent a man was, the more various the sins he was capable of committing. He drank his whiskey and threw the glass into a dying piñon fire. The powdery ashes muffled the sound and no one noticed. He stood there, quieter and seemingly unthinking in the almost empty room. After all, he told himself, he wasn't really going into the Church; there was nothing to fear; it was all silly, anyhow. He felt better.

5

THEY BAPTIZED HIM about ten days later, on a Sunday, in the church at Ranchos after the last Mass of the day. Sunlight streamed into the adobe baptistry as in a bad religious painting, giving Bain a sardonic pleasure and lighting the round and honest face of Father Gannon. Nunes was there, his acolytes, and Estevan Maes, the sexton, as godfather, with Natalia Lujan, Nunes' housekeeper, as godmother. Bain had asked Pedro Teran to be his godfather, thinking to thus obligate the man, but Teran had pleaded that he must go to Rio Arriba county with a load of late fruit. Nunes seemed preoccupied during the brief ceremony, smiling with his mouth when Bain's eyes happened to meet his own, but otherwise quiet and distracted.

So now Bain was being cleansed of the sin with which he had come into the world, his head inclined slightly and stiffly over the font while Gannon, his eyes closed as he spoke, baptized him in the name of the Father and of the Son and of the Holy Ghost. Bain's own eyes were closed and he did not see the pleased grins of his godparents. He thought the ceremony would be longer, and remained with his head inclined when it was over, so that Gannon said: "That's all, Spence."

Bain looked up, turning about and across the half-circle of faces around him. They all shook hands with him and his godmother kissed his cheek. He could smell the smoke on her hands from lighting fires that morning. She hoped that he would have much luck, she said in Spanish against his cheek.

They went into the rectory, where a large breakfast was laid on the table. The sun was bright here, too, and everything seemed lucid to Bain, objects of sight not less than the aim and intention of his work. He knew what was happening; it had happened before: the period of staleness and weariness was going and he would be strong again to go back to the mountains. He had felt the strength coming back into his body all week, the clarity into his mind. . . .

Nunes said grace and they sat down. Natalia and another village woman served them and they ate hungrily. Conversation was difficult. Gannon, they could all see, had trouble in controlling his pride. But the priest said nothing about the conversion; after all, the main thing had been accomplished; who was he to boast?

Mildly, Nunes said: "What are you going to do now in the work, Spence? I mean, are you going to stay around here or go into the back country for a while?"

"In a couple of days I'm going up around Peñasco, again", Bain said. "I want to go into those little villages near there, before the roads get too bad. You know, El Valle and Vadito? See how much clearer, if any, the Spanish strain runs there."

"You can always ride in," Nunes said, "even when the roads go bad."

"You know how good a horseman I am", Bain said and the Spaniards laughed.

"The thing in the mountains is not to get lost", Nunes said.

"I know", Bain told him. "I stick to the roads except when I have to leave them."

There was a silence as if each was too polite to ask why Bain should want to leave the roads. They were all good, kind people, he thought; even Gannon. He wondered why he should deceive them. He had never had any illusions

about science being his master, nor any deep sense of ded-
ication to its cause. It even seemed to him, at this moment,
that he was not ambitious. . . . That reticence and unsureness of intention, which is the true chastity of the scientist
or artist, was with him today; strongly for the first time.
His means were not only bad, he considered, his ends were
obscure. In what might have been only a reflex attempt
toward order, it seemed to him momentarily that his
conversion had been sincere. He felt the anger and frustration of a deliberately tormented animal, and he raised
his head as though to meet an enemy. But they were eating and talking one to another; they were not looking at
him.

Gannon said: "Mrs. Senton is coming to talk to me this
afternoon about the hospital."

"At the hospital?" Nunes said, mildly.

Gannon nodded vigorously. "I had virtually to insist on
its being there. She has practically no sense of propriety."

"To put it charitably", Bain said. They laughed again.
Today, he noticed, he could make them laugh at almost
anything he said. Even the Spaniards, who were not always
sure of what he said in English.

The acolytes and Maes departed and Gannon said that
he must go, too. But Bain stayed on after the others, sitting
alone and quiet with Nunes at the table. They could hear
Natalia in the kitchen, and Bain wondered if it were her
near presence that constrained them. It never had before,
he knew, and wondered if her imperfect English had ever
enabled her to understand some of the things he had talked
of here with Nunes.

In something like weariness Nunes said: "So now you
are going into the mountains in more ways than one." He
did not quite smile.

Bain experienced the same sense of shock he had once with Gannon—not at the remark but at its source. After a pause, he said, without looking at Nunes: "I never think of it in romantic terms. I have tried to be cold." His voice had thickened.

"I was not speaking in romantic terms", Nunes said.

Bain made a little gesture of simultaneous acquiescence and dismissal. "What do you think Teran will feel about my wanting to belong to the Hermanos de Luz?"

"I don't know", Nunes said. "I try not to interfere in their affairs except to see that they remain in the Church and pervert none of her doctrines. Although sometimes I think their penance helps atone for all—Do you think you really want to be a Penitente—or is it just your scientific curiosity?" There was no archness in the priest, only a pleasant gravity.

"I don't know. Maybe that's it."

"It would certainly be better for everyone if you waited a while", Nunes said. "Then you could be sure of your own intention as you were when you decided to enter the Church. After all, this Hermano de Luz business is a pretty primitive thing. . . . It is for men prone to sins of violence and of passion . . . to whom only a violent penance is a worthy one."

"About the violence I don't know," Bain said, "but I'm as passionate as the next guy. In the work—"

"Save your confessions for the confessional", the priest interrupted mildly. It was the closest Nunes had ever come to a rebuke in their acquaintance.

"I guess that's right", Bain said. Clearly he saw that the rebuke was also an admission by Nunes of the priest's own humanity.

"What does your wife think of this?" Nunes said.

"I don't know. I haven't told her." He wondered why she had not written.

"You think she may not like it?"

"It's possible", Bain said. "She's not religious."

"I thought that might be the case", Nunes said. "Very few intellectuals are these days. But she shouldn't be annoyed?"

"I don't think so", Bain said. "We love each other very much. There is nothing like a little enforced separation to renew love for one's wife."

Nunes smiled. "That's very good. I mean, being so in love. Marital love is degraded or denied so often these days. Especially by people in your profession. They do not seem to know where their first obligation lies."

"You certainly don't think much of my profession, do you?"

"Oh, I think highly of the arts and sciences", the priest said. "It's only that their practitioners so often lead such unpleasant personal lives. Look at the artists around here— adulterers and worse. Why does it have to be so prevalent among such people? Artists and scientists are supposed to be the salt of the earth."

"I don't know why", Bain said. Pride, maybe, he thought, saying: "Of course, they're all hypersensitive or they wouldn't be in the business. It's a kind of illness. You know, like the pearl being the product of the oyster's sickness."

"Would you say the oyster was hypersensitive?" Nunes said.

"Okay." Bain laughed with the priest. "You do well for a country pastor." He stood up.

"Oh, I was the archbishop's secretary", Nunes said with burlesqued pride. He puffed his cheeks and stuck out his belly.

They both still laughed easily, and more than the joke was worth. Bain put on his coat. "I'll see you soon", he said. "And thanks—for everything."

"Any time at all, Spence", the priest said. "Always glad to see you."

Bain felt good as he drove home. He had not had such a sense of well-being in a long time. He was home only a moment when the phone rang. It was Gannon, laughing and apologetic. They had overlooked his father's name, Gannon said; they wanted it for the baptismal records at Ranchos.

"It was James", Bain said. "Like my own. I was born James Spencer Bain." They exchanged some meaningless pleasantries, and Bain hung up and turned. Mirabal was standing in the doorway. His grin was mixed. "That why you have Santiago's picture on your wall?"

"What do you mean?" Bain said.

"Father Nunes or someone was just asking you what your other name was?"

"That's right."

"So it was James.... That's why you have Santiago on the wall."

"Hell's fire", Bain said. "I never gave it a thought! I've got *santos* all over the place."

"Okay, Spance." Mirabal sat down. "So now you belong to the great whore, eh?"

"José, you talk like a Protestant. Have a drink and relax. I'm not going to try to exorcise you and ruin your business."

Mirabal laughed without humor. "Now they got you", he said. "Next week they get Guadalupe."

"That's going to be bad for business, isn't it? First the man you work for goes into the Church and then your daughter. They'll think you're losing your grip."

Mirabal shrugged but retained his sick grin. After all, he was not displeased with what Bain had done. "In the mountains they won't know about it", he said. "It's only in the mountains I got much reputation, anyway."

"And after Lupe is baptized," Bain went on, "next comes the younger children. You don't think a good girl like Lupe is going to allow her younger brothers and sisters to remain unbaptized?" Bain was pleased to see Mirabal's grin fade.

"It's all about nothing, anyhow", Mirabal said.

"Oh, no." Bain pressed home. "Not at all. You have to believe in God, otherwise you can't be a diabolist." He started to laugh, inordinately, at Mirabal's stricken face.

"Say," Mirabal said, "they didn't have to work very hard to get you. You sound just like a priest."

"Why, I know more than most priests", Bain said. "Have a drink."

"All right." Mirabal's voice dropped to the politeness of the respectful, the attentive native assistant. Bain poured two glasses of the bad wine. The customary drink of the place, it made the Spaniards feel more at ease than whiskey; besides, whiskey cost more and did not sit well with either Spaniard or Indian.

They were a little time without speaking, drinking the wine. The afternoon sun reflected dully from the walls so that the room's dust and confusion showed clear and in all three dimensions. "I've got to get that Archuleta woman or someone to clean up the place. It looks like a badger's den."

"Now," Mirabal said, shaking his head, "you got to leave the women alone. No one but your wife now. Got to be a good Catholic." He grinned, showing his bad teeth.

"I never fooled around with other women much, anyway", Bain said. "Except in the work."

"Huh," Mirabal said, leering, "how about last Saturday at Mrs. Senton's? I heard how you stayed late. One of the maids told me. That in the work, huh?"

Bain shook his head. His face indicated mock, roguish denial, while his mind reflected that it had been a disappointment there. All they had done was sit around on hassocks or the floor, himself, Mrs. Trevelyan, and half a dozen of the regulars, and listen to Mrs. Senton talk about art. There had still been nothing to eat. Across the group Mrs. Trevelyan had smiled faintly at Bain, while into a respectful silence Mrs. Senton told of a great painter she had lived with in Florence. Bain had never heard of the painter.

So now Bain undertook the mock denial of that which had never taken place.

"Everything goes in the work. I know", Mirabal said, also roguish.

"You sound like Schapper."

"That's the fellow's like your boss?"

"Kind of."

"What you going to do now?" Mirabal said.

"Go up into the mountains in a day or two. Go with Teran if he's going then."

"He's selling all over. Has to, before the fruit goes bad. If he says he's not going one day, tell him you'll wait for the next."

Bain nodded, smiling inwardly. He thought that either he would have made a good diabolist or Mirabal a good anthropologist.

"What you thinking?" Mirabal said.

"I was thinking that I'd better tell you I'm going to Mrs. Senton's tonight. Otherwise you'll have to go ask the maids again whether I was there."

"I didn't ask. I just found out by accident."

"What are you going to be doing while I'm in the mountains?"

Mirabal spread his hands. "It's wrong time for selling fruit trees. And I haven't got the license for selling medicines. Otherwise I'd go up with Teran, too."

"You never used to worry about a license", Bain said. "Not that I want you to come", he added hastily, thinking, me with a diabolist and trying to get in with the Hermanos de Luz, but saying: "You stay here and check some things for me. Write me out a complete explanation and as much as you know of the card game you call monte. You know, not the poker monte but the other one?"

"I know—Spanish monte; it's very, what do you say?—"

"Complicated", Bain said. "You write it out."

There was a little silence in which Bain poured more wine. It apparently gave Mirabal courage, for after drinking it, he said: "Say, Spence, maybe you could let me have some money, huh? I mean before you go."

"I forgot", Bain said quickly. "I'm awfully sorry, José. I owe you for last week and this week, too." He stood up, and on the table, with the help of what singles and change he had, managed to make ten dollars. He wondered, conventionally, where his own money went to, and then he wondered, with enough force to frighten him, if Mirabal's children had gone hungry because he had forgotten to pay their father, whose sole virtue was his diffidence. He began to apologize again as he paid the money.

"You have your dinner yet?" Mirabal asked.

"I ate a late breakfast."

"Celebration, huh?" Mirabal's mirth was not yet over.

"All right, José. Let's skip it for a while."

"I got to go get dinner for the kids."

"Maybe I'll come over for a bite later", Bain said.

"Be ready in about an hour. Chile and beans."

"Chile and beans", Bain repeated, laughing a little. It was an old joke, not only theirs. Bain wondered again that such a dull and bad joke should contain so much, tell in itself the story of the boredom, hunger, and poverty of so many of the Spaniards.

Mirabal gone, Bain sat almost stupidly over the bad wine. He felt a letdown, similar to the periods of ennui in the work, but without the accompanying physical weariness. That was gone, not to return for six or eight weeks. He supposed that he should write to his wife, although what he would write he did not know. That he wanted to touch her, lie with her. But she knew that ... and he wondered if it were not a kind of masturbation, this writing down on paper of his obvious physical needs. And about the work—if she were interested in the work—there was not much new to relate. He saw clearly—but not more clearly than at other times—how they had romanticized their marrying, the two young and good-looking scientists, the pictures in the paper, the notices in the social columns (Elva's people were what is called prominent), the marriage of minds.... Elva had been virginal but he saw now that he had been surprised more than pleased: it had been a nuisance what with their fear of having a child. For the first time, he felt a thing more like revulsion than anything else he could name. He saw, as on a medal or coin, the marriage of scientists represented as a young man and woman approaching each other, a microscope in his hands, some vague kind of contraceptive in hers....

He yawned, stretching, displeased over nothing definite, perhaps only himself. Reaching for his notes, he began to page through them. A time of displeasure was a good time to go through notes, he had decided years ago: you could be ruthless. Perhaps too ruthless, he thought idly. What was a man's norm, when could he see things most truly? He had thought it was only after sexual satiation, but wondered now if that were any more a time of complete objectivity than its opposite, a chastity imposed whether from within or without. The page open in the notebook read: "Crimes of passion are excused more easily than in most cultures; crimes of injustice seem to inspire a cold rage. This, I think, is conventionally Spanish, although here the Anglos seem to share the attitude." He changed "the" before Anglos to "some".

He closed the notebook. The chastity, he saw, must be imposed from within, otherwise it was not good. He supposed Nunes' and Gannon's was imposed that way, but what of his own? He cursed and resented it continually, and yet he was amazed, now and finally, that only twice, here in the mountains, had he been unfaithful. He didn't know why he had not been more profligate. He certainly suffered enough in his chastity; there was certainly enough opportunity. Love of Elva, it seemed to Bain, was not a valid explanation, not valid enough, anyway.

He stood up. It was beginning to bother him again. There was a knocking on the door and he opened it. One of Mirabal's younger children stood there, looking at Bain with large eyes, with disturbing respect. "Papa says, you want to eat now?"

"Sure. You tell him I'll be right over."

"Okay." The child ran awkwardly across the mud road. Bain felt the thing like sadness again, but swore as he put on his coat. He looked around hastily for something to take with him, but there was no food worth the effort. He picked up a half-full jug of wine, but felt silly. Only he and Mirabal drank. He really shouldn't be eating their food. After all, he had eaten in enough native homes. His uneasiness stayed with him as he crossed the road.

Guadalupe met him at the door. He had forgotten about her, and now sighed inwardly in exasperation. "H'lo, Spance." Her smile was simple and respectful. He was disturbed more than he usually was by their constant respect.

"How is everything, Lupe?"

"All right. I hear you were baptized today."

He nodded. "You, too, pretty soon."

"Next week", she said, still smiling. "You like chicken tacos?"

"I love them", Bain said. "You shouldn't have gone to that much trouble."

"Oh, that's all right. You aren't baptized every day."

No, thank God, Bain thought. Why couldn't they just leave a man alone instead of almost literally doing a dance because someone not even related to them had been baptized?

The girl talked as he took off his coat. "Papa's been teaching me to cook, so I thought I'd try this for you."

"That's very nice of you", Bain said. He went into the kitchen where Mirabal and the younger children sat at a table obviously set for an occasion. Mirabal looked at Bain with Mirabal's equivalent of helplessness, and Bain began to laugh as he sat down. The children smiled through their constant awe of Bain, and for the entire meal he was light and happy as he had not been in his memory.

†

Mrs. Senton was unmistakably cool when Bain arrived at her home that evening. But Mrs. Trevelyan smiled at him from across the room to tell him not to fear, all would yet

be well. The two or three regulars there also greeted him
coolly. He did not remember their names, but found he
was, for some reason, amused by them.

Mrs. Senton sat in the large room before the inevitable
fire of piñon. Her shoulders were again hidden by a shawl;
it was, Bain considered, a long time for a fashion to last
with her. The others were grouped around her, four of
them, including Mrs. Trevelyan, near whom Bain sat. He
knew her best and found her least repellent of all in the
room. He wondered again why he came here: they were
not part of his work, nor of his life; they and their talk
wearied him; he had been to this place before, often: in
Greenwich Village, when he was studying at Columbia; in
Provincetown; in Woodstock—wherever bohemians justi-
fied their sicknesses and their sins by talk of art. He did
not like them or what they thought they stood for. They
were dirty and very sick and even the world had left them
behind. But he, Bain, returned to them. He wondered if
they did not represent, for him, an escape from reality.
But what reality?

Mr. McGaver, the portrait sculptor, said: "I was very
amused, Marsha, to note the other night how chastened
the women with the cinema people were by your shawl. A
totally unexpected touch." His laugh froze on his face as
the others maintained a silence. Unwittingly, he had spoken the truth: he would not do so again lightly.

Feeling sorry for McGaver, Bain said: "How are things at
the hospital, Mrs. Senton?"

She looked at him. "Oh, no better, Mr. Bain. I had a
long talk with your friend, Father Gannon, and I don't think
they will get better."

"What seems to be the trouble?" Bain said, almost
indistinctly, as he lit a cigarette.

"Oh, I don't think that's fair", Mrs. McGaver said. "Not at all fair to Marsha. She has so much on her mind, and she's talked about it once today." Without quite looking at Bain, Mrs. McGaver managed to convey the impression of glaring at him.

"That's all right", Bain said. His astonishment increased when he saw that all the regulars but Mrs. Trevelyan—and after all she was not one yet—were managing to simulate anger very well.

"After all," Mr. Barston, the non-introspective novelist, said, "there are certain things which should not be discussed in one's home." His voice was measured and assured, and he nodded to give emphasis to his words. Mr. and Mrs. McGaver nodded, too, as Bain smiled foolishly. He thought of Alice in Wonderland.

Mrs. Senton sighed and said: "Now, children", tolerantly.

Brightly, Mrs. Trevelyan said: "I've never been in such a glorious atmosphere to work in. Not even on Cape Cod. The very air, the—"

"Ruth, you know, Mr. Bain," Mrs. Senton said, "now has her own cottage." She nodded, watching him.

He felt stupid again. "I guess she can work better now, all right", he said. He noticed that Mrs. McGaver was scornful of him. He wondered if it were possible that they would expect him, or anyone, to be physically attracted to Mrs. Trevelyan? Still, the woman had a child. He noticed, seemingly for the first time, that Mrs. McGaver was large-boned and tall, with a wide, generous mouth that had somehow soured. He remembered hearing that she had children and wondered what they were like. Sorrow, he never recognized in himself, nor did he recognize it now.

"And very snug, too", Mrs. Trevelyan said.

Impatient with such trivia, Mr. Barston waved a hand to brush them all aside, and said to Mrs. Senton: "Marsha, you should see the latest chapter. Probably the best thing I've ever done."

"Then very likely the best thing ever done by an American", Mrs. Senton said, quietly. Her eyes, but not her head, moved about the room as though to challenge any possible dissenter. But there were none.

Whether by design or not, their conversation seemed to exclude Bain and Mrs. Trevelyan, and he found himself talking to her whenever he did speak.

"I discovered only yesterday that you were married", Mrs. Trevelyan said. Her features went through the movements of a wistful smile.

"Yes," Bain said, "I've been married six or seven years."

"Your wife—is she pretty?"

"I think so, but naturally I'm biased. And I miss her, of course, while I'm here alone."

"Why isn't she with you?"

He felt Mrs. Senton's eyes flash toward them, then quickly away, or he thought he did. Mr. McGaver was saying: "And there's nothing like it."

Bain said: "She's a teacher."

"Oh", Mrs. Trevelyan said. "High school, I suppose."

"No. She teaches philology in a college."

"Which one?"

"The University of California at Los Angeles." The name was still distasteful.

"What a ridiculous name", Mrs. Trevelyan said. "The college, of course, I mean."

"Yes", Bain said.

"You haven't any children, of course?"

"No", Bain said. He was bewildered again.

"I know how it is for professional people to try to have children."

You can't have children, Bain thought, if you're here and your wife is in California. On one level of his mind he realized the thought was obvious enough to be ridiculous but on another level it seemed to possess a brilliant logic. An obscure sadness came to him and when he did not speak, Mrs. Trevelyan said: "My own child is sort of an accident." She giggled. "One night my husband and I—that was before we were separated—" She stopped, to Bain's relief. The others, with their incredible faculty for listening to three or four conversations at once, had ceased talking and now Mrs. Trevelyan, in something like an atavistic harkening back to the elements of decency, stopped talking, too.

In the disappointed silence, Mrs. Senton said, smiling faintly: "Well, have you joined the Catholic Church yet, Mr. Bain?"

He did not answer at once. He saw with the new sudden clarity, the question, even the situation, repeated down many days: himself sighing inwardly in exasperation: the sadness, the confusion, and the lies. Speaking, he braced himself for shock, as a long time ago he had braced himself—long, ungainly legs and thin body—to meet the shock of a tackle in high school football. He said: "Yes. I came, or went, in today."

The regulars stared at him in what was, without exaggeration or acting, incredulous horror. Mrs. Senton smiled cruelly. "That means the end of you as a scientist."

"Oh, balls", Bain said. He had not meant to defend himself—certainly not the Church—or shock the others. He remembered—although he had never noticed it before—that whatever their thoughts or acts were, here, their language was meticulous, was what used to be called refined.

So that now the vulgar word rather than his own vehemence or any conviction it indicated that something ridiculous possessed grandeur, induced a silence in them. It might have been, he considered, a respectful silence.

"You disagree, I take it", Mrs. Senton said.

"I don't think any church necessarily has to interfere with honest research", Bain said. It sounded feeble to him: the reason for his outburst gone now and lost; it sounded like Gannon.

"Oh, come", Mrs. Senton said. "The scientist, like the artist, must be ruthless, and Christianity cannot tolerate ruthlessness. How about the mountain women you have to sleep with, the lies you have to tell or act, in order to get your information?"

"It's possible to have more than one method of research", he said. "Expediency is not the final criterion of a method."

"I'll be interested to see your study of these people when it's done", Mrs. Senton said. Her smile was amused, now. Bain wondered just how it was she had confounded him; he had always thought of her as stupid.

Brightly, Mrs. Trevelyan said: "Oh, he's going to check my detail for me, Marsha. In the book, you know, for authenticity."

Mrs. Senton looked at her coldly, then smiled. "Sort of the blind leading the blind. Now, if Milton here", she turned to Barston, "were doing a book on these people out here, the Spaniards and the Indians, we'd know it was authentic. In fact, Milton, I think your next one might very well be such a book."

"It could, it very well could, Marsha", Barston said. He looked around, smiling through the thick glasses, his teeth showing. "That's the way we get inspiration here", he said. "I tell you, there's no place like it." Then he shook his head once sidewise like an embarrassed country boy. That's all he really was at heart, he wanted them to know, just a country boy who had suddenly blossomed out as a genius.

Holy God, Bain thought, this cannot be as bad as it seems; some of them must have a sense of the ridiculous. He found that he was looking at the floor, one hand partly covering his face, as if he were embarrassed for something, perhaps them.

Mrs. Trevelyan said that if no one minded, she would go to her cottage, she was tired.

"I have to leave, too." Bain said. It was a chance to break away. As he stood up he saw Mrs. Senton was almost grinning. The old bag, he thought, she would think I'm after Ruth Trevelyan.

Outside, in the cold mountain air, Mrs. Trevelyan apparently also thought so. She brushed—he had not taken her arm—against him as they walked the hundred yards or so to her cottage. His emotion was pity again; he was puzzled by it; it was not common to him. At her door, she said: "Won't you come in? It's warm. I keep a heater going."

"I've got a heavy day tomorrow", he said. "Thanks just the same." If only she were not physically repellent. But pity, though!

She seemed disappointed and crushed, more than she should have been, so that Bain was freshly puzzled. He said, heavily: "It's been nice seeing you."

"You will come in, *sometime*, though?" she asked, querulous as a child.

"Why, why, yes", he said. What the hell, if she wants it that bad, why not some of the others at the old lady's house?

"Well, good night", she said. "And don't worry about Marsha. She really thinks well of you. I know." The starlight, the door closing on her coyness, touched the deep lines of her smile and gave her an oddly grim quality.

Walking back to his parked car, Bain felt unpleasant and bewildered. He would be glad to get into the mountains again. This place stank. From the car, as he started it, he saw a door in Mrs. Senton's house open and a rhomboid of light fall upon the ground. Mrs. Senton stood in the light. "Oh, Mr. Bain", she called. Her voice was pleasant, close to plaintive. He drove off, as much in sudden and unreasonable fear as in any other feeling. The figure barring the light watched him go.

6

AND NOW BAIN WAS GOING into the mountains with Teran.
Off the main road at Ranchos the wagon turned and headed
eastward along the way to Las Vegas. This road was dirt,
graded and firmed with gravel. It moved slowly upward
into the mountains, which rose heavily before the wagon
and gradually, as it came into them, to either hand. The
aspens were yellowing early; they showed in great, bright
clouds and patches in the deep green of the pines. Against
his will they stirred Bain. He had always thought them banal,
so often had the bad painters done them, and now he recalled
with a faint inward smile, the epithet Mark Coster, Billy
Gruber's lawyer, sometimes used—son of an aspen-painter.
It had struck them funny that time in the bar at Gruber's;
now it seemed only mildly amusing. It was an awfully big
country, Bain thought, bigger than any of those who lived
in it. He supposed it was a great credit to the Spaniards that
they had even survived in it for so long. The Indians were
dying and the Anglos impressed him as having no more
than a foothold on it and a slipping one at that: their women
frequently could not carry babies in the altitude; their men
often lacked endurance. All right, Zane Grey, he told himself, it is shor' a big country, mister, or sir, or pard, hom-
bre, or just plain, old-fashioned son-of-a-bitch.

For the second or third time Teran apologized for the
horse and wagon. "I am sorry", he said, in Spanish, "to
delay you so. But in the back country it is best to go by
wagon when there is a chance of rain or snow as at this
time of year. And besides I have no truck."

"I'm in no hurry", Bain said. "We see the country better this way."

The remark seemed to please Teran. "Most Anglos are always hurrying", he said.

"If I hurry I do not get the work done", Bain said.

After a little silence, Teran said: "This work of yours, it seems odd to some of us. To what purpose is it undertaken? It is not of an obvious usefulness like an agricultural agent or a county nurse."

"Clearly," Bain said, also in Spanish, "it is not; except that in knowing something of other people we know more of ourselves. In that some people think the usefulness of my kind of work consists. But it is also a pure if highly inexact science."

"Does it then frequently make for a respect for those you investigate?" Teran said.

"Frequently", Bain said. "Of course, it depends on the investigator", thinking of Schapper and the "brilliant irascibility" someone had once said ran through all the man's writings. A kind of hate, Bain supposed; he had never thought of it before as such.

"Clearly", Teran said. "On the investigator depends much." He seemed satisfied and they rode in silence for a while. Wild turkeys, five of them in a line, showed below them on the mountainside. They did not hurry or flee. It was not the open season and the side of the road they were on was part of a hunting preserve. Some confused and forced allegory came to Bain, concerning his own attitude toward sex fidelity now that he was "in" the Church. But he did not pursue the allegory.

"I would think", he said, in English, "that there would be enough apples in the mountains. Wouldn't it be better to bring them to a town?"

"Clearly", Teran said. "But there are not many fruit trees left. The droughts can be worse in the mountains than in the valleys. And over a certain height many fruits will not grow."

Teran sounded glib, as glib as Teran could sound. There was no central authority among the Hermanos, Bain knew, unless the Church could be termed such with its partial authority over them. Each morada was autonomous, but a loose and almost accidental communication was maintained among the different groups. It was because he suspected Teran frequently visited other moradas on his journeys that Bain had come with him. Mirabal was a good assistant, he told himself again. There was an enthusiasm in Mirabal's aid. Thinking of this made Bain uneasy.

At noon they stopped by a stream that ran near the road. The autumn water was very cold. Bain had no rod with him, but he stood near the bank trying to see trout in the swift, narrow flow. Sun was hot on his neck, and he stooped to put one hand in the icy water, staying fixed so for a moment, the hot and the cold contrasted in his body. In back of him, Teran said: "It is best to eat quickly if we are going to get to Trampas by dark."

"That's right." He turned to where Teran sat on a rock, eating from a paper bag. The man looked stolid and almost stupid in the white light, and Bain had the sense of ennui and one of futility: after all, what could anyone learn going into a semi-wilderness with such a man? He knew the feeling was frequently encountered in the work, particularly when it was dull, but he was never prepared for it or its intensity. He sat down and unfolded his own lunch. What did he expect of a simple people? he asked himself. He verged on dismay (perhaps even despair), wondering if he had acquired a masked hate like Schapper's. Almost hastily he took from his pocket a small flask of the cheap wine and offered it to Teran. But even this gesture was marred by his wondering if the Spaniard would refuse it, branding the man a puritan or its equivalent.

"Many thanks", Teran said. "*Salud.*" He took a good drink and handed the bottle back, at the same time offering Bain a tamale, neatly wrapped in corn husk.

"Many thanks", Bain said in Spanish. "If there is plenty?"

"A number", Teran said. "My wife always prepares me well for a journey."

"A good wife is a fine thing to have", Bain said piously. He found he had said it spontaneously, that he was sincere.

"You are married?"

"Oh, yes", Bain said. He realized as he spoke that Teran's knowing this could make for a complication: supposing he wanted to talk freely with some of the mountain women? Teran, ex officio, was a more than strict Catholic.

"I remember you saying so. Why is she not with you in Tarale?"

"She is a teacher. In a university in California."

"Truly?" Teran was impressed.

"Truly", Bain said. "It is not unusual among Anglo women, as you know, to do many of the things men also do."

"I know", Teran said. "It makes for a complication in the having of children."

"Yes", Bain said, without looking at Teran. "Frequently." He rose and brushed the crumbs off his clothes. Teran finished a tamale and also rose, throwing the husk into the stream. The sloppy bastard, Bain thought.

But as they rode upward, he thought that after all the mountains were not a park, to be guarded from picnickers: his own displeasure with Teran was unreasonable. . . .

The stream followed the road steadily. Across the water a few miles on, stood a log house, near it a slab-covered shelter for animals. Children played near the house and a one-armed man in dungarees sawed small logs with a bucksaw, held deftly by his hand and a steel hook fixed to the stump of his left forearm. He paused to watch as the wagon came into sight, then waved his good arm as Teran greeted him, and came down a little slope to where a footbridge of a log, split and planed smooth on the split sides, crossed the stream. Bain noticed the man had a round head, like Father Nunes, and a mustache that ran down the sides of his mouth to join his dark, closely clipped beard. The man smiled with the open joy of the simple, and the three children, dirty and poorly dressed, followed him. Bain walked after Teran, although he had not been asked to accompany him. He saw that his presence constrained the two men, their speech becoming short and of obvious things. The one-armed man could not conceal that he was puzzled at Bain's presence. It was not often, Bain considered, that the demands of the work and their conflict with ordinary decency, were dramatized, even as simply as this. He turned to speak with the children. With his back to the men, the stream running, with the children, he could not hear the talk. Teran had made no gesture of introduction, but then they seldom did.

Did they go to school? he asked the children, although the oldest was not more than seven. No, the oldest replied, but their two sisters went.

Bain wondered, as he frequently did, about girls growing up in this country. Some psychiatrists called the landscape masculine and considered it oppressive to women, but he didn't agree with them. It was the women from the east, Chicago and New York, the low-country women who became depressed and neurotic, and most of them were that before they came west. But still it was frightening to him to think of young girls growing up here.

He found that he was staring at the children and they at him, with a silence between them; that he had bent his long legs, squatting to be on their level. He straightened up, vaguely embarrassed for some reason, and turned to the men. They had moved nearer the stream and were talking earnestly. Bain turned back to the children. "Is there fish in the water?"

"*Sí, Señor*", two of them answered. "Always, except in winter."

Or when the summer takes all the water away, he thought. "And your father catches them?"

"*Sí*, with weirs."

It was illegal to catch trout with a net. . . . The figure of the one-armed man raising a family here was suddenly very meaningful to him: if he could convey somehow the quality of these people. . . . But it was not that, either. It was he and Elva and their continual excuse for having no children. He felt tired again and remembered with something like spiritual nausea the long and grave discussions of eugenics in classes repeating themselves infinitely . . . but the bastards never had any children. Either the work or money or divorce always interfered. He was one of the bastards. Self-pity again, he thought, and forced himself to talk to the children.

It was cold in the winter? *Sí*, very cold, *Señor*. But they were warm in their house? Yes, of a good warmness. He heard Teran call to him and he gave the children each a quarter. Their eyes grew round, their faces loosened: it was unpleasant to watch it happen. They were too stupefied to thank him. He turned to where Teran waited by the foot-bridge. The one-armed man stood a little way off, polite, slightly stooped; the conversation was finished.

"*Adios*", Bain mumbled, passing him.

"*Adios, Señor.*"

Bain climbed into the wagon. "Why don't you give him a bushel of apples?" Bain said to Teran. "For the kids. I'll pay you."

"He has some fruit trees on the slope", Teran said. He pointed upward and Bain saw the fruit, like a subtle design, half-hidden in the rusty green of the trees. The one-armed man did well; it would have been good to see what kind of a woman he was married to, Bain thought. The wagon started up the road and Bain unthinkingly asked if the one-armed man were one of the Hermanos.

Teran's diffidence was elaborate. He hesitated, then said: "*Como no?*" why not, or how could it be otherwise. Yet not all the Spaniards in the mountains were Hermanos, Bain knew. Teran meant something else: perhaps that the one-armed man being what and where he was, religion must be dramatic to him. Bain did not press him any further.

It was colder in the shade now. They had gone off onto an all-dirt road, narrow and winding, rising almost continuously through the pines and aspens. Neither man talked much. With Bain, it was the slight lassitude any height above that of Tarale induced in him. Perhaps it was the jolting of the wagon, perhaps his now, for him, long celibacy, but he began to think of Elva again. He wondered why he should think of her as unfaithful: he had never known her to be so. The sexual anarchy which was the norm of certain coeducational schools would not necessarily affect her. He supposed it was the cinema work that tempered and conditioned his thought about her. Of course, the people who would go to pieces there would be those who had never had money and who suddenly realized they could have virtually any experience they wanted now that they had money. Elva's

people had always had enough inherited money for it to be
no novelty to her. He knew a great deal about his wife, or
he thought he did, yet his mind sometimes pictured her as
gross, which his experience and knowledge of her told him
she was not. The human mind was a lovely thing, he told
himself sardonically, or maybe it was just his mind: a kind
of masturbation, perhaps. And yet it was only what they
called, in the classes in "creative writing", "imaginative
insight" functioning. The thing you were supposed to have
to be a good artist or even a good anthropologist. Like fire,
he thought, it depended entirely on the control of the person who used it. He smiled, inwardly and ruefully. Nunes
or Gannon or someone had certainly done an awfully good
job on him. He let his mind go, following its apparently
new logic: it came to a matter of self-control, something
laughed at by himself and virtually all the people he knew
in the universities. He personally associated it with being a
Boy Scout. In something not unlike terror, he saw how the
great truths had been made banal for the popular taste; how
the oversimplifying of them was a danger to himself and
others dedicated to the complex and the subtle. The terror
became real in him as he saw for a second time, with a
clarity equivalent to physical sight, how much more difficult it was for an intelligent person to be saved. He shook
the terror away (shaking his head): after all, he simply didn't
believe in that kind of salvation.

In the chill of the pine shade, he sweated, and he finally
noticed Teran watching him. "Are you all right?" the Spaniard said. "Not sick from the height?"

"I am all right", Bain said in Spanish. "It is sometimes a
thought that disturbs one."

"It is frequently so", Teran said, looking politely away.
"We will be in Trampas soon."

The road, for the first time, went steadily downward, and they were moving past adobe corrals close to small, adobe houses. The failing light was not all shade now and Bain turned his head to look for the color that came to these mountains at sunset. It was not here; the slopes were at a different angle from those near Tarale, and although the village was higher than Tarale, the mountains here were lower, below the tree line, and pine was heavy on them. In a shapeless and almost deserted little mud plaza, Teran halted the wagon and they got down. Bain noted that there were two other wagons, a buggy, and only one automobile in the place. The large, square, mud church dwarfed all the little village, which spread out, following the sharply rounded slopes of the valley that lay like a pocket in the mountains. A low, heavy, open fence, the white paint faded and chipped on it, enclosed the ground on which the church stood. The door of the church and the gate of the fence were closed and locked with padlocks.

There were beer advertisements on the post office. Bain and Teran went up the wooden steps. The woman behind the grocery counter greeted Teran happily and with respect, and two poorly dressed men came across the store to shake his hand. Bain had, more strongly and in his mind at last definitely, the sense of exclusion that had troubled him brokenly by the water that ran near the one-armed man's house. He was not of them: it was almost as though some extra sense had warned them on sight of his false enthusiasms and mock heartiness. Although so far he had only stood by. . . . Yet he had fooled the children—a feat in itself: or had he fooled them?

The others were about to drink at the little bar; almost as if it were an afterthought, Teran turned and called Bain over. As he moved toward them, another man, a Spaniard, came from behind the partition at the back of the store, and the others greeted him, so that Bain was seemingly ignored. The newcomer's name was Sandoval; he was the postmaster and the woman's husband. Irritated, Bain turned to look at the woman.

She had regular features that, properly taken care of, could easily have been beautiful, but there was no makeup on them and her skin had coarsened slightly. She stood erect and sure, a strong, easy grace in all her movements, her breasts round and hard under the cheap gingham dress. Bain wondered why she was married to the postmaster, an unimpressive-looking man. Well, well, he thought, here we go again—recognizing the conflict in himself before he knew its nature or meaning.

The woman was opening bottles of beer for them. Looking at her, obscenities ready to his mind, Bain passed them by. He was, in a way, shocked at his mind's doing that. He was not very tired, he was not distracted: none of the common anaphrodisiacs were present. He was puzzled and almost disappointed.

In Spanish, Teran was asking the postmaster if he could put them up for the night. "Your friend, too?" the postmaster said. His restraint was definite.

Teran gestured apologetically. "He speaks Spanish well", he said to the postmaster. It was both a warning to the Spaniards against frankness and a small justification of Bain.

"If it is a trouble," Bain said, "I can perhaps find another place."

The remark had the intended effect. The postmaster protested that he would never think of letting Bain go to another place. They stayed there, drinking beer from the bottles and talking. The woman had gone to the rear of the store, behind the partition. There was an odor of chile cooking and somewhere a child cried briefly. Outside it had become dark, the dimly lit windows of houses on the plaza hardly more than brown marks in the night. The single kerosene lamp overhead shed an uncertain and granular light. The other men left, so that Teran, Bain, and the postmaster remained alone in the store. The small talk almost died with the departure of the others. Teran said he must stable his horse.

"You know where the barn is?" the postmaster said.

"From previously", Teran said.

"I should have remembered", the postmaster said. "And now, Señor," to Bain, "we can go upstairs to supper."

"A thousand thanks", Bain said. "If it is not a trouble."

The postmaster did not answer but led him up the dark wooden stairs behind the partition. The smell of chile grew stronger, even in the cold passage of the stairs; they entered a brightly lighted room, furnished in bad, comfortable taste. Two children looked at Bain from the set table; they ought to be in bed, he thought.

"Please to be seated", the postmaster said. He brought a bottle of anisette out of a sideboard. Behind a half-wall or partition in the Spanish manner, the woman tended to her cooking. From the change to the warm room or from the chile, Bain sneezed repeatedly and the children stared in surprise, then in amusement.

"You will be very lucky", the postmaster said. He raised his glass. "*Salud.*"

"Or something", Bain said. He drank some of the cordial. "After dinner I will finish it", he said. It was too sweet. He continued to hold the glass.

"As you wish", the postmaster said. "There is plenty, though." He rose and went over to his wife.

Bain looked around the room, wondering automatically why people always brought children into poverty or dirt or bad taste or something, maybe only just being. His mind wandered and seemed unsure, as though lacking faith in the infallibility of his logic or even his knowledge. . . . The children continued to stare at him. He had never become used to the inevitability of children in the Spanish homes. He noticed the round heads of these, confirming his old knowledge that there was a strain in northern New Mexico of straight Spanish. Nunes, the one-armed man, now these children confirmed this small part of his knowledge. He grew distracted over the little glass in his hand and saw himself as one grown avid for knowledge as other men for money, and not less grossly than they. The concept disturbed him as had his mind's turning away from his thoughts of the woman. A repetition of some sort was involved: his mind sniffed and pointed like a bird dog.

Teran came into the room, breaking Bain's thoughts. The children, Bain saw, were not notably more friendly toward Teran than they had been toward himself: he felt relieved. The conversation at the simple meal was polite: they talked around and for Bain. The children were less shy toward him and the woman pleasant, although she would not meet his eyes. As much from politeness as from his constant and by now egregious pursuit of the detail in other peoples' lives, Bain excused himself and went down into the little plaza.

Outside it was very dark except for the oil lamps behind brown paper shades in a few of the houses. Bain stood still in the quietness, waiting for his eyes to become accustomed to the starlight. Gradually, he could see the low buildings and the square bulk of the church solid and black against the stars. The white carved fence around it, in the darkness seemed a lighter shadow. Somewhere in the plaza a horse stamped and moved, the carriage creaking. The bastards, he thought, leaving the horse out in the cold air; it was almost freezing.

He moved—aimlessly, he told himself—toward the church. His hand on the wood fence felt the paint, dry and flaky against his palm. He tried the gate. It moved slightly and held, fastened with the chain and padlock. He wondered irritably why it was locked. He supposed there was no priest nearer than Peñasco, and—his mind going easily off on a tangent—God knows they needed him there, with their average of a killing a month. This town was too small to have a priest resident in it; no wonder they had a morada adjacent to their church. . . .

He began to think about Peñasco again and the often terrible violences of these Spaniards in the mountains. He didn't know whether it was despair or poverty or the nature of their race that moved them so frequently to violence. It was almost never premeditated. The Church again, he supposed, wearily. If there was ever much premeditation of violence among them, Billy Gruber would be dead by now, Bain knew. The Spaniards despised Gruber as much as they feared him, not only because he had killed one of them but because they had a vague and erroneous notion that he had enlisted the law on his side in the person of Mark Coster. Yet Coster had saved more than one Spaniard in court.

The horse in the dark plaza stamped again in the chill. The horse was uncovered, Bain knew; his annoyance with those who had left the horse uncovered was similar to his annoyance with Teran by the stream: a—now, here—transparent attempt to make their petty faults balance his own grave ones. He sighed and, like the horse, moved his feet in the darkness. His hand remained on the wooden fence, on the wooden gate, rather, that was locked against him. It seemed to him that for the first time he knew his own loneliness; not merely his strangeness here, nor anything so obvious as his separation from Elva; rather the essential loneliness which every man brings into the world with him, here at last made tangible and even dramatic. He saw himself as a hated prier into the homes of strangers, a kind of intellectual charlatan rationalizing his own prurience into scientific curiosity; someone at once lower and more pretentious than a professional social worker. He told himself that it was the night and the weariness from the altitude speaking in him. But fright and despair remained strong, and as much to seek a haven as the nearness of even sleeping people in another room, he turned back to the postmaster's.

As he walked, his mind resumed automatically its continual labors: the brown paper shades on the houses, the brown paper bags the Spanish towns used for *luminarios* set on the edge of roofs at fiestas: was there a connection? He spat thought out of him before his mind told him that any relation of the two things was preposterous. You weary hack, he told himself, climbing the wooden steps to the post office. He let the self-pity remain.

†

Sleep and morning returned his old arrogance to him: riding on the wagon with Teran, he felt keen and assured in the fresh light, the morning's soft coolness; he was doing a job here as good as anything Schapper had done on South American Indians. Why, Schapper, with his open scorn, could never have gotten into any of the Indian religions as he, Bain, had here.

Teran said: "These brothers we will see this morning are very poor. At times, they sell some of their worn-out things from the morada to someone who gathers such articles."

"Perhaps I would buy something myself", Bain said.

Teran shrugged. "Do not do it as a charity, but only if it can be of service in your work."

They topped a little rise in the dirt road and looked out on a small valley or pocket in the mountains, less than a mile square. The pocket in turn had its own hills, low and softly rolling in contrast to the harsh angles of the mountains. Teran left the road, driving over two faintly marked wheel ruts. They wound left and right about two of the small hills and quietly and suddenly came on the low, windowless building.

Three men sat on the south side of the structure where the sun had not yet reached them. The door near them was open and the interior showed only as a blank and dark. The men rose slowly to their feet as they recognized Teran on the wagon. They came less slowly to meet him across the little intervening space as he descended from the wagon. Their greetings were quiet, but their respect for Teran was clear, although it was a respect completely inexpressible in words. Bain thought—and he was right—that many people would not have noticed it.

Teran introduced Bain to the other men but not they to him. It was understandable, Bain knew. He was more intruder than guest. "This man here", Teran said, "is the Señor Bain, not one of the Hermanos, but a student of people and not without respect for our customs."

It was a pretty good recommendation, Bain knew, and Teran had been under no compulsion to make it. He saw some of the respect the others had for Teran conveyed in their faces to himself. He moved with them to the north-west corner of the building, between the sun and the shade,

and for the first time saw the *carrete de muerte* standing in
the shadow. The little cart, pulled by a penitent in the Good
Friday procession, was not greatly different from others Bain
had seen. Instead of a skeleton, the less common statuette
of a cowled hag sat in the body of the cart, a drawn bow in
her hands, an arrow mounted on the string and pointed
toward the shafts of the cart. Yet it was none of these things
that had depressed Bain when he had first seen a carrete. It
was the two solid wooden wheels, the wheels made not to
move, so that, with horsehair rope, a penitent must drag
the cart, its wheels unturning, while Death waited, its arrow
drawn at the penitent's back. He had known, even that first
time, what the unturning wheels meant, although all anyone else had written of them was that they were apparently
just one more penance. To Bain they had immediately meant
all man's work.

He had, in an unconscious movement of the mind quite
common among his contemporaries, never again let himself think of this. Now, seeing the carrete in daylight, for
only the second time in daylight, he told himself it did
not bother him. The practice was barbarous, this particular carrete not even particularly well carven, and though
old and in need of repair, not old enough to be an antique.
One of the Hermanos saw Bain looking at it and broke
off from the others' talk of the bad growing season to ask
Bain if he knew of the cart's use. Bain nodded and the
man said: "This one is old, so that we are selling it. Perhaps today, if not tomorrow, some from Sante Fe will be
here to see it."

"Be sure to get a good price for it", Bain said. "Those
of Santa Fe are often rich."

The man grinned, showing bad teeth. "It is not that we
wish to sell it for profit, but that one of our Hermanos has

made a newer and better one, and by selling this one we can make repairs to the morada."

"Clearly," Bain said, "it is not for profit. I should like to see the new carrete."

The man shrugged, his face becoming sly. Bain saw that his own indirection had not deceived this Spaniard. Turning to look at the others, he saw they were a little ways off, still in the shade but out of earshot. Annoyance mounted in him at their continual, polite evasion. Consciously rude, he approached the group and asked Teran if he could see the new carrete.

Their hesitation was slight. Then Teran and one of the others turned to each other and also shrugged. *"Como no?"* the other Hermano said. "How could it be otherwise?"

Almost simultaneously they all moved toward the door of the morada. Teran came closer to Bain and said: "You will be disappointed. There is not much to see."

"I've been in moradas before", Bain said. He knew that only during Lent did the windowless little houses take on life or much meaning. Ducking to enter the low doorway, he was blinded in the sudden darkness and stood still, hearing the others moving about him. Their noise conveyed to him their familiarity and their boredom with the place. Gradually, shapes emerged upon his sight: the rough, slightly raised table that could scarcely be called an altar; two or three simple and equally rough benches; stacked on their sides along a wall the tallish crosses the perhaps more sinful of the Hermanos, their faces hooded, dragged in the Good Friday procession. Thus far, nothing new or strange.

One of the men lit a kerosene lamp. By its vague light, Bain saw more clearly the essential bareness of the place. There were no dark splashes on the walls of *terra blanca* nor whips of any sort hanging or standing in corners. Bain told

himself that he had not expected any: he was no friend of
Mrs. Senton's, nor did he believe in the stuff her friends
had written. . . .

"Here," said the tall Hermano, the one to whom Bain
had first spoken, "here is the new carrete."

It stood against a sidewall near the rear corner farther
from the doorway. It was very new indeed, for the smell of
its wood filled the unmoving air of the place. It was not as
well done as the old one, although it was slightly larger and
the figure in the cart was that of a skeleton and not a hag.
The skeleton was more common than the hag, Bain knew,
and thought that Schapper, if he were to perceive the change
in the carrete of this morada, would attribute some profound or gross sexual meaning to it. Bain wondered why
he himself did not find such meaning. He experienced again,
like something heard over a distance or felt through partial
anesthesia, the sense of intellectual weariness, of mental ennui;
he and Schapper, all of them, so continually went by the
same unchanging and often degrading standards: Freud was
mighty and must prevail. All right, then, my pious friend,
he told himself, you give the class the answer.

He didn't know the answer, if there was an answer. (It
was about this time in his life, too, that he began to realize
that sometimes the answer must remain unknown.) He had
never known an Hermano who was or even seemed to be
homosexual. It was an affliction almost unknown among
the Spaniards here. He wondered if its absence had anything to do with their attitude toward sex, an easier and
much less puritanical one than that of most Catholics he
had known in the east. It was something he must ask Gannon about. Priests could talk about statistics gathered in the
confessional although not about a specifically named case.
It was not strange, he thought; it was even scientific that

they should be allowed to do this. He was disturbed that he should be so solemn about the obvious, as though he had evolved a subtlety.

"It is artistic, don't you think?" the tall Hermano said. "Much more so than the old one." They had been waiting for Bain to speak.

"Much", Bain said. "It is a fine bit of carving."

There was a silence that grew, in which his own professional glibness failed him. The statuette was badly carved and it happened in him, strangely, that he simply could not raise his usual false and easy enthusiasm. Teran tried politely to make conversation; here, in this place, the man was concerned suddenly with the amenities. "The Señor Bain," he said, "unlike most Anglos and scholars, is a Catholic."

The others murmured their surprise and pleasure. What startled Bain was the pride in Teran's voice. That part of his mind avid for gain in the work, forever hawklike and ready, seized on this new knowledge of Teran: he had not known Teran thought so well of him.

"I know little about the Church", Bain said. "I am only a recent convert." The false and appropriate modesty flowed easily and as of old.

"Here," said the shortest and most silent of the Hermanos, in a sudden burst of confiding that was close to joy, "here, when the drought was so bad in August, our pastor had all in the village go to Mass on three weekdays and pray for rain, and only two days after, rain came. Of course," he said, "it did not save much, but perhaps if we had prayed sooner—"

Bain saw the other men stiffen as a car drove up outside; he found that he had stiffened, too. "It is perhaps those of Santa Fe", the tall Hermano said, without enthusiasm. The other two local men started for the doorway, then stepped aside to let Bain precede them. He in turn insisted on all the others preceding him. He was about to follow them into the light when he saw the car and its occupants, and he stopped inside the doorway. He knew, though not well, the three women in the car.

They were typical of many of the eastern women who lived sporadically in the fashionable parts of the west. A little older and less unhappy they might have been in Tucson or perhaps Denver. But they lived, so to speak, in Santa Fe and looked at the twin hills called Los Natales and waited. Their waiting they broke in various ways, sometimes by these trips into the mountains, for some of them excused all their desires and aberrations by saying they were writers or painters or even scientists. Now that they were alighting from the car in their twill slacks, their suede jackets, and dark glasses, Bain felt constrained to stay within the walls of the morada. So that he found himself in shadow and darkness looking out, unseen, upon the others in the light. Perhaps it was this self-imposed segregation from them, perhaps merely his almost continual lust, but he found himself watching one of the women, a Mrs. Vasseur, that he knew better than the others.

"*Buenas dias, Señoritas*", the tall Hermano said. He smiled mechanically and Bain wondered if it were barely possible that the man's thinness was due to hunger.

"We are very glad to be here in your beautiful valley", Mrs. Vasseur said in bad Spanish. Bain's lust diminished, but only slightly.

The Hermanos stood dutifully in the sun and waited. Although they had gone out of the morada promptly enough when they had heard the car, Bain saw they did not like the business at all. Teran was out of Bain's narrow range of sight. The women had obviously expected a better reception and now stood uncertainly in the strong light. They could not be afraid of sex violence, Bain thought; indeed, they might rather be hoping for it. Pity was in him again, completely unexplained.

The Hermano who was of middle height looked at the ground and rubbed the edge of one sole uneasily, so that Bain wondered if the man were disturbed, too. It was unlikely, Bain felt, that he was not. He could hardly know the Spaniard merely thought these women funny-looking.

"In your beautiful valley you must have had many fine crops this fall", one of the other women said in the bad Spanish.

"No", the little Hermano said in bad English. "The rain not come in time." It was a simple statement of fact, but everyone in the group became embarrassed. Behind the women's dark glasses, Bain knew, the eyes must have gone blank in that peculiar way they had of going blank when something was mentioned that did not concern them.

"Oh, I see", one of the women finally said. Bain wondered if it were possible.

The silence was resumed, to be broken again by Mrs. Vasseur. "We understand you have an antique carrete for sale?" she said, uncertainly.

"As you see", the tall Hermano said. He looked at the cart but did not gesture toward it.

"Oh, it's lovely", one of the women said. When no one said anything, she said: "I mean its impressive, kind of, like."

"It'll look wonderful in that studio of yours, Muriel", Mrs. Vasseur said to the third woman. "So typical of the southwest."

In the darkness, Bain choked. With the rage and the scorn, pity still remained, so that he was very confused. It was a little while before he could see or hear clearly. Then Mrs. Vasseur was bargaining to get the carrete for her friend.

She couldn't possibly give more than fifteen dollars, she explained.

The way it was, the tall Hermano explained, they were not trying to make money. They simply had to have so much in order to repair their morada.

"Fifteen dollars", Mrs. Vasseur said, smiling.

"From forty dollars we would descend to thirty", the tall one said.

"After all, Tina," Muriel said, "they are hard to get."

"Oh, hush, Muriel, you'll ruin everything," Mrs. Vasseur said, as though the men spoke no English. To the tall Hermano, she said: "Fifteen dollars."

"It is not something we like to bargain over", he said. "If we were more rich here, we would dispose of it in some other way. But we have no money to—"

"Oh, that's an old story", Mrs. Vasseur said.

"I know", the tall one said. "We have always been poor here."

"I meant—" Mrs. Vasseur said, then caught herself. "Twenty dollars", she said. "That's final."

The tall one turned to the other men—Bain could see only him and the women—and made a questioning motion, so that to Bain it was as if the man were gesturing to the invisible or to God. The Hermano turned back to the women. "All right", he said to Mrs. Vasseur. Her face relaxed, became almost shapeless. Bain watched the change with sudden disgust, remembering the party in Santa Fe a year ago and how he had stumbled into a bedroom, and Mrs. Vasseur and the drunk on the bed, and the way her face had changed then, too, the same, in the five or six seconds he had stood in the doorway.

Two of the Hermanos were lifting the carrete into the rumble seat of the car, and Muriel was paying the tall one in cash. "When you have another one, let me know", Mrs. Vasseur said.

"It will be a long time", he said, smiling over the money, but Mrs. Vasseur thinking he was smiling at her. She smiled back as the car drove away.

The four Hermanos stood there in the sun. The pity in Bain was toward them, now. He moved out of the morada, to be nearer.

"One would think", the middle-sized Hermano said, "that such as they would not worry over five dollars or ten."

"Here," the short one said, "with the drought—" He stopped talking, seeing that the others did not like to hear about the drought. They might all go hungry this winter, but only the short one had enough imagination or enough lack of control to keep talking about it.

"Still," Teran said, smiling oddly, "they have taken one worry off us. They have bought Death."

Irony being not common to Teran, Bain turned to him, thinking the man had been literal and superstitious. Teran, half-smiling, met his look. "And these are your people, my friend", he said to Bain. "God must indeed be merciful to spare them."

Again the glib and pious word failed Bain. In something like terror, in a literal and partial failing of the sight, he could only speak what he felt to be the truth, shaking his head slightly and as a man distrait. "You don't know", he said thickly. "God hasn't spared them."

7

BAIN CALLED THE AIRPORT at Albuquerque four times on the eighteenth of December. The plane from Los Angeles was down in Arizona because of weather conditions, they told him each time. The fourth time they told him that the passengers were proceeding east by train. He cursed and hung up. The mind, making concessions to his precarious continence, had kept promising him for days that Elva would be with him tonight; and now he must wait until tomorrow. He put on a coat and went out into the early dark.

Hesitating aimlessly, he told himself that he was debating whether to go in and see Mirabal or not. He had not seen much of his assistant since coming back from the mountains. Mirabal had made a needed, though not altogether honest killing at monte while Bain was away. He had paid some bills, gone on a drunk, and, Bain suspected, was spending a good many of his days with a widow north of town near the Colorado line. He had been gone this time for three days and if he had come back would have been over by now to see Bain. Knowing this, Bain still went over to the mud house with its ugly and inappropriate porch. It was not until Lupe opened the door that he knew why he had come to Mirabal's house.

She did not seem the young, fresh, and virginal figure he always thought of her as being. With her father away, most of the housework fell to her, and now she looked slovenly, her cheap dress not very clean and her long hair unwashed and only roughly combed. She seemed older and less impressed by himself. He wondered again—at times he wondered continually—if she were still virginal.

He said: "How's things, Lupe? Your father home yet?"

She shook her head. "Not yet. Maybe tomorrow." Not until his silence made her uncomfortable did she say: "You want to come in? I got two of those kids in the tub. They haven't had a bath in a month."

"All right." He stepped inside the doorway, feeling the heat of the low-ceilinged place rise around him, his head lowered as if in a kind of shame. The only light came from the kitchen and he walked toward it. Mirabal's two youngest children—Bain had known it would be they, a boy and a girl—grinned up at him from a metal washtub full of soapy water.

Lupe bent over them. "These kids", she said. "They're worse than I don't know what." She was embarrassed, but whether because of the dirtiness or the nakedness of the children, Bain didn't know. He knew, now, how fully he had intended to use, first, Mirabal's absence, then, after he had known of it, the children's nakedness. Lupe was confused by it and embarrassed. This, added to her usual respect for him, should be enough.

The children stood up dripping in the tub, giggling at the unusual pleasure of warm water against their skins. Their sister would not look at Bain as she dried them.

"Where are the others?" Bain said.

"They're at their aunt's for supper."

"Your father made some money", Bain said. "He ought to get some neighbor in to help you while he's away."

"I don't know", the girl said. "He maybe didn't mean to be gone so long."

"Did all of you have supper? I mean, was there something to eat?"

"Oh, sure", she said. "He bought some canned stuff after he made that money at Billy Gruber's while you were away. You could have eaten with us if you wanted. We only finished a little while ago."

"I'm going to eat in town. I was expecting my wife."

"Can't she come at all?" For the first time since Bain had entered the kitchen, the girl looked at him. She was sorry for him, he saw, as he had probably intended her to be. It was more than he had intended, though, and transcended sorrow: it was pity.

Now he could not do anything, he thought; old Bain, the boy Casanova. He wondered how she could possibly have known of the depth or perhaps just the intensity of his desire. He stood up. "She'll be here tomorrow", he said. "Her plane is down in Arizona."

"You mean a wreck?" the girl said, blanching.

"No, no. It was just bad flying weather, so they couldn't fly." At times she was stupid, even for a kid, he thought. She stood there, pitying him and distrait over the children she had finished clothing in ragged pajamas.

"Maybe your wife could be my godmother when I get baptized. And you my godfather?"

"My wife couldn't be", Bain said. "She's not a Catholic."

The girl stood there silently, nodding and still distracted. "That's right", she said. "I mean, you've only just been baptized yourself—"

"And the way it is with me," Bain went on, hurriedly, "I may not be here long, not more than another year, probably. A godfather is supposed to be near enough to help bring the child up in the Church, if something should happen to the parents."

The girl nodded, still uncertain. "I didn't know that. I thought it was like just having another cousin or aunt."

"That's the way it usually is", Bain said. "Although the Church intended the obligation of the godparents to be more strict than that." Oh, sure, the Church intended a lot of other strictnesses, too, you son of a bitch, he thought: that a man should be faithful to his wife; that other men should pay their workmen enough; even that people shouldn't say Mrs. Senton was an old bitch and her protégés often various and unspeakable. He trembled as if suddenly sick. In something like terror, but complex and full of many clarities, partly seen, he knew that there was no argument: on the basic things the Church was always right. By what extraordinary sifting of experience she had become so, he could not understand: it had always amazed him that this basic accuracy and rightness, achieved through some realistic process and over a long time, should be attributed by the Church to anything as ridiculous as what she called revelation. It was not that he and some of the others were ignorant of the Church's being right so often, as that they could not bring themselves to subdue their incredible pride long enough to do what someone else said they should do. Of course, if they believed in God, he thought, it would have been something else again.

"You all right?" the girl said.

"Oh, yes", he said, not looking at her and sidling toward the door. "I'm fine. Tell your father I want to see him when he gets back."

"Good night, Spance", the children said to his retreating back.

"Good night, kids." He closed the outside door after him.

There was no wind, only the still mountain coldness, dry and stinging the nostrils. He got heavily into his car, turned it, and went off toward Tarale. He wasn't hungry and he thought he would go to Gruber's. Saturday nights, even at this time of year, there would be dancing and the dice table would be going. You played it, even though you knew the dice were sometimes loaded. As with some of the things the Church taught.... The annoyance such thoughts often engendered in him, new and unsubtle as they were, passed over him again. He recalled one or two other anthropologists who had found themselves believing in religions they had pretended to adopt. "_____ them all", he said, and pushed the accelerator down.

The neon signs at Gruber's welcomed him in the night. There were only three or four cars in the parking lot, one of them Mark Coster's, mud-splashed. Coster had been in the mountains on legal business or for the early skiing. He must get some of the skiing himself, Bain thought idly.

Inside Gruber's the lights were not all on yet and in shadow was the dance floor beyond the cheap tables that stood nearer the door and in front of the polished bar. Just beyond the bar was a doorway that led to the dice room.

Two tables had young Anglo couples from the town seated at them, drinking Cuba libres, and Gruber himself sat at a table near the far wall, talking to Mark Coster. They both moved their heads to see who had entered, and Coster raised a casual hand in greeting. Gruber half-rose, his stocky body and square, lined, ugly face bent and twisted into the caricature of affability and good humor, the whole illusion mocked and made more terrible by the small, black, and triangular eyes of the man. It was a phenomenon Bain had noticed several times since Gruber had killed the Spaniard: this short man, Billy Gruber, by nature sullen and intemperate—he had been a professional bronco rider in his youth at the big rodeos—trying to be affable, well-tempered, and kindly now that he must stand trial, perhaps for his life, before a jury not yet chosen. "Hello, Mr. Bain. Glad to see you", he called across the room.

Bain moved a hand in greeting and turned to the bar, embarrassed. "Scotch and water", he said to the barkeeper. He noticed that the man was new and an Anglo. The old barkeeper, a Spaniard, had left Gruber, too. The new barkeeper was diffident, a stranger with thinning dark hair and the somewhat flabby but immobile face often seen on bartenders in the city. Bain guessed that the man was here from Denver or Kansas City to guard Gruber. He made the drink without speaking, took Bain's money, and moved off down the empty bar. Bain felt rebuked. The watered whiskey tasted good. He had not drunk much for the past week.

He stood there, the whiskey warming his empty stomach. Brokenly in the mirror, partly obscured by bottles, he saw himself, a melancholy and studentish figure: the glasses, the hollowed and bony face, the corduroy coat. Self-pity stirred again and he spat it out: a thing for children, but one with which he and his contemporaries romanticized themselves. He saw, in amazement, that it had been with him even recently, usually unrecognized, and that it was now as distasteful to his mind as stale beer to his mouth.

More people had begun to come in and the four-piece orchestra was tuning up. Turning to a hand on his shoulder, Bain found it was Coster's. The lawyer was short and had to look up at Bain. His face, with its regular and undistinguished features, held a kind of permanent flush, which most people attributed to hard drinking, although it was due to the time he spent in the open, for he had come to the western mountains for his lungs. "What you drinking?" he asked Bain.

"Scotch. Have some."

"No, thanks. I'm drinking bourbon. When in Rome— Why, I'm practically a Roman. I've been here fifteen years this month."

"You seem to have stood it well." Coster still retained some of the bumptiousness of the undergraduate athlete he had been, and Bain resented it. (*Who had stood on long legs in the ring at school, tottering before the flailing arms of a shorter man: the nose clogged with blood, the puffed lips, and the defeat?*)

"Stood it well?" the lawyer said. "It saved my life. They took me out of college—I weighed 130 pounds and was playing in the Fordham backfield—and clapped me into a san in upstate New York and after I'd been there a few months, my old man came up with a specialist and the old man said in front of me that he wanted a frank opinion. So the specialist said I had six months to live and I began to cry. And my father said, 'Oh, for God's sake', and I shook my fist at the specialist and I was still crying and I said, 'You goddam old butcher, I'll live to piss on your grave.' I did, too. That is, I outlived him. Where's that bartender?"

The man was finally approaching them, after serving a couple at the other end of the bar. "A little bourbon, Alfred," Coster said, "and some more Scotch for my friend, here."

"Alfred", the bartender said, shaking his bent head. "Do you have to tell people?" He turned away to get the bottles.

"What's he?" Bain said. "Kind of a bodyguard for Billy?"

Coster looked at him. "How did you know?" His manner broke and changed. "I forgot, though. That's kind of your business, isn't it, knowing about people from the way they look?"

"I don't know", Bain said. The flattery glowed in him as whiskey never had. He hadn't known he needed it so badly.

"They sure have poor Billy in a bad way, haven't they?" the lawyer said.

"You don't think you can get him off?" So doth intimacy make lawyers of us all, he thought, mocking many things, but most of all, himself.

"Oh, I think I can take care of him all right. It's the months before the trial that I'm afraid of. Billy's so scared, he wouldn't shoot at a burglar. He's even stopped hitting his wife. Some of the wise guys around here are going to sense it pretty soon and begin to make life pretty miserable for him."

"I've noticed what you mean", Bain said.

The bartender placed the fresh drinks before them. "Okay?"

"Everything's fine, Alfred", Coster said. The bartender moved off, shaking his head.

"I noticed a funny thing", Bain said. "That barkeep had on a Knights of Columbus ring. He must be a Catholic. Isn't that an odd business for a Catholic to be in?"

"Why is it? There's nothing immoral about tending bar. There's nothing wrong, even, about being a bodyguard. The man's got to make a living. I brought him out here from Kansas City."

"I see your point", Bain said. "It just did seem a bit odd."

"You converts are all like that", Coster said. "You think all Catholics should be in pure, wholesome businesses like small loans or real estate."

"How did you know I was in the Church?" Bain said.

"I get to know almost everything that happens in the county. As a matter of fact, Father Gannon told me. There's another one. He wanted the Indians not to dance in front of their chapel this Christmas. But Nunes slowed him down. He told him that David danced before the temple."

"Gannon is no convert."

"No, but he comes from the same background that has influenced most converts and even most of the Church in this country. The Irish-French kind of Catholicism that's managed to bitch the Church up over here. It's why a few people have come here or stay here, where Catholicism is still pretty close to what it should be. Although I'm not much of one myself. I'm in the Church because I have to be, not because I want to be, like a lame man has to have a crutch." Coster paused to drink and Bain felt the lawyer was waiting for him to say something about his own coming into the Church. There seemed nothing to say, although a kind of fear played in Bain. He said, finally: "My wife was supposed to arrive today. But the plane's down in Arizona on account of the weather and she won't be here until tomorrow."

"That's too bad. I guess you've been missing her. What did she say about your coming into the Church?"

Where did the bastard think he was? Cross-examining? "She doesn't know yet", Bain said. "She's not very religious and I've kind of been wondering how to tell her. She's certainly going to be surprised."

"Man", the lawyer said. "That's putting it mildly. You certainly must have known what you were getting into. What are you going to do about birth control or abortions or half a dozen other things? If you were dumb, it would be different, but you're not, and you automatically assume moral responsibility for things that the dumb can't, or don't."

"I know, I know", Bain said. That bastard, Mirabal. "My wife and I have led more or less separate lives. Not that we're incompatible or anything like that, but simply due to the nature of our work."

Coster drank as Bain spoke, but even after he put his glass down neither of them talked for a little while. The orchestra had started to play, but it seemed a long way off. Reflected in the bar mirror, Bain could see Billy Gruber, greeting people at the door, the toothed smile, the gestures become by now actually fawning. Usually the man sat at a table and spoke only if spoken to, even on Saturday nights.

"Hello, you little son of a bitch", a big man said to Gruber.

"Ha ha", Gruber said, just like that, saying the sounds. "I'm sure glad to see you, Jake."

"You little bastard", Jake said. "You were never glad to see anything but a Denver pimp after a rodeo."

"You said it, Jake", Gruber said. "Go over and sit down and I'll be right with you."

With a faint, cruel smile on his mouth, Jake moved on. Watching Coster in the mirror, Bain said: "I never thought I could be sorry for someone like Billy."

"He's no worse than a lot of other people", Coster said. "Of course, a man that kills people is more of a danger to society at large than a woman that peels off an abortion every year or two. But actually—"

"You certainly have that on your mind tonight, haven't you?" Bain said. He and Elva had been lucky, he considered, they had had to have only one.

"Well—" Coster said and paused defensively. "I was just thinking that when an intelligent person comes into the Church, it's a great complication for everyone concerned. I suppose you think the ordinary parish priest likes the job of trying to decipher the Kraft-Ebing case histories that intellectuals bring into the confessional?"

"I wouldn't know", Bain said. He rapped his empty glass on the bar. Over Coster's shoulder he could see the dancing couples, most of the girls close up against the men. We manage to be so obvious and unsubtle about our sex, he thought. Now, the Indians and the Spaniards in their dances, if they don't exactly give sex dignity, at least raise it above the status of a game or a sport. The close-packed bodies in the line of the pueblo's deer dance were no aphrodisiac to the beholder.

Coster said: "That gun he used. You see, he wasn't trying to shoot anyone. He was just trying to knock out this
drunk Spaniard by hitting him over the head with the barrel of the revolver. The Spaniard ducked and the end only,
that is, the muzzle hit the side of his head and the jarring
discharged the gun. It hardly touched the guy, the bullet
just ran along the bone, just breaking it in one place. It
never even went into or through his skull."

"I heard about that gun", Bain said. He could not look
at Coster as he spoke. "Only trouble is, that kind of revolver
is made not to go off unless the trigger is pulled."

"Oh, now, listen", Coster said. "No gun can be guar-
anteed not to go off accidentally. We've gone into that a
lot. It was a double-action revolver and it wasn't cocked.
It—"

"The cartridge was marked by the firing pin", Bain said.
He still could not look at Coster and felt embarrassed for
the man.

"God," Coster said, "you sound like an assistant D.A. I
think you'd have made a good one at that. You wouldn't
buy very easy."

"Oh, I buy easy", Bain said. *Sure—every day your integrity
for a sentence, for even a well-known fact. . . .* He had learned
nothing new since coming into the Church. . . . "Scotch,
again", he said. The barkeep had returned. "And bourbon
for the barrister, here."

"Thank you, thank you", Coster said. "It sounds so like
bastard—and that they are always saying."

The place was almost crowded by now. The door leading outside opened and closed several times a minute, the
cold air rushing into the low-ceilinged and noisy room.
The band had swung into the Varsoviana for the first time
that night, and Bain turned to watch the couples wheel

and stamp. It was a good dance, he thought again, and apparently the dancers thought so, too. They laughed and grinned as they moved in the vigorous, controlled, and formal patterns. Bain began to hum and move his head to the music. Suddenly and gravely, he wanted Elva here to dance it with him. He kept forgetting about what else he wanted her for, distracted with what seemed curious ease. Now, willfully and consciously, he made himself recall the details of her body and her—there was no other name for it—considerable skill. The new drink was in front of him but he had lost all taste for it. In something like embarrassment, he saw that only now and here and after a long abstinence did he finally consciously recognize her amazing physical quality: the innocence and even virginity of expression, the sweetness and gentleness of speech, contrasted with her bodily attraction. He wondered how conscious she was of the paradox, if in her heart she smiled always, fondly and slyly?

"Drink up", Coster said. "We're going to get our ears bent. Here comes Father Gannon."

The priest stood in the doorway, his overcoat buttoned high so that his Roman collar did not show, a faint and easy smile on his flushed face. He moved his head in recognition, seeing Bain and Coster, and approached them slowly, with an elaborate unhaste, a formal reluctance. "Good evening, Padre", Coster said, with irony. "What are you doing in this den of iniquity?"

"The cold alone brought me in", Gannon said. "I needed a drink. It was positively warm in Albuquerque today."

"What were you doing down there?" Bain said.

"Oh, just seeing what it was like." The priest seemed cool, Bain thought. "Where have you been, Spence?" Gannon went on. "Haven't seen you since the night we played cards at Father Nunes."

"Why, you baptized me."

"But that wasn't exactly social."

"I've been pretty busy with the work", Bain said. "And I was in the mountains for awhile."

"You've been back a month or more", the priest said. He loosened his coat and they could see the Roman collar between the folds of a heavy, white silk scarf.

"What'll you drink, Father?" Coster said.

"Brandy. And a little soda on the side. It's cold out."

"Did you drive?" Bain said.

"No. I came by bus. Something was wrong with the heater, though, and it wasn't warm. By the way, Spence—" The priest stopped talking as Billy Gruber came up to the little group. "Hello, Father", Billy said. "Glad to see you here." He turned to the bartender. "Don't you go taking any money from Father here for any drinks, you hear me, Al?"

"That's right", Al said.

"Now, look, Billy", the priest said. "I can't have that. I only—"

"Now, you listen to me, Father", Billy said.

They went on like that for a moment or two while Bain studied Gruber. Now Coster turned his head toward the bar in embarrassment. It was, Bain supposed, a kind of sanctuary for Gruber. No one would call him a son of a bitch while he was talking to the priest. Bain wondered if Gannon was aware of this service to Gruber, and if he was, whether he was pleased or not. It was difficult to tell. Gannon stood there, a slightly pained but otherwise ambiguous expression on his full face. Bain turned to look at Gruber. The man was a living caricature, but at the moment too complicated to serve as one. The twisted face on the stocky and slightly misshapen body, where the vague spinal injury he had suffered in his last ride at Amarillo forever marked him, the creased face and triangular eyes, the leaden mouth in the leaden and ghastly smile. It was not often, Bain considered, that so many things showed at once so clearly in a man: rage and terror, both, and frustration; the long life of bodily strength and skill, and their equal opposites in the mind. Even the bodily subtlety and the mind's lack of it; the body had to be subtle (cunning? incredible balance?) to ride the horses Gruber had once ridden for a living. So that all the qualities that Bain admired and thought should be in a mind, he saw in Gruber had gone into the body; and now the body was twisted, too.

"—all a time, Father", Gruber was saying. "I don't go to no church, but all a time I'm glad to see any Father here."

"Well, thanks. Thanks", Gannon said. His reserve had increased till everyone, even Gruber, was becoming uncomfortable.

"Well, ha ha, glad to see you", Gruber said, and moved off, his head turning away before the body completely had. Bain saw, as the man departed, that the fierce little eyes were really dazed, and in amazement, felt pity stir in him for the killer.

"I wonder what all the cordiality was for?" Gannon said. "The once or twice I was in here before, he hardly noticed me."

"I don't know", Coster said and drank and put the glass down. He left his shoulders hunched and studied carefully the circles of wet on the bar near his glass.

"It's his form of getting religion, I guess", Bain said. He had intended it as a deliberate, if white, lie, but immediately wondered if it were the truth.

Gannon nodded. "Some men come into the Church while they're in prison and I suppose they're sincere enough at the time. Of course," he added hastily, aware of the scientist and lawyer near him, "more leave it when in prison."

Bain and Coster nodded moodily. In the light, noise, talk, and heavily played music of the place, they formed a sombre little island. Gannon said: "Oh, I almost forgot. I was starting to tell you when Billy came over. There was a young woman on the bus. I think her name was Bain, too. I heard someone at the Albuquerque depot—some passenger agent, I think it was—call her Mrs. Bain. I didn't know but what she might have been your wife. I had to finish reading my office, though, and I didn't speak—"

"Blonde?" Bain said. He almost choked.

"Why, yes", the priest said, startled and bewildered.

"Holy God!" Bain said and started for the door. He heard Coster laughing behind him and he saw as he strode toward it that the door had opened. In its frame stood Mrs. Senton in evening clothes, backed by a small group of regulars and strangers that included Ruth Trevelyan; all about to enter Tarale's nearest approach to slumming. Mrs. Senton's flat face moved and changed, smiling with pleasure and incredulity. In fury and in pity, Bain saw that she had mistaken his violent movement toward the door for a gesture of welcome to herself. "Why, Mr. Bain", she said. Her feet moved in tiny steps a little to one side, her body, enshawled in mink, drew in on itself. The strangers with her smiled expectantly, the regulars erased their smiles.

Bain did not hesitate. "For God's sake, get out of the way", he said. It was then, now past her and them and going into the darkness beyond the neons, that pity struck upward in him, not displacing but accompanying his passion. The poor old bitch, he kept thinking—even saying it once, as he got into the car—the poor old bitch.

The motor started heavily under his suddenly clumsy foot, and he swung the coupé sharply and impatiently twice to clear the parked cars. He could see the lights of Tarale ahead and like a child or the very young of heart he began to think and mouth paraphrases out of deep and old memory. "Come where my love lies shining", he thought. "Or dreaming", he said. "Who has beheld fair Venus in her pride", and "at the round earth's imagined corners blow your trumpets, angels, and arise, arise from death, you numberless Infinities." Donne, he knew, hadn't meant what he, Bain, could now think he had meant.

The car backfired as he braked to enter the plaza. The bus still stood before the station, and Eddie Bleese, the driver, was talking to the agent. They both looked up as Bain came out of his car, greeting him. He moved a hand in recognition. Opening the door to the station, he saw what the stickered windows had prevented his seeing clearly before, that Elva was not in the station. Rage beat through him, formless and aimless, and then he saw her coming out of the phone booth—the fair and brightly colored face between the small hat and the beaver coat, the eyes first annoyed, then changing abruptly as they saw him.

"Elva", he said.

"Oh, Spence."

The two or three other people in the station put restraint on him. He kissed his wife lightly and he noticed that she wore no scent. He said: "I didn't know you'd be here so soon", and then he said, even lower: "Let's get the hell out of here."

"Why, yes, but my bags. I checked them. I mean, didn't you get the wire?"

"No", he said. "Let's get out."

"Here", Bleese said. "I'll put them in the car for you, Spence."

"Thanks", Bain said. He had Elva outside in the cold now, and her arm in his hand seemed heavy and somehow reluctant. Bleese walked ahead of them, a heavy, middle-aged Anglo, while Bain whispered to his wife: "My God, am I glad to see you."

"But, Spence", she said. "I—"

Bleese turned to them. He wouldn't accept a tip, Bain knew, but with the slightly faked hospitality of certain western towns, would insist on meeting Elva. Bain introduced them, helping Elva into the car, and got in himself,

"This is sure some country, Mrs. Bain", Bleese was saying. He grinned.

"Oh, I've heard", Elva said. Bain thought she sounded more distracted than she should be. He started the car and told Bleese in his cowboy hat, ridiculous over the soft face, that they would see him. Starting to swing around the plaza, he felt Elva take his arm. Her pressure was at once more and less urgent than that of affection. "Spence, look", she said. "I've forgotten something."

"What?" he said. "It can't be important. All the important things you carry around with you all the time. I mean, you can't help it; you can't forget them."

"Oh, hush, Spence", she said, her smile beginning and fading as she forced it from her lips. "I mean have you a friend in town that's a doctor?"

"Why? Are you sick?"

"No, I've forgotten something."

"What?"

"You know. You don't want to have a baby."

"Oh, hell", he said. "That." His mood changed. "I thought you carried it around in your purse all the time. You know—to take care of sudden emergencies."

"Oh, you're mean, Spence", she said. "I lost the old one. When you left last summer. I mean—Oh, Spence, we're out of town. You've got to go back. Isn't there a friend that's a doctor? I mean we just can't—"

"Only Atwood", he said. "And he'd laugh too hard. I don't think the drugstores here carry them. I—"

"Oh, Spence, what are we going to do? We—"

"We're almost home", he said. "I'll start a fire to warm you."

"All right", she said, with that measured and almost prim firmness in which neither of them ever knew the exact proportion of delicate mockery. "You'll see."

"I certainly will", he said.

There was a silence between them for the few minutes it took to reach the house. Bain smiled into the darkness as he pulled up by the wall, cut the switch and lights, and turned to his wife. She felt wooden and unyielding under the heavy beaver of the coat. "I'm mad", she said, unconvincingly.

"I know," he said, "but you won't be long."

"I think you're terrible, Spence", she said. "I'm getting out."

"The door to the house is straight ahead of the door in the wall around what we call the patio. But you might stumble in the dark. You'd better wait for me." He laughed silently in his throat. She waited on the other side of the car in darkness. He put his arm around her waist and started to walk toward the house.

"My bags", she said.

"How passionate and unrestrained you are", Bain said. "You're like a child", she told him as he turned back to the car.

"I know." Sadness was with him, in the sudden manner so many thoughts, moods, and emotions had come to him lately. He would be like a child with her, but only tonight and tomorrow, probably. Then she would be common to him again, her glory a matter of relief only. Fumbling in the blackness of the car for her luggage, he felt the sadness flow through him, dominating the other things that had been in him. When he straightened up, a bag in either hand, he felt even a little weary. She moved ahead of him, visible in the starlight now, her high heels catching and wabbling on the pebbles Mirabal's children had left in the rough patio. This little physical unsureness, this unpreparedness for a world that was not hers, renewed and deepened the sadness in him. "Oh, Christ", he prayed, aimlessly and to himself.

In the cold house he put the bags down and snapped on a light.

"Electricity, eh", she said. "I didn't think you had such luxuries."

"That and a cold-water bathroom are about all." He turned from her, almost diffidently. The passion—childish, as she had said—was gone. The room—he had had the house cleaned the day before—was clean and orderly. If there were only a fire. He stooped and blew in the ashes hopefully and some of the coals glowed. Putting piñon splinters on them, he blew them into a fire, then stood larger pieces of the wood on end, leaning against the blackened clay walls of the fireplace. The flame licked along them, in the rough grooves of the split wood, and he stood up and turned to Elva. She had taken her coat off and stood with her back to him, looking at the *santo* hung over the bed. Her hat was still on her head and she held a lit cigarette.

"Take your hat off", Bain said. "Aren't you going to stay?"

"Who is the little gentleman with the pointed beard?" she said, her back still to her husband.

"Santiago", he told her. "The Spanish Saint James. That's a pretty good *santo*. I got it in Vadito this summer. I'm going to give it to the collection back at the University."

"Saint James", she said. "That would be your patron saint, if you believed in such things."

Well, well, he thought, my sins are finding me out already. He said: "There's a lot to talk about", and sighed and came close to her back and put his hands on her breasts.

"No", she said. "I think you're very mean. You wouldn't call your doctor friend and I told you." Her own hands moved upward to his, engaged the fingers, and pulled gently on them.

"Oh, hell, Elva", Bain said. "You're just being coy."

"No, I'm not. I'm just protecting myself—and even yourself—from you. You wouldn't think much of me or my intelligence if I gave in now."

"Why, I think you have a wonderful intelligence", he said.

"Spence!" she said. "Stop. Don't be a fool." Something like mirth accompanied her anger, so that it was the anger that appeared simulated.

"It's too late to stop", Bain said and picked his wife up. Still holding her like that, he put the light out and stood still for a moment, conscious of the firelight on them. "Like a movie", he said.

She lay quietly, too quietly, in his arms as he stood there. She felt heavy to him. "You do love me, don't you?" he said.

"Yes, Spence. Very much."

†

It was only a little later, while they lay quietly together, that Bain began to weep and Elva asked him why.

"I don't know." He shook his head. "I just started to think of that . . . baby you carried for a while."

After a moment, she said: "Yes?"

"I began to feel terribly sorry for it. It was a boy . . . and you know how a fetus is, all head and belly and genitals. And I began to think of the boy dead there, so small . . . and, oh, Christ, I don't know, I felt like my brother or someone close to me had died. I just don't know." He sobbed again.

After a moment, she said: "I don't know, either, Spence. It's more than that, though. If you were religious, it—I suppose Schapper or someone like that would think it meant you had a homosexual tendency or—"

"Do you?"

"My God, no. Not after just now." She laughed. "You're very nice, Spence", she said, and held him closer to her, but she could not console him and he shook his head again, and again wept.

†

The knocking which so often awakened Bain, awakened Elva one morning. Out of half-sleep she groped twice for her husband's body, feeling two fears, the first at his absence, then remembering he had gone early into the mountains for the day, another fear at being here alone in the near-dark. The knocking persisted, tentative and itself almost fearful so that her own fear left her. She tried to settle back to sleep and the warmth of the blankets, but the knocking came again. Why in the dark? she wondered, and turned to look at the clock. It was almost nine. Knowing how much storm the darkness might presage, she grew fearful again for her husband in the mountains and rose and shivering put on her robe.

Looking out a window before opening the door, she saw a girl waiting. Unease she did not try to give a specific name, filled her. Certainly the girl did not seem cheap. The faded skirt, the dark shawl over the head were hardly the apparel of wantonness. Opening the door, Elva said: "Yes?"

The girl seemed surprised to see her, "Spance", she said. "He's not here?"

"Why, no. Mr. Bain is away. Is there something you want?"

"My father, he——"

"Who's your father?"

"José Mirabal. He——"

"Oh, you mean my husband's assistant? Come in."

The girl entered and followed Elva into the bedroom-sitting-room. "Sit down", Elva said. "You've had your breakfast?"

"Oh, yes, ma'am. My father just said before he went away the other day to ask Spance for some money if I needed it for the house."

Elva looked out the window, then decided to light a cigarette. "But why did he say that?"

The girl grew puzzled. Still holding the shawl with one hand under her chin, she looked sidewise. "Well, my father he works for Spance."

"Yes, I know."

"Well, Spance, he pays my father five dollars a week."

"Oh, I see. . . . And you want some money in advance, is that it?"

The girl drew a little breath. "No ... it's like for last week, the week before the last. I mean——" She stopped, confused over something, or perhaps embarrassed.

Elva felt herself color. "Spence shouldn't be so careless", she said, then regretted saying it. She stood up. "How much does my husband owe your father?"

"I don't know. Two weeks, I guess. I'm sorry. If—"

Looking in her purse, Elva waited for the girl to continue speaking. When she realized that she was enjoying any embarrassment the girl might feel, she herself felt a sudden, sharp, and almost unaccountable shame. Starting to raise her head and turn to the girl in some vague sort of apology, she noticed first that she had only some change and a dollar bill in her purse. So she paused, as in midair, realizing that whatever little gesture of apology or kindness she had been going to make to the girl would be empty now that there was no money to give her, for who would not think, under the circumstances, that kindness was not being substituted for the money?

So, her coldness again on her, Elva turned back to the girl. "I seem to be out of cash. Could you get a check cashed if I gave you one?"

"I don't know", the girl said. "Maybe. It's all right, though."

"What's all right?" Elva said.

"About the money. I guess we could wait until Spance come home." She started to rise.

"What did you want it for?" Elva said. "Sit down."

"I was going to the grocery store."

Again Elva felt the faint color rise: any fool would have known, she told herself.

"But you ought to be able to charge it", she said.

The girl also colored but did not move other than to draw down her upper lip.

Elva felt exasperated, then realized the exasperation was with herself.

"We'll work something out", she said. "I'll walk in to town with you or perhaps Spence has some provisions in."

They sat there for a moment, looking away from each other, Lupe at the floor, Elva at the gray window. She wished the girl would go. On the edge of consciousness she sensed in dismay, in fear, an avoidance of obligation that had been there a long time, that underlay much of her existence and her friends', that informed with almost fantastic subtlety the abortions, the adulteries, the lies.

She said, as rising from sleep, from dream: "I'll dress. And then we'll go in to town."

"It's all right", the girl said.

If it was all right, why didn't she go, Elva thought again. "Do you go to school?"

The girl nodded once. "Not always. Those kids, you know—I got to watch them when my father's away."

Elva, too, nodded, distracted suddenly. "You must be alone a good deal of the time, then?"

"Only those kids", the girl said.

"Do you see my husband much?" Elva felt her mouth twist as she spoke.

"Spance, you mean? No. He's away a lot like my father. Sometimes they go away together." The girl had missed whatever she had implied, Elva saw. How could anyone that old—fifteen? sixteen?—be so stupid.

"I see", Elva said. She rubbed out her cigarette slowly. She could not look at the girl and a little, heavy silence grew between them.

"I am going to be baptized soon", Lupe said.

"Oh, yes. Aren't you rather old?"

The girl nodded dumbly. "My father, he wouldn't let my mother get me baptized when I was a baby."

"Why was that?"

The girl's eyes seemed to lose focus. She's going to cry, Elva thought. But the girl didn't. "Oh, never mind", Elva said. "I'm very glad you're finally going to be baptized."

"I'd like you to be my godmother", the girl said. "If you were a Catholic, I mean", she added quickly, seeing Elva's face go blank.

Elva found herself breathless and unaccountably shaken. "Well," she said, "that's very nice of you. What gave you that idea?"

The girl looked at the floor and wet her lips. "I don't know", she said, indistinctly.

"Well," Elva said, "this isn't getting you anything to eat, is it? You just wait here while I dress, and then we'll go in to town together."

But when Elva came back into the kitchen, the girl was gone. Annoyed, Elva did not bother to go to Mirabal's house after her.

8

SNOW FELL also the morning of the day before Christmas. They could see it drifting down from where they lay in the cold bedroom. "You must be pretty lonely here at times", Elva said.

"I miss you", he said. "Outside of that, it's not so bad. No one you can talk to ... but in fieldwork that's the way it is, usually."

"I meant just living here in this place", she said. "Adobe can be pretty bad in certain lights, and if no one cleans the house regularly—I mean it must affect your viewpoint in the work."

"I can't live in a hotel", he said, "if I'm going to work closely with a native people."

"No," she said, "but I wonder how much the depressing effect of their quarters on anthropologists working in the field, is reflected in their notes. I mean—"

"Of course, it's not like your nest in Hollywood. That's the contrast—"

"Spence!" she said. He could feel the bed move as she stiffened. "That's the second time you've made that crack. And I won't have it."

"Oh, all right", he said. "You're losing your sense of humor, though. On the other hand, who else but me would think as good-looking a gal as you had such a soft job in Hollywood without having earned it in the bed."

"I'll give it up", Elva said. "I mean it, Spence. If you—"

"Oh, hell", he said. "I wasn't serious." He turned to her, seeing she had begun to cry, but she sat up and put her

legs over the edge of the bed. He put a hand out to her
bare shoulder but she was already rising. "Heavens, it's cold
in here, Spence. Isn't there any way of keeping a fire going
all night?"

"When in Rome", he said.

"You justify everything by that", she said. "I think you
could allow yourself some kind of stove."

"We could leave the electric plate on all night."

"Oh, you're very funny", she said. Her nakedness, as she
moved hurriedly out of her nightgown and reached for her
clothing, interested but did not greatly attract him.

"Anyhow, you've been here a week now," he said, "and
you ought to be used to the cold."

"Like you're used to me", she said. Her smile was almost
imperceptible and he wondered how she had known he
had been thinking about that, too.

He sat up, feeling not unpleasantly the cold on his naked
skin. Elva was putting on a gray wool dress with red pip-
ing. As it dropped about her, her eyes avoided his, and he
knew she was ashamed of her little outburst.

"What did Atwood say when you went down to get your
what-do-you-call-it the other day? I bet he died laughing."

"Why, not at all", she said. "He was very polite."

"I bet he wondered what you did without one the first
night."

"I don't know", Elva said, thoughtfully. "I just hope nothing went wrong." Her back was to him as she spoke and
she moved into the next room where he could hear her at
the electric plate. He got out of bed and put on his shorts,
bending to peer out through the window at the snow. Mirabal was in the patio, sitting on the chopping block, from
which he had swept the light, wet snow. It lay nearby, breaking the even whiteness of the new snow on the ground,

and Mirabal, the uneasy red markings on his face clearer than usual, stared quietly at the broken white.

Why, he's crazy, Bain thought. Their diffidence could still catch him off guard and amaze him. It was clear to him suddenly: he hadn't paid Mirabal in two weeks and the man needed the money. But he wouldn't knock on the door while Bain and his wife were presumably sleeping: he would wait in the snow until they arose from sleep and found him there.

Still clad only in his shorts, Bain went to the outside door and opened it. "What's the matter with you, José? You trying to catch pneumonia?"

"Just looking around, Spance", the diabolist said.

"Come in, for God's sake."

Mirabal came slowly toward the house. In it, he removed his hat, bowing slightly and almost formally to Elva, whom he had met once, two days before.

"How are you, José? Well, this morning?" she said.

"Yes, ma'am", he said. His diffidence toward Elva puzzled Bain.

"Sit down", Bain said. "We'll give you some coffee right away. You think it's going to stop snowing?"

Mirabal shook his head gravely. "Snow all day, Spance", he said. Bain realized that the question was something of a professional one for Mirabal.

"They won't call off the dance at the pueblo, will they?" Bain asked from the bedroom as he dressed.

"If it snows a lot, they will."

"Do you like your coffee strong, José?" Elva said.

"Yes, ma'am", he said.

"I do, too", she said, as if making mock-thoughtful conversation with a child. Bain did not like it, even in her; it was a thing that had to be overcome in his own work, although some were never able to overcome it. He wondered if Schapper was ever able to eliminate this constant, curious tendency—a subtle form of pride?—to patronize; if Schapper wasn't able to, his success was incredible.

"Would you mind making a fire, José," Bain called out, "while I dress."

"Sure, Spance."

The Spaniard was on one knee before the fireplace when Bain came out. Bain grinned, seeing the picture of Saint James above Mirabal and a little to one side. In Spanish, he said: "You're not kneeling before Santiago, are you, José?"

Mirabal rose stiffly. "Not me", he said. "You wanted a fire."

"I don't like this talking in Spanish over my head", Elva said. "I'm a big girl and I can stand to hear anything."

"Oh, you're a fine big girl", Bain said. He was surprised at the depth of his feeling as he said it. He had intended lightness, even a kind of mockery. In Spanish again and to do away with his sudden feeling of unease, he said: "I've got some money for you, José. Right after breakfast."

"I meant to tell you—" Elva began.

Mirabal shrugged as if it didn't matter.

"Now both of you sit down", Elva said. "What a time to be eating breakfast."

"Spance didn't get up to go to Mass this morning", Mirabal said.

"Why, no", Elva said. "Why should he? Although," she went on, not seeing her husband's stricken face, "I suppose he has to occasionally in the work."

"Why, didn't you hear?" Mirabal said, grinning brokenly. "You husband, he become a Catholic."

"He what?" Elva said.

"Goddam it, José", Bain said. "Why don't you keep still?"

Mirabal laughed quietly and Bain wondered why the man had said it.

"I mean, why the secrecy?" Elva said. "If you want to lose your mind in your old age, that's all right with me." It wasn't all right with her, of course. It was annoying and even frightening to her, Bain could see.

He said, "It's not that simple. It's the work. I mean I had to for the work."

"Oh," she said, "that's different. I was wondering. But why didn't you tell me?"

Well, why hadn't he? Bain asked himself. It was quite a question. "I didn't think you'd be particularly interested", he said, knowing immediately how weak it sounded. "I mean we had other things on our minds", knowing, also immediately, that his own and Elva's satiation had robbed those words of any rough humor they might possess.

"We always have other things on our minds", Elva said, turning to the electric plate, the cigarette in her lips almost muffling her words. It took Bain a moment to be sure of what she had said, and he could wonder, reluctant and amazed, if she meant what he thought she meant.

It could seem to him that not only he but Elva were saying things, truths, neither of them liked nor even recognized except as something different from, if not opposed to, whatever it was they themselves lived by or for. It was unreal, he thought, but knew that was like saying torture was annoying. Nunes, he thought, illogically; Nunes and Gannon and their gibberings about Grace. But immediately he knew it was not they: they had been, each separately and in his own way, diffident. What he knew about the Church, about Grace, he had read, reluctantly and only because of the peculiar nature of the work.

He had, for an unmeasurable time, been oblivious to the others in the room with him. Now he saw that Mirabal had finished his coffee and risen, disturbing Bain's own thought, and that the cup on the arm of his own chair had stopped steaming.

"See you later, huh?" Mirabal said.

"Wait a minute." Bain moved toward the unused kitchen and the door leading outside, fumbling in his pockets as he moved. He stopped to one side of the door and gave Mirabal two five-dollar bills. "I'm sorry I held you up on this, José."

"That's okay. See you later, huh?"

"Sure", Bain said. He opened the door for Mirabal to go out, and as the man moved past him saw that the weather had undergone one of those swift changes peculiar to the country here. The sun was shining strongly, the snow melting already, except in the shadow.

Grinning, Bain closed the door behind Mirabal's back. In the room where Elva sat, he said: "Stand up."

"What for?"

"Never mind. Get up."

She rose, indicating she might be favoring an idiot, and he put his arms around her and kissed her, then released her. She had not responded. "What was that for?"

"I don't know", he said. "Just let it go."

"Dear, dear", she said, sitting down.

He was embarrassed, but it could not destroy the faint, steady flow of happiness or benevolence in him. He said: "After the dance this afternoon, you want to go to Mrs. Senton's? We were asked."

"I don't care", his wife said. "What's she like? Do you want to go?"

"Not very much", he said. "I thought you might want to see what there is of literate people around here. Although,

God knows—" He stopped talking, thinking amazingly that it was useless or something to heap one more uncharity on Mrs. Senton's head. Or his own soul.

He found that he had shaken his head as though to clear it from a blow.

"God knows what?" Elva said.

"I don't know", he said. "If you want to go, we'll go."

"All right."

He picked up a notebook. He remembered his medicine, but he couldn't be bothered to get it. Why Elva didn't question him more closely about his pretended conversion, he did not know. In something he did not quite recognize as horror, in a dismay at once bottomless and translucent, he saw that she had accepted his own casual explanation as a complete justification of what he had done.

"The sun's out", Elva said. "Mirabal was a bad prophet."

Bain did not look up from the book. "I was thinking that", he said, gravely.

†

In the late afternoon they drove west to the pueblo. Clouds were overhead again, but a clear space in them to the west, much like the mouth of a cave, let the last sunlight through so that it made the usual change and color in the mountains over their shoulder.

"I feel excited", Elva said. "Don't you?"

"I've seen them dance before", he said. "Although I think this tonight will be one of the really good ones, maybe the best, the Matachines. God, it's a wonderful, stately thing."

"Stately?"

"Well, oddly enough," he told her, "it's a dance *they* borrowed from the Spaniards, and the Spaniards in turn seem to have gotten it from the Basques."

She nodded, preoccupied, cigarette smoke drifting about her face. Ahead, Bain could see the brownish mass of the pueblo rising above its haystacks and corrals. Cars had already gathered in a field to the north, and an Indian in a pink-and-white mail-order blanket was going from car to car collecting a quarter from each one. Bain started to say something scornful but the now recurring sadness moved through him like a wave.

"There's Mark Coster", he said to Elva. "He's the best lawyer in town."

"Uh huh. I suppose Mrs. Senton will be here, too."

"Usually", he said. "If it's not too cold." He parked the car and the Indian came over and put his head in.

"Hello, kid", the Indian said.

"What do you want, a quarter?"

The Indian nodded once, squinting in a kind of grin. "What's it going to be today?" Bain asked. "*Los Matachines?*"

"May be", the Indian said.

They got out of the car and Coster came over with his wife to meet them. "Just in time, Spence", the lawyer said. "Father Gannon is saying Vespers or something at the chapel before the dance." Coster's smile faded as he saw Bain's face become blank and the eyes evade his.

"I don't think you've met my wife", Bain said.

"No", Coster said. They introduced their wives and Bain stared a little at Mrs. Coster, a still pretty, slightly faded woman about forty. She was rarely seen in public although she was part of the legend her husband had become in the north of the state. She rode with him on his sometimes risky investigations in the mountains, and for a long time she had carried a pearl-handled .22, empty, in her purse. She said: "I hope it doesn't get too cold", her voice thin and even delicate. She had two children.

Now, thinking of these children, thinking of the small legend, of other things even more unrelated, even nameless— like Coster's sickness, like Coster's cold homage to the Church—Bain could see a devotion and a love in the wife, both largely ineffable, that amazed him and shamed both himself and Elva. Bain said, "You want to go over to the chapel, Elva?"

"All right. If we don't miss any of the dancing."

"Oh, you won't", Coster said. "It's timed so that Vespers are over just about the time the dancers come out of the kiva."

"That's thoughtful, isn't it?" Elva said. Bain saw that she was embarrassed without knowing why, without any of them quite knowing why.

They walked toward the mud chapel. The doors were thrown open in spite of the cold, and the crowd, mostly Indians, had filled the place until a few of them had to stand outside. But you could see over their heads and Gannon, in cassock and white, lace surplice, kneeling before the altar.

Standing in back of the crowd, a little space outside the chapel, Bain could see easily over the heads of the shorter Indians. Gannon prayed in what Bain thought of as the priest's "official voice", a sonorous, rhythmical, but undistinguished utterance—like the repeatings of a record on a phonograph—of what Bain was sure were now platitudes to Gannon. His own attention held, but once his eyes moved to where Elva stood near him. The skin of her face had been stung to a lovely freshness by the cold, and against the dark faces near it, had some of the quality of a cameo; a curious one, though, for instead of the placidity of expression such carvings have, Elva's face was pained slightly, as though she were being subjected unwillingly to a bad smell. Dismay for nothing he could name struck upward through Bain like nausea or hurt. For a moment he felt like an animal, bewildered for no reason it could understand. He had, clearest of any thought, though not very clear, an unreasonable feeling that Elva, too, was the enemy ... although why she was or what the enemy might be, he did not know.

Gannon had finished on a note Bain did not hear. The Indians about him had started to turn and come out past Bain and his wife. Bain's thought was changed by this and by the first sound of the string music on the brokenly blowing wind. His heart lifted strangely and even wildly. It was the Matachines. They were going to dance the Matachines as he had hoped they would.

He took Elva's arm to help her through the first of the dusk toward where the crowd was gathering in two thick, short lines with the masked dancers between. On the darkening air the string music rose, thin and brave, breaking the heart. "It's the Matachines", he said to Elva. "Let's hurry."

"You sound like a child", she said, but let him force her into a half-run.

In a kind of phalanx or oblong of two lines, six men deep, the dancers moved, grave and stately, the masks hiding all but the front of their faces, little three-pointed objects, like shaftless tridents, carried delicately in one hand. Bright ribbons fell down their backs over the spangled shirts.

Bain hurried his wife to the front end of one of the lines which enclosed and kept pace with the dancers. Gravely the dancers moved, in ranks serried and exact, their faces grave, although the clowns called Delight Makers gibbered and feinted in and out of the phalanx. The dancers raised their knees in a kind of skipping hop which somehow contained solemnity, too, and after an advance, retreated almost imperceptibly, while the Delight Makers grimaced and yelped like animals. But always, in the general motion of the group, the dancers moved forward.

They moved past Bain and Elva now, turning solemnly in the brief retreat, then resuming the grave skip forward, the little trefoils in their hands held still and as though they or their stillness were precious. Three Spaniards followed them, playing two violins and a guitar. Bain knew one of the Spaniards as a Hermano de Luz, the others by sight only.

Twice, behind the line Bain was in, other, younger Indians fired rifles into the air. And now another fat Indian had dragged over toward the crowd a torch fully eighteen feet long made of pine splints bound together, and was trying to light it in the wind. "Hey, kid," he said to Bain, now at the end of the line, "you got any matches?"

Reaching into his pocket, Bain heard Atwood laugh near him and turned to see the doctor walking past with his son perched on one shoulder. "Give him your cigarette lighter, Spence", the doctor said. "Nothing like the modern touch in these little festivities."

"Okay, sport", Bain said to the doctor. He gave the Indian a paper of matches and moved after the dancers. Elva was ahead of him, just back of Atwood and the child. Beyond the dancers, beyond the farther line of the crowd, another torch, flaring, was raised. Against its light in the darker dusk, they could see it had begun to snow in small flakes and then felt the snow, which had been falling steadily for minutes.

Bain hurried after Elva, running. "Come on", he said, and she ran, awkwardly, with him. They got to the front end of the line again in time for one of the pauses when the dance did not move forward but the movements took place over one piece of ground for perhaps as long as a minute.

What Bain noticed now, although never before, was the intense, strained gravity of the dancers' faces; and he wondered if it came from their own feeling about the dance or from their annoyance with the crowd, now mostly tourists, who pressed on the ranks of the dancers in spite of two or three older Indians who tried to act as policemen. The tourists were the real distraction, the Delight Makers the symbolic one. Gravely the dancers turned from both, making sometimes the movements of the dance the occasion or excuse for the turning. It was an almost incredible exhibition of courtesy and discipline.

The rifles of the young bucks sounded more often now, and Bain wondered if the tourists knew of the more than passing danger from the deer guns of those of the Indians who had been drinking. But he himself forgot about it as he saw the snow falling against the raised torches and heard the string music on the turning wind. So, gravely under snow and to the violin music, the dancers moved and turned. It was the gravity, he thought, the grave stateliness in the midst of tourists and under snow, the heeding of the music and the discipline under snow and between the foulnesses of an alien, ignorant, and scorning people. "Holy God", Bain said to his wife. "Did you ever see anything like it?"

"It's very lovely", she said, and he supposed it was that, too. In the opposite line of the crowd he saw Teran in the shifting and tenuous light, and it reminded him he had work to do, that he had not yet established himself with the Hermanos. After Elva went back he had work to do.

In their round of the pueblo, the dancers had reached the place where they would stop. So long had they danced, so strictly held to the exact and arduous pattern, that there existed in many of those who watched, the impression of never-endingness. So that now as the dance stopped abruptly, the serried ranks dissolved, the torches lowered, the music died on the air, the costumed dancers walked away with bowed head, stooped vaguely in weariness—there was a kind of astonishment in Bain and many of the others. The rifles only continued to sound, and Elva said: "It's as if there was a hollow in the night or the air, isn't it?"

Bain nodded, pleased with his wife again. "You still want to go to the old lady's?" he said.

"Why not?"

"I know", he said, nodding with emphasis. "That same question and that same answer have ruined lives around here. People are so goddamed bored or so curious or so avid that they'll go there. She's built a reputation strictly out of the boredom and curiosity of people."

"Oh, Spence", Elva said. "You're being very silly."

"All right," he said, gloomily, "you'll see."

"You're just tired", she said, taking his arm.

"Maybe you're right", he said.

†

They were all regulars at Mrs. Senton's when Bain got there. Mrs. Trevelyan was there, too, but she was a regular by now, Bain decided. They seemed friendlier than ever before toward him, although he was amazed—why amazed, he never knew—to see that their warmth did not extend to Elva. Now Elva was the outlander and he—his uneasiness suddenly increasing—one of them.

"So nice to see you", Mrs. Senton was saying. "So good of you to come." Elva was trying to say something, but Mrs. Senton went on. "Dear Spencer," she said, "he's so

busy with the work, but he finds time to come to my little
gatherings."

"Oh, yes", Elva said. Her small, fixed smile indicated to
Bain her awareness of the hostility. But he knew she must
be puzzled by it, as any normal person must be puzzled
and perhaps alarmed that there should appear to be such a
bond between himself and the others. Wondering, *do they
really expect me to recognize a relationship with them that I do
not share with her?* in a curious mingling of anger and love
and a kind of grief, Bain said: "This is only the second or
third time. I—"

Mrs. Senton looked at him, all amenities dissolved from
her face, the face blank again and characteristically hopeless. Instead of the anger he had expected, there was only
despair in Mrs. Senton. Pity for her came to him again,
amazing and horrifying him.

Mrs. Senton said: "We'll eat soon. Just two or three more
people coming. Intimate acquaintances. We—" She turned
her head, "Oh, Ruth", then turned back. "I won't bother
with general introductions. But this is Mrs. Trevelyan.
Spencer's wife, Ruth, Mrs. Bain."

Mrs. Trevelyan smiled broadly with her mouth. "So glad
to see you. Spence has spoken so much."

Bain never heard his wife's reply. In a continuous but
now no longer nameless horror, he saw that Mrs. Senton
had stepped back a little and was surveying the three of
them with a quiet smile, knowing and pleased, as if the
first step in a complicated series of operations had now been
completed to her satisfaction. He thought: she must be thinking "trio" or "triangle" or "triplicate" or some other god-
damned word that gives her her kind of pleasure. For the
first time he realized clearly how strange the woman's pleasures must be (like sins the Church had never named),

for now the eyes had lighted, not unlike some large, semi-precious stones, and in the still somewhat blank face, shone with pleasure and fascination.

Mrs. Trevelyan was responding to her patron's surveillance with something close to fervor. Her lips tried to move in the kind of rich and knowing smile that women with riper bodies and lovelier faces might use. There was a sort of nameless obscenity involved, as if a cat were trying to sing, and Bain was relieved to have Mrs. Trevelyan say: "The work is going awfully well. I'm half-finished with the book."

"Good", Bain said.

Elva's face was quite expressionless. This apparently enraged or excited Mrs. Senton again, for she abandoned the role of spectator and again became a participant. Coming closer to the three, she said: "How do you feel about your husband's entering the Catholic Church, Mrs. Bain?"

Feeling despair again, Bain could still be astonished at this incredible accuracy the woman sometimes showed. Nothing else she could say would have confused him more.

"Why, I think that's one of the few things that's strictly his business", Elva said.

Mrs. Senton smiled tolerantly. "But how quaint, my dear."

"Oh, balls", Bain said.

Seeing her patron at a slight disadvantage, Mrs. Trevelyan said: "You know my daughter is here, Spence. I'm going to show her to all of you before she goes to bed." She smiled broadly again and Bain thought that even she had unerringly spotted a weakness of Elva's.

More people, including Atwood and his wife, were entering the room. The doctor gestured in greeting to Bain, and Mrs. Senton, turning, again thought it was to herself. She grinned, thinking Atwood's partly concealed dislike of her had passed. Ruth Trevelyan left the room, and Bain, turning to his wife, said, "Coming here was your idea."

"You want to go?"

"It's too late to eat out", he said. In the little silence that fell between them, in which they evaded each other's eyes, he knew that Elva was thinking of the same thing he was: that what might be called Mrs. Senton's influence was largely based on such little things as people's not wanting to leave her house at nine o'clock because the restaurants were closed; and the incredibly subtle sloth which every person carried in him led them to avoid going home and preparing a meal. He wondered if the Devil used such trivialities. But then he didn't believe in the Devil.

Atwood and his wife, a quiet, darkly pretty and tired young woman, came across the room toward Bain. "Well," the doctor said, "here we are again, all gathered like flies around the honeypot."

"Not me", Bain said. "I may be a fly, but this isn't my pot."

"No", Atwood said, seriously. "But that makes you almost the sole exception here. The only one here that it isn't that for."

"Charles' English is atrocious", Mrs. Atwood said. "I think he gets it from trying to talk Spanish to his patients."

"Spence's language is atrocious, too", Elva said. "But not in the same way. Spence has no excuse."

"I get that way from talking to people, too", Bain said. "But not the Spaniards."

They laughed conventionally and just then Mrs. Trevelyan came into the room bent slightly as she poised over a three-year-old child in a white party dress, who walked with a dainty uncertainty ahead of her mother. The regulars in the room began to smile and even move with a kind of automatic similarity: obviously the child was a favorite of Mrs. Senton's. There was, too, an element of fright in their actions. None of them had ever had any children: none of them ever would. But they crowded dutifully around this one.

More slowly and with their own unease, Bain and Atwood and their wives approached the group. They had to stand on its outer edge. Already, before they had reached it, the little girl was being put through her paces, while Mrs. Senton smiled broadly down.

"—And the little progressive school Marsha's so good to send Sylvia to, just thinks of *everything*", Mrs. Trevelyan said. She grinned coyly up from where she stooped and Mrs. Senton grinned benignly down. "See", Mrs. Trevelyan went on. She put her hand on the child's knee, moving the hand slowly up the thigh. The child brushed the hand away quite sharply. Smiling, Mrs. Trevelyan repeated the process and the child reacted in the same way.

In the fascinated silence that had fallen among the regulars, Mrs. Trevelyan's voice sounded almost shrill. "You see, they teach them everything. How to protect themselves."

"It's too bad someone didn't teach the kid's old lady the same thing", Atwood whispered to Bain. But the silence of the regulars, broken whenever Mrs. Senton finished speaking, was quickly resumed, in the manner of the house, just before Atwood spoke. So that they all heard the whisper and each face took on its own kind of bewilderment: believing sedulously in sexual anarchy, talking forever of it privately, but now dismayed—why, they might never know—by what Atwood had said.

"Dinner", Mrs. Senton said, suddenly imperious. So had she quelled other uprisings. "We must eat." She clapped her hands twice, but it was several moments before some

Spanish girls came into the room, carrying dishes. The group moved slightly apart as they waited.

"I don't imagine you're very popular in these parts", Elva said to the doctor.

"Gosh," Atwood said, "I didn't think they were going to hear. The old lady is my best customer."

Standing a little apart, Bain was not surprised when Mrs. Senton came up to him and in a normal tone, heard by anyone fairly near, said: "Your wife—why is she so cold? Ask your wife why she is so cold."

Bain turned to face the woman fully and in an anger so icy that it amazed him. "She's not cold to me", he said.

He had thought of himself as being on the defensive and of his reply as weak, so that he was surprised to hear her say: "Well—" and repeat the word and then, as though thinking of something she had forgotten, turn and hurry away.

The brittle case that held his anger cracked and he felt his knees begin to shake. The adrenals were pumping in him as before a race or a fight. He became slightly sick to his stomach and, turning to his wife, said: "Let's get the hell out of here."

"Whatever you say."

"I'd go with you," Atwood said, "but—"

"I know", Bain told him, but got no satisfaction from the doctor's stricken face. Walking toward the door, his wife's subtle odor telling him she was close to him, he wondered what the old lady's hold on Atwood might be. Merely being Atwood's patient did not seem enough to keep the doctor at heel. And yet, Bain remembered, he himself had once felt constrained to pass a girl student in his course because he knew she was having a brief affair with Schapper.

Outside in the dark it was windless but quite cold. He felt immediately better. "Did you *hear* that old bitch?" he said.

"I heard her, all right. That was the idea, that I should hear her."

They walked a little way through the dead garden and without speaking Bain stopped. "Come here", he said. She came into his arms and he kissed her, so violently that he could feel her teeth through the flesh of her upper lip. It was a gesture of defiance and of a rage he had not known since he was a boy. "I love you", he said.

Elva nodded against him.

"That dirty old bitch", he said, and took Elva by the shoulders and shook her. "Well, say it", he said.

"She is one."

"What are you crying for?"

"I *am* cold and she knows it."

"Like hell", he said. "Even if you were, look at that dried-out Trevelyan thing. What am I supposed to do—toss you over and play with her?"

Elva took his arm and made him begin to walk again. "Oh, you're very nice", she said, her voice still a little broken.

As they walked he felt a kind of nobility on him, never experienced before in his adult life, and ridiculously like that which he had felt after victory in some high school game of his youth.

In the darkness, he heard someone approaching them on the gravelled walk, from the direction of the entrance outside which the cars were parked. Bain drew his wife into the deeper shadow of the patio wall. Gannon walked past them; outlined against the sky, it was easy to recognize the tailor-made chesterfield, the expensive homburg hat. After the priest had gone, they resumed their walking toward the car. Elva asked who had passed them.

"Father Gannon. He baptized me." Bain realized that a little laugh should have accompanied his last words, to set them off, give them their true value. But he hadn't laughed.

After another silence and just as he started to open the car door, Elva said: "Spence—"

"Yes?"

"Sometimes I think maybe you really went into the Church." Her voice was low and what might have been called humble.

"Don't be a damn fool", he said, rather unpleasantly. Then, repenting a little, slapped her on the buttocks as she got into the car.

9

ELVA HAD BEEN GONE almost a week, and Bain sat once more in the littered and dirty room in which he lived most of the time that the weather was cold. He was still experiencing one of his rare spells of physical well-being. It had begun imperceptibly shortly before Elva left and had continued longer than usual. He had made notes during most of it, and lately had begun to grow alarmed that this bodily sanguinity might give to his notes an optimism or gentleness that was false.

Now, he wrote:

> Most of them die intestate and the farms are usually divided among the several children, with the result that immediately or eventually the individual pieces become of little value to the owner, even should he want to pursue the difficult farming of the country. These small pieces of land are eventually sold for two or three hundred dollars, which goes to pay debts or is squandered. Thus, particularly in the back country, there is a group of young people who literally have nothing to do. There are few local industries other than mining, and for some reason or reasons—perhaps an actual love of the country—many do not leave to work in the cities or as sheepherders in Wyoming. The resulting longterm idleness is responsible, along with their Latin blood and enforced winter seclusion, for the more than average amount of killings, venereal disease, and petty thievery.

He paused, feeling rather pontifical, and then went on:

> Sporadic but actually increasing attempts to remedy this and other attendant or resulting evils are being made by

the state or national governments and by groups of indi-
viduals. Even the Church has sanctioned a few such
attempts at co-ops or the like.

He stopped writing and smiled; the last sentence had been
written without conscious thought. "Out of the fullness of
the heart, the mouth speaketh", he thought. He felt much—
the word was his own—safer. He felt relieved. Putting his
pencil down, he thought that he had done enough here for
the day; he would go skiing, perhaps even see Teran on the
way to the run. And he thought of Elva and her concern as
he said good-bye to her at Albuquerque. She had put her
arms up around his neck briefly and with surprising strength
in the crowded station and said: "Honest, Spence, you don't
believe in that, do you? The Church, I mean?"

"Why, hell no", he had said. "What makes you think
that?"

Instead of answering him, she had kissed him, trembling
a little against him, but whether from passion or something
else he could not be sure. Bain himself was always affected
profoundly by partings, and had grown sullen that desire
should come to him so strongly at that time and in that
place. "You worry about the damndest things", he said, when
she didn't answer him. Her eyes, as they turned from him
to follow the porter to the plane, were wide and turned in
the gesture called walleyed, perhaps with fright.

Bain did not know why he should think of this incident
now, as opposed, say, to the usual thoughts of a husband
separated from his wife. Perhaps some law of opposites jux-
taposed it in his mind to his random decision to see Teran.
But for weeks he had been going to talk to Teran. Yesterday, Sunday, he had seen the man at Mass in Ranchos but
had somehow missed him after the service.

†

Teran's farm lay on the road to the ski run. It was not untypical of the farms of the place—the roughly fenced fields,
the stacks of deeply golden straw, canvas-topped; the low
house, from some angles difficult to see, for like many adobe
houses it seemed to cling to and be still a part of the earth.
There was no activity near it as Bain drove into the yard,
only two or three horses moving slowly from one scant
clump of the last grass to another. Ice, frozen solid at night
in the irrigation ditches, was porous now in the sun; but in
shade the cold was uncomfortable. Standing in shade as he
knocked on the door and waited, Bain felt the chill, but
some nostalgia for this way of life seized him with unaccountable sharpness. He recognized it for what it was, an ata-
vism, much longer and deeper than his dim memory of his
grandfather, who had farmed near Columbus, Ohio.

Teran's wife answered the door. She was a quiet woman
with good eyes, her body made solid but not shapeless by
her four children. Bain had met her once, and now she was
pleasant and civil, but no more. (He had noticed lately, with
vague alarm, that he had come to half-expect the frequent
and more or less vague subservience that their economic
state imposed on many of the Spaniards.) Her husband was
not in, she said; she did not know just where he was, but
he would be back for supper.

Perhaps he would return later, Bain said. He found that
he was both embarrassed and disposed to linger for a
moment. He saw in Teran's wife the same quality he had
seen in the postmaster's wife at Trampas: an assurance and
blunt spiritual solidity—as though God were literally and
visibly at their right hand—that neither he nor Elva—nor
indeed very many people at all—possessed.

"Lent will be early this year", he said in Spanish. "I suppose Pedro is busy with the affairs of the Brotherhood?" He knew it was a mistake even before she said she knew nothing about the affairs of the Brotherhood.

As he stood there, fumbling although he neither moved nor spoke, he saw her scorn for him become pity, and he turned and went away.

His spirits picked up quickly as he drove to the ski run. Skiing now and fishing in the summer were the last pleasures of their kind to interest him. There were not many things in which someone like himself could lose thought completely, but the quick-dropping, the slowly looping motion over snow was one of them. He enjoyed, more than he admitted, the bird-motion, as though the body ran ahead then of thought, was only caught again by thought at the base of the run.

Passing it on the way to the parking space, he saw there were not many people on the run; this pleased him inordinately, for he was bothered by crowds and liked to ski as solitary as possible; the tow was all that made him use the public run here. His mounting pleasure or joy was diluted by his seeing, as he got out of the car, Mrs. Trevelyan's red ski jacket on the slope. He saw, then, the McGavers' car, and wondered how many of the regulars were here.

His joy almost gone, he strapped on his skis and pushed himself over to the tow. On the way he saw Ruth Trevelyan come twice down the slope. She skied well; it was rather strange that she did, for nothing about her, her appearance or her thought, prepared one for this. He went to the bottom of the tow, around the base of the hill from the open slope of the run, and Mr. McGaver, swooping awkwardly around the base at the end of his run, came up suddenly in back of him and said, "Ah, there you are, Bain. I half-expected you here, today."

Bain was about to ask why, when Mrs. Trevelyan came gliding around the base along the path through the aspens. "Why, hello, Spence", she said. "You haven't been here in quite a while, have you?" She came up alongside him, quite close, and he could smell her scent, *Cuir Russe*—made to be worn on outdoor clothing, he thought, and wondered how she could afford it. He noticed, directly ahead of them, Mrs. McGaver had taken her hand off the towrope she had been about to use, and was staring at them with what could only be called an avid smile.

"I've been busy", he said to Mrs. Trevelyan. He greeted the McGavers as politely as he could, watched them go upward on the tow, and waited for Ruth Trevelyan to precede him. She giggled as she passed by. "Oh, Spence," she said, "I'll be so conscious of you watching me from behind as I go up."

"Don't worry", he muttered, but saw that, wrapped in her own joyful contemplation of something or other, she had either not heard him or did not understand him.

He followed her up the tow but lingered at the top to tighten his bindings, hoping thus to avoid the others, to be at the top when they were at the base, and to keep as best he could between them the entire slope of the hill.

Feeling strong, he gave himself to the skiing. Dropping down the slope the first time, he did not stem, but let himself gather speed quickly. Thought fled backwards from him as he had anticipated. He felt something like a grin break the mock-ascetic lines of his face, felt what he knew only now to be a host of nameless concerns and sorrows leave him, and follow like the tail of a kite.

The thing repeated itself for him, over and over, seeming not to stale through repetition or anticipation. Between runs downhill he sometimes noticed and even spoke to, vaguely,

the McGavers and Mrs. Trevelyan but did not know what
they or he said. Finally, in these periods at once of exhil-
aration and blankness as he shot downhill, thoughts began
to occur as though released from deep in him by the pressure of still other thoughts lifting as he skied. He considered, first and in something like amazement, that he had
not yet been to confession, although this was nothing Nunes
nor anyone could check on with any certainty, even if they
were disposed to anything so egregious as checking. And
secondly, in one of the times he let himself swing downward as fast as he could over the snow, he remembered
again Elva's face at Albuquerque and thought he knew now
why she had looked as she did: she was afraid she was
pregnant.

It was at the end of the run during which he had seen
this, and when he had paused near the tow in a kind of
half-stunned confusion of thought, that Ruth Trevelyan came
circling around the base of the hill and in a curiously awkward gesture for so expert a skier, ran into Bain. The con-
tact was not a hard one, and her skis went to either side of
Bain. He apologized although he wasn't at fault, and waited
for her to move apart from him. Turning his head, he saw
her face held a look of childish triumph on it. She hardly
noticed him, it seemed, but clung to one of his arms awkwardly while she called over his shoulder to the McGavers
by the tow: "Oh, look, Betsy and Carl, I bumped into
Spence, and my legs went one on each side of him."

From the tow and slightly above them, the McGavers
beamed and nodded approval. "Look, Ruth," Bain said, "you
sick?"

"Why, Spence," she said, moving by him finally, her large
eyes blinking in the apple-like face, in a kind of obscene
coquetry, "don't be so coy."

His anger, returning, was not with her; it was more with himself for forgetting something. . . . He turned and pushed himself slowly back to his car. The skiing was spoiled, but finally, as he knelt by the car to loosen his bindings, he knew that he had been angry over having forgotten Elva's fear of a baby. And he wondered, with a most curious and illogical sense of fear and foreboding, why something so obscenely sick and even ridiculous as what Ruth Trevelyan had done, should be chosen as the means of his distraction. And he wondered then why he had used the word "chosen". If there had been a choosing, who had made the choice? Certainly not Ruth Trevelyan. He knew enough—indeed, a great deal—of the Church's teachings about not only Grace but the Devil, to recognize a phenomenon in whose validity he might not believe himself, but in which a legion of otherwise reasonable people did believe.

Getting heavily into the car, he began the drive home. He thought that given certain premises, believing in them, the logic was inescapable. If you believed in a God, you believed also in a Devil, and people were horribly important to both of them. Himself, Elva, the new life in her, which she would want to abort and for whose destruction she could argue with a logic he could not counter, even should he want to. He discovered, quietly and terribly, that he did not want her to abort, that this feeling had been in him deeply and unrealized. And that the beginning of his realization of it had been his thinking of Elva's fear. And, finally, something had not wanted him to think of the fear and the other thoughts the fear would open up to him—or else why the distraction of Mrs. Trevelyan's obscene and pathetic gesture?

Coming to Teran's home again, he drove into the barnyard. The mountain dusk was already in the valley, although the Sangre de Cristos still held their color from the last sun. It was almost suppertime, Bain knew, and he had been trying lately to avoid the various rudenesses into whose habit he had fallen, such as thrusting himself upon the Spaniards for meals. It was—he could hardly believe it—as if now he wanted to enter Teran's home as a sanctuary rather than a place for Teran to be deceived and for his own lies.

Teran was home, opening the door for Bain and even greeting him with some warmth. "Come in, my friend", he said, in Spanish.

"Thanks", Bain said. "I'm glad to see you, Pedro." He had to stoop, as always, to enter their doorways. Automatically, he noted that the room's furniture was crowded and in the usual poor taste. The heat was in this room, a wood-burning stove, and all the children were there. Teran's wife was in the kitchen beyond; Bain could see her dipping tortillas in hot fat to soften them. Teran showed him into another room and called for one of the children to bring wood for the corner fireplace.

"It's a long time since I have seen you", Teran said, when they were seated.

"My wife was here for the holidays", Bain said. "We saw you at the dancing Christmas Eve at the pueblo."

Teran nodded; he did not seem pleased at the reference. "I did not go there for pleasure", he said. "It is just that the dancing is also a way of respecting God."

"*Verdad*", Bain said. "Truly." His glibness was not with him today. He thought, too, that Teran was something of a prig or a puritan; but either or both were implied in Teran's position as *Hermano mayor*, and Bain knew that he himself should not be disappointed or surprised, nor feel a sense of discovery at finding this quality in Teran.

Teran nodded and seemed to wait. "As you know," Bain said, baldly and awkwardly, "I have become a Catholic."

"I had heard something of it", Teran said, no more than polite. "You are to be congratulated."

"With the example of the people here," Bain said, "I could not do otherwise." Don't worry about your glibness, old boy, he told himself.

Teran expressed surprise with his eyebrows. "That is strange", he said. "We are a violent people, with many passions. It is the reason for the penances of the Brotherhood. We do not feel that the ordinary penances imposed by the priest in the confessional are enough."

Bain nodded, as much in satisfaction as in anything else. He knew already what Teran had just told him; the thing that pleased him was Teran's being so frank with him. He cleared his throat, thinking that Teran had saved him from being devious, from a long and possibly embarrassing process of breaking the ice. "That's one of the things I wanted to see you about", Bain said. "Now that I am in the Church, could I not also become one of the Hermanos? That is—" He stopped talking. Incredibly, some excitement had started to beat in him.

Teran was looking at him oddly. After a little silence, the man said: "Do you think it necessary?"

"What do you mean?"

"Do you think your sins are such that they require—strong penances?"

Bain had begun to sweat. "I—I think so", he said. To conceal his unease, he went on hurriedly. "I thought that principally the objection might be that I was an Anglo. . . ."

Teran did not move or change his expression. "It would be unusual", he said, after a moment. "The other thing is more important, though." He waited.

Seeing nothing else to do or say, Bain finally said: "I am a more than ordinarily sinful man, if that's what you mean."

Teran shrugged disparagingly. Bain almost smiled; their sins here were mostly tangible, physical ones, and they had difficulty in seeing how anyone like himself could commit grave sin. Teran voiced this thought immediately.

"It is difficult", he said, "to see how a man in a profession as refined as yours, could commit serious sin. With us, who are always prone to violence from our bargaining and hard labor and ignorant nature, it is different."

"Each profession has its own particular sins", Bain said, politely. He saw Teran break and almost visibly wilt. At the same time the man was pleased by something. Without conscious plan, Bain saw, he had yet hit on a certain method or manner of approach that was moving things along more rapidly than he had hoped. "After all," he went on, "is it not the sins committed in cold blood that are more grave than those done in passion?"

"True", Teran said, almost reluctantly. "But our fallen nature needs to be disciplined against the sins of passion as well as to do penance for them."

Bain felt now the curious intellectual unease that he knew most priests felt toward the Brotherhood; all of them, including those most sympathetic to it, recognized in it some sort of heresy. It was more curious, still, that *he* should also experience the unease. Perhaps it was because he knew how the Church tried to guard its elect against scrupulosity as against the more common sins. . . . He had not spoken after Teran's last words, and Teran went on. "We are not as you," he said, "but ignorant men. With someone such as yourself it is doubtless enough to be told of the wrongness of a thing, but—"

"What makes you think that?"

Teran shrugged; almost slyly, Bain thought. "Is it not so?" the Spaniard said.

Bain shook his head, the motion tense and just perceptible. Watching Teran, he saw that the man seemed at a loss
if not altogether bewildered; but by what, Bain could not
tell. "It is not enough", Bain said. "Ignorance or knowledge doesn't seem to have too much to do with it. After
all, the more intelligent a man is, the more sins he can
think of."

Again, Teran gave that muffled impression of being shocked
or stunned. "I had not thought of that", he said. Then:
"You are not satisfied with the penance given you in the
confessional?"

Feeling the shock transferred somehow to himself, Bain
could still find time to think, before his answer, that such a
reversal of their positions was hardly conscious or inten-
tional on Teran's part. More desperate than he knew, he
told almost the exact truth. "I have only been once to confession", he said. Then, his glibness returning with a rush:
"I think the priest knew it was a first time and gave me a
light penance."

Teran nodded, as if still puzzled. From the floor, the child
who had been blowing the fire into being, turned her head
and looked at Bain solemnly, then rose and left the room.
There was an uneasy silence for close to a minute, before
Teran said: "Then it is still not clear to me why you wish
to become one of the Hermanos. If it is only so that you
may know about us for the records you keep in your work,
we would be glad to tell you. It is only the unhealthily
curious or the scornful we do not want near us."

Bain was shaking his head automatically. "After all, who
is best suited to know what his own penances should be
than the penitent himself? And perhaps it is only that I
wish to follow in Our Lord's footsteps on Good Friday, as
do all of you."

Teran tried to conceal how much he was impressed. "That is possible without being a member of the Brotherhood. The way it is with some moradas, whole villages follow in the procession on Good Friday, women, children, even dogs."

"But only two carry the crosses?"

Teran shrugged once more. "Sometimes more."

"And earlier in the week, when the *carrete de muerte* is—dragged?" He had almost said "pulled", but remembered, as he would all his life, the unturning wheels.

Teran nodded again, this time moodily and uneasily, Bain thought. Finally, the Spaniard said: "I could ask the Hermanos. I don't think they would like it. There are some things I am sure you would not like."

"The lashing?"

"But naturally", Teran said. He watched Bain closely.

"There is no point to the lashing if one likes it."

"Still," Teran said, "there are some so sick among your people that—"

"I know them well", Bain said. "That is, I know of them." It took so many forms, he thought, frightened again.

Teran nodded. "And for them, penance must certainly be a difficult thing to achieve."

"The thought of penance never occurs to them."

Again, Teran could not conceal that he was impressed. He tried to, by saying: "Then, there is the matter of the cuts in the back."

"But that is only to prevent the worse scarring of welts from the lashing."

"True enough", Teran said. "And none of these things are compulsory. We recognize that some are too frail, in their minds or their bodies, to endure them."

"I am not too frail", Bain said. He saw that unconsciously but nonetheless willfully he had clinched things.

Teran could no longer conceal his feelings. He nodded and said: "Still, I would have to talk with the others. . . . And I am not sure it can be arranged. It is most unusual."

Bain shrugged, politely and with just the right amount of disinterest. His own excitement he could still not account for. After a moment, Teran said: "You know, we are a very old Brotherhood. Since we came from the Third Order of Saint Francis, we go back very far. And Saint Francis is really our father."

Bain nodded. It had always been an amazement to him, even at his most scornful, that the Hermanos should have stemmed from a group founded by so gentle a saint. It was an example of a mystery of opposites that, if it gave him and his confreres little satisfaction (none of them were ever at ease to call a thing a mystery and be done with it), gave them pleasure from the frustration and anger such paradoxes induced in the churchmen. And yet, he knew—and now thought again—it was the churchmen who recognized the dual nature of man and his own people who denied or ignored it.

Teran had been talking rather solemnly about the Brotherhood, and Bain, while preserving the appearance of listening, had not been. Teran's wife stood in the doorway. She was waiting for her husband to finish talking. Bain studied her face to see if there was in it any of the evidences of physical dissatisfaction he thought he could sometimes find in a woman's face. But there seemed none. She was a solid and handsome woman; somewhat placid, perhaps, but what another generation had known as "a fine figure of a woman". Of course, Bain thought, it could always be someone other than Teran—

"Supper's ready", she said, when her husband glanced up at her.

"Good. You will stay?" he asked Bain. "It's nothing much. Beans and some ranch meat—"

"All right", Bain said. As they rose, Teran slid his arm easily and casually around his wife's waist and gave her hip an almost imperceptible pat. On her face, turning away, Bain saw the faint, the pleased and secret smile.

He followed them into the dining room where the children were already seated. Indicating a place for Bain on a bench with two of the children, Teran said, casually: "Tomorrow is the First Friday of the month. There will be confessions tonight if you want to go with us after supper."

It was not much of a shock to Bain, but he could think that so, sometime, casually and unexpectedly and much more terribly, death would come to him. He fought down something like terror and said: "I have an engagement early this evening. To see some *santos* a friend has brought down from the mountains. Saturday I am going to confession."

Teran nodded, convinced. "A few beans?" he said.

When Bain reached his own house an hour later, there was a letter in the mailbox from Elva. As he had expected, it said that she was very much afraid she was pregnant.

10

MIRABAL WOKE BAIN the next morning by his knocking. It had taken Bain some time to get to sleep, and he was irritable coming out of the warmth and deep unconsciousness. Grumbling as he let the Spaniard in, he hurried back to where he had been sleeping and the sun had made it less cold than the shaded kitchen. Following him into the room, Mirabal said: "I didn't think you were asleep, else I wouldn't come over this early."

His back to the man as he dressed, Bain said: "What's on your mind? I was up late working and I was going to sleep this morning."

"I'm sure sorry", Mirabal said. "It's after nine o'clock and I—"

"It's all right", Bain said. "What's up?"

"Oh, not so much." Mirabal spoke slowly as he sat down. He was not often hasty with his information.

"You have breakfast?"

"I had coffee when I got the kids off to school."

"You better have some toast or something."

"Okay." Mirabal stood up to help as Bain put the coffeepot on; there was a vague urgency to Bain's movements, for he could still taste the wine that had been all there was to drink in the house last night.

Mirabal said: "Things going all right?"

"So so. I was talking with Teran yesterday."

"How was he? All right with you?"

"He was all right. I wouldn't be surprised but what he gets me into the Hermanos."

There was a little silence before Mirabal said: "He say anything about you going to confession?"

Bain turned. "How'd you know?"

"I didn't. It's only that some of them are beginning to wonder how it is that someone who is come into the Church, they never see him at confession."

"I see." Bain felt relieved. He should have thought of it himself, he considered; he knew how closely they watched strangers in their churches, not in suspicion particularly, and even less in any joy that someone else had held or embraced the Faith, but in something that included both amazement and concern that one from outside—an Anglo, a *rico*, a stranger, or all three—should deliberately and willfully have chosen a way of life so difficult that they themselves might not have pursued it had they not been born to it.

It had been a mistake in tactics, he saw, but not irremediable: tomorrow was Saturday.

Mirabal thought so, too. "Best thing for you to do", he said, "is go to confession tomorrow. You don't have to tell much. Tell him you said some bad words or you missed Mass. Something like that. They don't give you much penance, anyway."

"Where do you think I'd better go?" Bain said. His hand shook slightly on the coffee pot handle, waiting for the coffee to boil.

"Father Gannon, he'll be hearing out at the pueblo. You don't want to go there. Nobody'd see you there but Indians. You want to go in Tarale or Ranchos, where plenty of people will be sure to see you. Father Lanigan here in Tarale, he'd be stricter than Father Nunes, but he doesn't know you so good as Nunes. He probably wouldn't recognize you there in the box."

Bain found himself nodding in agreement. With a momently remote level of his mind, he also found himself admiring Mirabal's weighing of the possibilities. But he himself knew there was only one thing to do, go to confession to Nunes in Ranchos, where Teran or some of the Hermanos from the local morada would be sure to see him.

†

In the old church, once a mission, only a single oil lantern was lit; with the ever-burning sanctuary lamp it made the place one of shadows rather than light. The three or four sets of pews were arranged roughly in the middle of the church, almost as an afterthought, making the place seem bigger than it was. Bain stumbled once on the rough, board flooring and knelt in the nearest of the pews. He was tense—always so, lately—and even in the cold building was sweating thinly. The church, familiar to him, seemed strange now. He had rarely been in it except by daylight. The once or twice he had been to Vespers or Benediction by evening, candles had added their light to the oil lamps', and he could see faces that he knew.

Now, strangers, faceless, moved in the shadows near the altar rail, and Bain, in the unfamiliar and distasteful position of kneeling, sweated steadily in the cold. The confessional was in the deep shadow of the left transept, and people passed from and to it at irregular intervals and almost silently. The line of waiting penitents, most of them women, knelt at the altar rail and was never more than three or four long. Sooner or later he must join it, Bain knew, and wondered at his reluctance and unease. Of course, he told himself, it was part of the almost formal pattern he must follow: the penitent knelt in a pew before joining the line, so that he might pray to know his sins and confess them fully and contritely. Then followed the "examination of conscience"—he had looked in the Baltimore Catechism again before coming here tonight—and finally the taking of one's place in the line.

Bain did not pray while he knelt in the pew. He did not even try particularly to discover the reason for his state of nerves. He thought—as he had almost continually since her letter—of the many possible complications of Elva's pregnancy. She had been afraid in her letter and she had been angry. He had never been able to determine just what it was she so feared about pregnancy—indeed, he had never tried very hard to find out—but the anger was at him. It was during or shortly after these rare occurrences of anger in her that he himself experienced fear; he realized then how much he needed her, how much a part of his own fiber she had become; and he experienced sick fear at the thought of her leaving and divorcing him. She had never threatened to do so—indeed, threat making was not part of her nature—but he knew how easily their friends and confreres made divorces of convenience—more easily than an earlier generation had made marriages of convenience— and he knew, with curious terror, how easily Elva could make one, with how little troubling of her conscience.

She was not some Polack factory worker, she had written, to have an abortion one day and be back at the punch press the next. She had been unable to do much of anything for two or three weeks after the last one. And how could she take two or three weeks off in the middle of the school year? While if she waited until May and the end of school, she would be too far along for an operation—as she called it—to be anything but dangerous.

It was quite a dilemma, Bain told himself solemnly, and the nearest he himself could come to resolving it was the rather pathetic thought that it was still pretty early for Elva to be so sure she was pregnant.

Someone coughed in the church, recalling him to his surroundings. Two men passed him on their way out; in the shadow he could see the faint, white flash of their eyes as they looked at him. There was only one person left of the line at the rail, and Bain knew that he would have to get up now, or risk Nunes coming out of the confessional, thinking that all the penitents had been heard. And if he should have to speak to Nunes, ask the priest to go back into the box to hear his confession ... A fear, more nameless than that inspired by Elva's anger, caught at Bain's belly and throat. He rose and left the pew, stumbling over the kneeling bench, and walked up to the altar rail, where an old woman, her head covered by the conventional black shawl, yet remained, waiting her turn.

He knelt close to her. The terror and the sweating had gone, but the tension still held him. The old woman prayed audibly in Spanish. She was short of breath, and some parts of her prayer, repeated over and over, came clearer than others. "Hail Mary, full of grace ..." and "Holy Mary, Mother of God ..." the beginning of each part of the Ave Maria, each beginning quickly lapsing into a breathless mutter.

He wondered what she could possibly have to confess. That she had said bad words to her husband or daughter; that she had told a lie, petty, of course. If she were not invincibly ignorant, he thought, as were most people, she might confess a sin of uncharity or of envy or of passing malice.

He himself was not invincibly ignorant. The thought came to him, quiet as a knife in the dark. The sweating began again, although now he was unaware of it. He was annoyed additionally and angered by the recurrence here of a phenomenon he had noted repeatedly before now, his occasional and as it were conventional reaction to the precepts and customs of the Church, as if he, too, believed in their validity and was subject to their disciplines.

There was no explanation of this that satisfied him, save possibly one. He knew that in certain monasteries or convents, when a monk or nun was experiencing a period of spiritual dryness, their superior or confessor would advise the making of all the indicated gestures of prayer or penance or good works, even though the heart was not in them ... and in time the heart would be in them, the time of dryness or doubt would pass away.

But he himself had made only a few gestures of the kind, and always coldly and as a spectator, and often unwillingly and with annoyance. It was not a good explanation. But any other explanation not only displeased but frightened him—if there was an explanation, he thought.

The old woman leaned toward him and said, in Spanish: "If you want to go ahead of me, it's all right. I'm not ready, yet."

"Oh, no", Bain whispered.

"It's all right", the old woman said. "Go on. I don't mind." She turned slightly and plucked at his coat to make him precede her.

Someone was leaving the penitent's box, and as much in fear of Nunes' coming out if the box remained empty as for any other reason, Bain rose and walked, stiff legged, toward the confessional. As he opened the warped door, its squeak seemed louder than usual, and he turned, perhaps to see if it had attracted any attention. But he could not see the back of the church, and only the old woman remained in the front. He closed the door after him, quite firmly,

and was in the narrow darkness of the place. His foot touched
the little kneeling bench, and he knelt on it. His long legs
did not fit well in the place made for people of a shorter
race. Behind the screen that separated priest and penitent,
Nunes stirred—impatiently, it seemed to Bain—and spoke
in Latin not quite intelligible.

Bain wet his dry lips and began the formula: "Bless me,
father, for I have sinned ..." then realized Nunes' Latin
had been the blessing, uttered too soon, whether in ennui
or distraction, or in an effort to speed the process.

"It is—" Bain said and stopped. He was supposed to say
it was his first confession, but if he did, Nunes would surely
know who he was. Conversions were rare things here, and
Bain's voice and odor were hardly those of a child. "It is six
months since my last confession", he said, then realized that
was a mistake, too. No man could go six months and have
for his confession only the innocuous, the virtually pious
little sins Bain had half-consciously planned to confess. In
the silence, Nunes moved uneasily but did not speak.

Blindly, in anger and sudden rage, partly with himself,
partly with Mirabal, in incredible bitterness and with an
equally incredible feeling of having been trapped, Bain began
his actual confession. "I lied", he began, and paused.

Old-fashioned in many ways, Nunes spoke for the first
time. "How often?"

"Many times."

Nunes seemed satisfied with this, and Bain went on. "I
committed fornication—twice."

"Neither of you were married?"

"I am."

"Then it was adultery and not fornication."

Anger, now almost objectless, came up once more in Bain.
When he didn't speak, Nunes said: "Is that all?"

"No." Then: "I was uncharitable—also many times. I also take pleasure in certain thoughts. I think that's all", he ended, in what amounted to a rush of physical effort. After all, he thought, it was Elva who had the abortion that time, not he. . . .

Now Nunes hesitated, as if he did not know whether to give the bit of counsel or advice that was customary. Finally, he said: "The principal thing is to avoid the occasion of sin, not less in such matters as lying and uncharity as in more carnal ones. If your business makes for such occasions, or for lying, say, you should try to go in some other business. That is all, then?"

"Yes." He was very bitter. So much so that he forgot to try to say the Act of Contrition while Nunes finished the Latin formula. Nunes paused in the middle of the formula. "You should say your act of contrition now", he said. "Some say it later, but I think it best to say it now, so that there will be no danger of forgetting."

Bain knew only a few phrases of the prayer. While Nunes finished the Latin, Bain ran the phrases over, making a pretence of catching his breath during the parts he did not know. ". . . I detest all my sins . . . firmly resolve . . . to do penance and to amend my life, amen."

"Go in peace", Nunes said.

Bain stumbled, still sweating, out of the box. "Like hell", he thought but wasn't sure whether he meant his own last words or Nunes'.

The old woman hobbled past him on the way to the box. She was still praying breathlessly. Bain, passing the center of the church, forgot to genuflect. He picked his hat up from the pew he had knelt in and started out of the church: there could seem nothing wrong with that to any watchers: many people said their penances later on, for one reason or another.

In the faint and powdery light of the single oil street lamp that burned before the church, two or three men waited, as if casually or aimlessly. They wore the ranch clothes and flat hats of the Spaniards native to Ranchos. One of them moved slightly, so that he faced Bain, who must pass him. As Bain came closer, the man touched his hat respectfully and asked if he were the Señor Bain. Despite the respect in the man's gesture and tone, Bain felt fearful. "Yes", he said in Spanish. "What do you want?"

"Nothing of great importance, sir", the man said. "It is only that Pedro Teran thought you might like to meet with himself and some others tonight."

Bain felt the fear leave him, and the thing that he and his friends called scientific curiosity—that possessed even its own degrees of intensity, so that it, too, could become avidity—come again to him, strong and sure.

"Why, yes", he said. "I would like to very much", noticing how his tone and speech cleared, even in those few words.

"Then be so good as to come with us, sir", the Spaniard said.

Bain followed the men to an old car parked nearby. Something he could only call triumph flowed in him: such respect as these men showed was not common to them; it could only mean that he had convinced Teran, and Teran perhaps the others, of his sincerity.

He sat in the front seat with the man who had spoken to him, the other two men sitting in the back. He knew where they were taking him and he sat there in the creaking car, feeling what he called triumph now quiet in him. It wasn't more than ten minutes ride to the local morada: he knew the two ruts they were in now as the road to it.

They were at the building, a low, dark block in the night, before he realized it. He had seen it before, rather often, by darkness and by day, and from one of the little nearby hills had watched the processions during Holy Week of the year previous. He had again, more clearly than ever before, the sense of wantonness and of waste; everything had been written about the Brotherhood that could be written: he himself, for some months already, had been able to distinguish between the honest and accurate accounts of them, and the lies and distortions. Nothing he had yet found out for himself had added to or been at variance with what the honest accounts had stated. So he could wonder again why he was here and doing what he was doing. (And what of the urgency he felt?) As he got out of the car, his mind gave its old, its inevitable and omnipotent excuse again: scientific curiosity, the healthy and gentle doubt of all that had gone before. *Either that or to find out if these bastards were masochists.*

The driver of the car knocked on the recessed door, while Bain and the other two waited (silently and not unlike men guarding him, Bain could think). The door opened promptly and Bain could see into a lighted room that he knew must be the chapel. Half a dozen men sat around a cheap, square table toward the front of it, beyond them the altar, so-called, and on it the crude, antique *bulto* of Christ staring out over His woodenly outstretched arms and over the men. He wore a red robe with tarnished golden trim.

Some of the men at the table rose and others half-rose as Bain came uncertainly across the room. Teran was one of those who stood up and Estevan Maes, the sexton and Bain's godfather. Curiously, Bain discovered, he had virtually forgotten that Maes existed.... Now, the old man smiled at him, kindly and generously, his expression more that of a father than an uncle. For some reason he might never be able to analyze, this smile of the old man's struck terror into Bain such as actual physical danger never had.

Teran shook Bain's hand while old Maes left his place at the table and came and embraced him. "Welcome, son", the old man said. "I am glad to see you here."

"Thanks", Bain said. "Thanks." He remained stiff in the loose, dry clasp of his godfather's arms. His eyes avoided those of the old man as he stepped back, and for their excuse surveyed the others at the table. He knew all of them by sight, one or two by name. Teran made no attempt at introductions. Turning to the others at the table, he said, simply: "This is the Señor Bain, of whom you have been told. He is a Catholic and one sympathetic. He wishes to make us Hermanos part of a report he is making. There can be no harm in him listening to us tonight."

From some of the faces, there were those who did not agree with Teran, but no one spoke. The driver of the car motioned to the wall behind Bain. Perhaps a dozen other men, poorly dressed, whom Bain had not seen, sat against it on rough wooden benches. In that wall was a closed door. Bain knew it for the room—it corresponded almost to a sacristy—where the *carrete de muerte*, the crosses, and the whips were kept, with the masks or hoods to be worn for the mind's humility (for who is so ignorant as to take pride in public penance?) as the horsehair rope was worn for the body's.

Bain was quite sure he would not be admitted to that room tonight; with a little, inaudible sigh he sat down in the narrow place they made for him on the bench.

It was a very dull meeting and his tenseness, largely unexplained, made it a difficult one to endure politely. After he had surveyed every detail of the room, finding nothing new or strange in it, nothing he had not known about before through reading or his own observation, he listened to the talk.

They were discussing their local charities: whether a certain injured Hermano could best use two sheep or ten dollars; whether another's widow was as poor as she pretended to be.

The meeting ended half an hour after Bain's arrival. At a simple gesture from Teran, the others knelt on the floor; Maes took from his pocket an old copybook and began to lead them in a sequence of prayers.

So the old man was the *rezador* or reader here, Bain thought, and smiled inwardly and sardonically, wondering what Nunes would think if he knew his sexton was an officer of the Hermanos. Still, it was unlikely that Nunes did not know.... So Bain directed his sardonic smile toward the Archbishop in Santa Fe ... wondering then what His Excellency would say if he knew the local sexton was also the local *rezador*.

Now that the prayers were finished and the group breaking up and departing, the restraint of the meeting on himself eased, Bain felt freer to look more openly at those about him. He had seen almost all of them before, although he knew less than half of them. Most of them were farmers or wood gatherers or adobe plasterers, with a scattering of small tradesmen and clerks from Tarale among them. None of those here surprised Bain by his presence, with the exception of a moron of about twenty-eight whom Bain knew only by the nickname of Garbanza. He was a rather gentle man, who dragged one foot continually in a more or less spastic motion, and whose lips were always ready to a polite and consciously false laugh. Bain had long known of, although he had not yet been able satisfactorily to account for, the fondness or affection—it was certainly more than a tolerance—of the Spaniards for those mentally afflicted. But he had not thought that it extended to such locos being admitted to the Hermanos de Luz. He must look into it.

Teran and Maes were coming toward him and the former put one hand on his shoulder, while old Maes gently and absently touched Bain's arm. "You see," Teran said, "we have many charitable enterprises, too." For the first time, Teran seemed to lack dignity. He felt that something new and important had been revealed to Bain tonight. Bain was annoyed, but in his annoyance he sensed how the two were on either side of him, in a kind of guarding, or even— though less likely, he thought—in a gesture of sponsoring. . . .

It did not take a sensitive man to feel the unease his presence had induced among many of those here. Two or three walked stiff legged as in anger. Some others that he knew, avoided his glance. But a few seemed pleased that he was present.

He noticed that they did not linger here, as was their habit in other meeting places. They moved toward and through the narrow door. It was very cold outside and windless. Behind him, Bain could hear someone—the *celador* or warden, he knew—padlocking the door.

"You could ride home with me if you want," Teran said, "or with those who brought you."

"It doesn't matter", Bain said. "I'll go with you. My own car is by the church in Ranchos."

He crowded into an old car with Teran and some others. Outside, he heard Maes bidding them good night, and he tried to answer him above the noise of the motor. Not knowing who else was in the car with them, he was afraid to talk freely to Teran. He felt eager and hopeful. . . . He was almost sure that Teran and Maes were doing what they could for him. And then he began to wonder if that was why he felt as he did.

They left him at the church in Ranchos, with conventional good-nights. In the sleeping village he was alone by the church. He stood a moment looking at the square, solid bulk of the building, standing as if its gray-whiteness in the light, its blank or bland sureness were rooted there forever, in darkness or in sun. Something, some mood, perhaps, eluded him there in the cold, and he got into his car and drove home.

†

He was not sleepy when he got there, and he thought he had better answer Elva's letter now while he had nothing else to do. He wrote to her that he was sorry it had happened and that he'd try to get West to be with her when she had the operation, but naturally couldn't be at all sure of this. He suggested Easter vacation for the time. Easter was early this year, he told her, and she oughtn't to be too far along by then. Late March wasn't much more than three months. Of course, that would be a bad time for himself, he wrote, as he wanted to be here at Easter time for the processions and so on. But she had had the last one without him.

He told her that the work seemed to be going well, and that he thought he'd be finished by late spring, so they could have a good and restful summer together, perhaps on Long Island if she wanted to be near her folks; if not, any place that she wanted.

When he finished the letter he found that he was inexplicably weeping. It was the tiredness, he told himself. Of course, these spells of physical weariness were common to all people, such as teachers or painters, who used up tremendous quantities of nervous energy. And his own reserves had the added drain, Atwood had told him, of living the—to him—strenuous life of a native, with unusual stresses and simplicities.

Yes, sir, he told himself, it was the tiredness, the weariness. A fine word, weariness, he thought. Right out of the *Ladies' Home Journal*. Like charity, it covered a multitude of sins.

How he happened to be kneeling in darkness by the side of the bed, he was never sure. Perhaps it was because if a man was going to weep, that seemed the most appropriate place and position for it.

HE HAD BEGUN ABOUT THIS TIME, in mid-January, to work up some of his notes. By now, he knew that certain parts of his subject had been exhausted, that nothing he could discover in the future would mute or change what he knew of the Spaniards. Perhaps it was only his desire to concentrate on his work, perhaps this desire was itself a mask for a new and curious reticence or physical diffidence, but for two or three weeks he left the house only occasionally, having his communications with the outside through Mirabal, letters, and the telephone.

Mirabal, considering what he was—or perhaps because of it, Bain thought—seemed to know a good deal about the activities of the Hermanos. It was through him that Bain learned it had become quite possible he would be accepted into the Brotherhood. He was sitting in the warm, cluttered room on a day both cloudy and cold when Mirabal told him of this. The normal questions did not occur to Bain: How had Mirabal found out? How had Teran and Maes managed it? Instead of triumph or accomplishment, Bain experienced a sense of unease. Yet along with this a mental excitement and anticipation.

He sat there in the room, Mirabal forgotten, and tried to analyze his feelings. It was Elva, he finally knew, and nothing else. She had answered his last letter after a wait of almost two weeks and she had been surprisingly—even strangely—bitter. He talked so blithely now, she wrote, of an abortion. Had he forgotten how he carried on that first night they had been together during the Christmas vacation, had he forgotten about the last abortion, five years gone? He must be crazy to think he could say one thing to her, then write another. It was *he*, not herself, she was worried about. And for better or worse, she did love him and even needed him, so that she was not going to go lightly into something which might estrange them. If he really wanted to know, she had been pretty badly upset by what he had said that night, and now she wasn't going to do anything until he had made up his own mind about what he wanted.

Surprise was hardly the word, he told himself, for what he felt on reading the letter; that was like exclaiming "touché" after being hit on the head with a club. The word was shock, and the shock remained in him and would not go. It was as though a new, an almost religious concept had been transmitted to Elva, not by, but *through* himself.

Mirabal cleared his throat to reclaim Bain's attention. When Bain looked at him, Mirabal said: "So I guess you going to be all right now, huh?"

Bain nodded, absently. "I guess so."

There was a little pause in which Mirabal made what Bain knew was the man's sole nervous gesture, a wetting of the lips. "One thing, you know," Mirabal said slowly, "you got to be careful of some of those guys in the Hermanos. They're pretty tough, some of them."

Bain nodded automatically.

"I mean," Mirabal said, "they might think they're holy and all that, but some of them are, you know." He tapped his forehead. "If they found out, they might get tough."

Bain shrugged. He had been in South America on one expedition and he had not been afraid among headhunters. Like Schapper, he had long ago established his physical courage. So he shrugged now as would any man who had had his courage thus both publicly and privately attested. But this gesture of his only served to emphasize and make more strange the fear that lay in him, heavy and increasingly less shapeless. If he was being used, what was using him? He said, at last: "We'll know pretty soon, won't we? I mean Easter and Ash Wednesday are early this year, and if I'm going to get into the Hermanos, it'll have to be the night before Ash Wednesday."

Mirabal nodded. His face looked grim from some unusual strain around the mouth. "You're glad to see me doing this, José", Bain said. "Why? Did you used to be an Hermano?"

"Not me", Mirabal said. "I just want to do—to make trouble", he amended.

Bain knew that the man had been going to say: "—to do evil", as he had said once before, early in their acquaintance. Bain felt the light sweat on himself. Something apparently showed in his face, for Mirabal said: "I mean, what do they think they are, thinking they're so holy and all? We don't owe them anything."

Bain nodded, almost imperceptibly. "I've got to find out about them for the work. That's all I care about."

"Sure", Mirabal said. He, too, was uneasy and rose and moved a step or two toward the door. There he hesitated and shifted his feet. "Hey, Spance, you got any money you could spare? I mean—"

Bain rose hastily. "Say, I'm always forgetting, José. I must owe you for a couple of weeks."

"Thanks, Spance", Mirabal said when he was paid. "See you pretty soon, huh?"

"Any time, José."

The man's spirits had so obviously revived with the money, that Bain went to the window and watched him go away. He moved quickly, even happily, and Bain wished there

were something that could as easily raise his own spirits.
He searched, eagerly, his own mind for what that thing
might be, but could not name it.

†

At the end of January, Teran came to see him. The man
was alone and some of his old diffidence seemed to have
returned. He made small talk until Bain's uneasiness was
almost unbearable and Bain finally and bluntly said: "Pretty
soon it will be the beginning of Lent, and you will be
busy?"

Teran nodded, suddenly easier, so that Bain was reminded
again of the deep respect the Spaniards had for the learned,
fake or real. Teran, it was apparent, had a mission either
delicate or unpleasant, and his respect for Bain or Bain's
learning made it embarrassing to perform. "In two weeks
it will be Ash Wednesday", he said. "And on the night
previous the novices come into our order." He hesitated
painfully, then went on. "If there can be a good explanation of one thing by you, our morada will be glad to have
you as an Hermano."

Bain found it a little difficult to conceal his pleasure; yet
it was something other than the nearing satisfaction of his
old curiosity that he felt. "I'd be glad to answer anything
you wanted to know", he said.

The strain showed clear in the Spaniard's face. Bain felt
moved, and guessed that the man, sponsoring himself and
therefore believing in him, must have jeopardized his influence among his own people. There were, Bain knew, several questions that could be asked by any person not an
idiot, any of which could embarrass himself or his spon-
sors. But he did not expect the one Teran did ask.

"Many of the Hermanos", Teran said, "cannot understand how an intelligent and devout Catholic like yourself can employ one such as José Mirabal in your work."

In the moment before the again glib and pious word should rise to his lips and save him, Bain considered, not ruefully but in a kind of pure wonder, how he himself had overlooked anything so obvious. "Why," he said, "you don't mean this business of José being a diabolist, do you? Myself, I just don't believe he can be one."

"You believe in the Devil, don't you?" Teran said, a little sharply.

"Naturally", Bain said. "I just don't think José is a diabolist. He's never—well, accomplished anything in that line. At least, not that I know of."

Teran stuck out his lower lip. "Perhaps", he said. "The point is that you did hire such a man; a man with such an intention. And surely one so intelligent and observing as yourself must have known of his reputation?"

Bain shook his head automatically. "At first, I did not know", he said. "Then, when I found out what he was supposed to be, I felt sorry for his large family—he has five motherless children, as you know—and I could not with a clear conscience discharge him."

Teran wilted visibly. He closed his eyes and nodded. "I suppose you might perhaps have thought of trying to change him?"

Relaxing but still alert, Bain said: "I could hardly hope to accomplish that. It is enough if I can save myself."

Teran was beaten and convinced. "I think the others will understand. But you are not afraid of the man's influence? I mean of his possibly being an influence for sin?"

"I believe in the Devil." Bain shrugged. "But I don't believe that poor José is a diabolist. He was just made bitter by some things, and left the Church."

"Leaving the Church is one thing," Teran said, "or even no longer believing in God. But when a man says he is for the Devil, it means he believes in God, still, but is against Him."

"Honestly," Bain said, "Mirabal hasn't done, or even said, anything about it lately."

Teran stared moodily at the floor for perhaps half a minute. "Oh, I guess it will be all right. If it is not, you will know soon. Otherwise, our Novice Master will visit you in a few days and prepare you for admission." He seemed disposed to linger, silent and uneasy in the crowded room, and Bain offered him wine. To his surprise, Teran accepted it, saying as a kind of excuse: "Soon it will be Lent, with no wine."

Under the wine, they both grew relatively cheerful. Bain, for a little while and by some curious process, could think that there were no lies here, and that he himself was present in this place in all simplicity and truth and even honor . . . a farmer here or perhaps the county agent . . . a helper of these people. For some reason he might never know about, he again almost wept. There had been too much weeping lately; he wondered if he were about to have a nervous breakdown.

†

The Novice Master was a farmer whom Bain knew only by sight; relatively well to do, he was about sixty years old, with eight children and many grandchildren. His name was Eloy Sandoval and he was a tall, erect man who managed to convey an impression of severity without being severe. He sat in the dirty room, refusing Bain's wine, and almost formally, but movingly because of his restrained intensity, gave Bain a little history of the Hermanos de Luz. Knowing all and more than the old man told him, Bain was yet stirred.

Their father was Saint Francis, the old man said, and at
one time the Hermanos were all members of the Third Order
of Saint Francis, of which the Señor Bain doubtless knew,
since it existed even to this day in other parts of the country.
Their purpose was to do penance for their own sins, so that
they would have to do less penance later on in Purgatory,
and also to try to insure their not going to Hell. Many per-
sons misunderstood the purposes of the Order, especially
Anglos of a frivolous nature. The Hermanos were convinced of Bain's sincerity, of his lack of a frivolous intention,
and they were happy to welcome him into their ancient society.

The old man followed this with detailed instructions as
to what Bain should do. He should go to confession and
on the morning of the eve of Ash Wednesday attend Mass
and receive Communion. Some men fasted all or most of
that day, the old man said, but in general this practice was
not recommended.

Bain could guess why it was not recommended and felt
the little sweat on himself.

For the rest, the old man said, he recommended a bath
to cut down the danger of infection from the cuts the *sangredor* made in the back. The Señor, of course, understood
the reason for the cuts?

Bain nodded. They were not for themselves alone, he
said, but so that the lashes of penance would leave no welts.

The old man nodded, as though pleased that Bain should
be so well-informed. Then he seemed to hesitate, before
asking Bain if he could truly say that he did not look forward to his penances with pleasure?

Truly, he did not, Bain said. That certainly was the truth,
he thought, with some fervor.

Sandoval seemed again pleased and half-apologized for
the question. They had learned, he said, from watching

certain Anglos occasionally admitted as spectators to the services, that some of them took pleasure from another's penance. He hoped Bain was not offended by his questions, but it was unusual for an Anglo to be admitted to the Brotherhood.

He understood perfectly, Bain said.

The old man took his leave and Bain sat there watching the quick mountain dusk blank out corners of the room, and the fire show clearer and redder in the white and sooty fireplace. He had a strong desire to pack and go away. After all, he had gotten almost everything he could get here. He did not see quite clearly why he was entering the Hermanos. . . . He did, too, though, he told himself. Like all his confreres, like all readers of Proust, he could never quite convince himself that people did such penance for other than sick reasons, or that the Hermanos should be as honest and simple and God-struck as they seemed. Yet the excitement he had newly felt—at the meeting he had attended, at Teran's last visit—was with him, now . . . as though approaching, finally, something possessed of meaning.

†

So, a week later, Bain waited with four other men, all younger than himself, in the cold outside the morada. He knew only one of them, Nunes' acolyte, Alfredo Sanchez, who had been at his baptism. Bain had driven his car to within a hundred yards or so of the morada, then walked the rest of the way over a little rise to where the low mud building was almost hidden in a dip of the land. There was no moon but the stars were very clear and sharp. Coming down to the morada, he did not at first see the little group of four where they stood against the wall, as if to get out of the wind that blew intermittently and broken, like the sounds of grief, by silences. Bain had thought he was early and the first.

Then he saw the novices, darker shapes against the mud wall, and he wondered, aimlessly, if others might also be arriving. Alfredo recognized and greeted him. "Hello, Mr. Bain. You are here, too?" the voice rising in wonder.

"Who's that?" Bain said.

"Alfredo Sanchez, sir."

Not recognizing the name, Bain peered silently in the dark, but could not distinguish the face in shadow. "Who?" he said.

"Alfredo Sanchez, sir. Father Nunes' altar boy."

"Oh", Bain said. Then: "What are you doing here? You're too young, aren't you?"

"No, sir. I am seventeen."

Bain was not very surprised; he knew they went into the Hermanos as young as sixteen, but he was mildly shocked and uncomfortable. By now, he could see Alfredo standing there, not particularly tense. The boy's unease showed only in a faint, too ready smile under his glasses, but he stood against the wall, or rather leaned, as if consciously or deliberately making himself untense. The others nearby, whom Bain could now gradually see, were not doing so well as Alfredo. They were men in their twenties, grave, tense, with drawn mouths and tightly-squared shoulders. One of them, Bain was sure, did not see him, did not see anyone. His eyes, fixed and dark, stared almost blankly outward and upward.

Seeing these others, and their manner, Bain considered his own. He still sweated lightly under his clothing, in the cold, but then he had always sweated easily. He was neither tense nor relaxed; he did experience a certain amount of unease or perhaps fear, but it was probably due to the pain he knew he must undergo. Knowing this, he yet tried to establish once more clearly in his mind his reason for being here. He had an illogical feeling of his own life being closer to meaning than ever before. . . . And he was almost sure there was nothing new to find out. From watching the others, from his own feelings during the ceremonies, he might find out—well, what? How sick they might be? But he was not they, nor they himself. Easily and without conscious humility he made the amazing concession: he was the sicker, the sick, even; he and his people. Yet, standing there, waiting in the cold, he feared pain. He had not experienced it in years, certainly not in the intensity with which it came in, say, a footrace or boxing match. He wondered—and grew almost nauseated—if the child, cut from its mother untimely, knew pain, and if so, how much? It was ridiculous to think that it did, he knew, but his own feeling would not go away. Quite suddenly, he wanted Elva to have her baby; quite suddenly, he felt that some payment must be made for the one they had deliberately killed.

"I think it is time", Alfredo Sanchez said.

Bain wondered if it would be best to go first if he could, go now to end the waiting, to experience without seeing or hearing first anything to condition him.

"You are the oldest, sir", Alfredo said. "Although, of course—"

"I'll go", Bain said. He wet his lips and approached the recessed door and knocked.

There was a slight sound of movement within, as of a group settling to silence, but no answer. Bain began the formula in a voice so dry and low and uncertain that he hardly knew it for his own. "God knocks at this door for His mercy", Bain said.

From inside, a group of voices said, indistinctly: "Penance, penance, who seeks salvation."

Bain wet his lips again and said, his voice even lower: "Saint Peter will open the gate for me, flooding me with light in the name of Mary, with the seal of Jesus. I ask this gathering: Who gives this house of light?"

His voice had dropped even lower as he spoke, and in back of him, Alfredo said: "Louder, sir."

But inside they knew what he had said, whether they had heard him or not. The answer came: "Jesus."

"Who fills it with joy?" Bain said.

"Mary", they answered.

"Who keeps it with faith?"

"Joseph", the Hermanos said.

The door opened for Bain and he stooped—as always to pass their lintels—and entered into the room he had been in once before. Now, to either side, in two kneeling rows, the Hermanos were arrayed, three or four times as many as before, the full membership. Their faces, Bain saw, were as various in expression as those of the men who waited outside. Some had clasped their hands, others folded their arms, while from some of the hands rosary beads depended. Between the kneeling rows, the officers stood, vaguely formal in the thin light. Teran was empty handed, while Maes held only the dog-eared copybook as perhaps, a long time ago, someone had first held one of the Gospels. Others of the officers had rosaries or nothing at all in their clasped hands. Over their hands, Bain's eyes lightly and even frantically skipped, knowing what they were searching for before ever Bain's mind caught up with them, and finally resting fixedly on the hands of the *sangredor* and the small piece of flint the man held. It was a relief to Bain to see that it was flint, and that the *sangredor* was an old man, the oldest of the officers.

Apparently, Bain hesitated a little longer than was customary or seemly, for the master of novices, old Sandoval, stepped toward him and placed a hand on his shoulder to indicate he should kneel. "The coat", he whispered. Impatiently, perhaps, the old man waited while Bain removed his coat, a sweater, and his hat. Kneeling stiffly down, Bain found that of all objects and faces there from which he might possibly draw confidence or what was generally called courage, he had looked to the face of his godfather, Estevan Maes. The old man nodded repeatedly and almost imperceptibly to Bain, smiling a kind of distant and sorrowful smile, as if to tell Bain that every man must bear fully and alone the burden of his own penance.

Seeing the *sangredor* move toward himself, Bain felt panic and a kind of anger rise in himself. Feeling the need of something to fight these with, he knew that his scientific curiosity was not enough, that it was pathetic, like a man going out to hunt bear with a BB gun. If he could simulate, he thought, in himself deceive the emotions to an illusion of penance.... Because it was the keenest, as well as the deepest and most recent, because he could think that regret for the child gone, for the manner of its going, was all he had ever repented for in his life ... Bain fixed his mind on that, and felt, incredibly, the tears form at the back of his eyes.

"*La camisa*", the *sangredor* said in a flat voice. "The shirt."

Bain removed his shirt and undershirt. The *sangredor's* hand on his shoulder indicated he should bend slightly forward. Doing so, Bain felt the muscles harden and the skin tighten. He wondered if his trembling was perceptible and if the others would think he was very afraid. It was much quicker and less painful than he had thought it would be. The old man took only five or six seconds to make the three horizontal cuts, no longer for the three vertical ones. Each separate sting was no more than iodine in a scratch. Bain straightened up; he felt easier. It was not over yet, it had only begun, and still he could feel reassured: he had not flinched from the pain, but more heartening still, he had taken no pleasure in it: he was not that sick; he felt almost joyful over not being that sick.

The *sangredor* had put aside his flint on the rough table near which the officers stood, and had picked up the rawhide lash. Quickly, the fear returned to Bain; he felt everything but the fear leave him, and again he could think only of the lost child for something to sustain him now and justify what he was doing. Feeling, as he resumed the formula, how dry his lips were, he said: "For the love of God, the three meditations of Christ's passion."

Now, kneeling entirely upright, but with his head bowed slightly, Bain heard the old man utter an almost inaudible sigh, heard the whistle of the leather in the air and braced himself for the shock. But not enough. If the pain of the flint had been less than he was prepared for, this pain was immeasurably greater. It struck like fire into him and he fell forward onto his hands with a choking sound. While he was so, the *sangredor* hit him twice more with the leather, making three times in all.

That's enough, Bain thought. His mind was blurred, as if he had been clubbed, but cleared as he straightened up slowly in the silence. He looked for and could see them watching him, the drawn faces and the blank. Ordinarily, this part of each individual's induction went on through most or a large part of a formula, until the penitent collapsed. It would not be so with him, Bain thought. Yet when he started to rise to his feet, it was as if some deep, ancient, and willful part of his soul would not have it so. His voice croaked and dryness had split his upper lip as he said: "For the love of God, the Five Wounds of Christ—" and the leather fell again. Whether it fell less heavily or whether he was more prepared, he did not fall forward this time. But before the fifth stroke he thought that he might break in some fashion under the pain. Then, when that had ended, he knew he could endure no more and got heavily to his feet. Staggering once as he straightened out to his height, he felt himself caught on either side, and looking at his helpers saw they were Maes and a melancholy little man, one of the officers, whom Bain guessed to be the coadjutor or infirmarian.

"You're a good boy", Maes said in Spanish.

In his own bewilderment and hurt, Bain knew it was an unusual thing to be said here and now. He had, he knew, endured less than any of the others would; but more than that, no one came here to be complimented on his fortitude or called a good boy. . . .

He let the coadjutor help him toward the back of the room. As he walked slowly next to the little man, he looked, more by accident than intention, at the others ranged to either side of the room. But none were watching him. . . . Some looked into old copybooks like Maes', others toward the door, where already another had knocked and said that God was knocking, too.

There were half a dozen little three-legged stools back there in the dimness, and Bain sat heavily on one of them. His mind was blank and curiously at ease. He had forgotten the remainder of the formula until he smelled the rosemary when the coadjutor began to bathe his back in a solution of the herb. It eased his pain and the smell was good and heartening.

Sitting there, with his back deliberately to the room, he heard the voice of the next novice clearer as the man entered, but Bain still did not turn. The coadjutor had left him, and Bain sat there quietly, without thought, and what might have been called at peace. In a little while, certainly tomorrow, he would have to think again—of Elva, of her baby, of Schapper, of his returning lust—but now he just sat there on the little stool and at peace as would a man whose sins are forgiven him. So some men feel after leaving the confessional; so, others when they leave the psychiatrist's dimlit chambers. But Bain, who had been to both these places, had not felt so until now.

12

BAIN LAY IN HIS OWN BED, with its dirty sheets, in the cold room, and waited for the doctor. His back was stiff and painful; not more than it should have been, but he had the idea it might be infected. It had taken him almost three days to decide to call a doctor; he had wanted no one to know of what he had done. Now that Atwood was coming, Bain was annoyed with himself, with the doctor not yet here, more obscurely with things he could hardly name: Santiago over the foot of the bed on his ridiculous horse, with his ridiculous sword; the letter from Schapper that had come in today's mail; an unreasonable feeling that he was nearer to purpose in his life than ever before.

Schapper thought he would like to take a look at the great, open spaces; he would be out to Tarale during the spring holiday with some friends: the publisher, Jeremy Kendal, and his wife. Bain told himself that the annoyance was with someone like Schapper not knowing better than to distract a fellow scientist trying to live and work under field conditions, but even he knew finally that he was also disturbed by *both* Mr. and Mrs. Kendal accompanying Schapper. He had heard that Schapper was interested in Mrs. Kendal, and there were stories about Mr. Kendal—Bain knew neither of these people, only that Kendal was also a trustee of the University— that were part of what some people fondly called the "legend" of Jeremy Kendal. So that Bain was annoyed by Schapper's letter and tried to explain all his unease by the letter.

Someone knocked on the outer door and Bain called to enter, expecting Atwood. But it was a lighter step in the

intervening room, light and careful . . . so that Bain moved
uneasily on the bed. The door from the kitchen opened
slowly and Guadalupe Mirabal stood in the doorway, a covered bowl in her hands. "I thought you'd like some soup,
Spance."

Oh, hell, he thought; his voice cracked suddenly, like a
boy's: "That's awfully nice of you, Lupe, but you shouldn't
have bothered. I'll get up probably for supper."

Putting the bowl down on a table near him, she said:
"You want me to make a fire? It's getting cold."

It took him a moment to answer. "It's all right. I'll be
getting up." His head was turned to the fireplace while slant-
ingly he looked at her where she stood within, if he stretched
a little, his arm's reach. He could not determine whether
she had placed herself there in simple trust or as an excitement. This uncertainty or conflict took on extraordinary
proportions as he lay there, seemed to be determining by
its solution the course of his conduct. Still, if she had deliberately placed herself so—and he was reasonably sure she
had not—there was always Elva to consider. It was an unusual
thought for him, he knew. Lying there on one elbow, he
possessed again the sense of wonder and chagrin he had
experienced these last few months, while his eyes yet held
their oblique and natural glance.

She hesitated a moment, as if fearful to displease him by
moving, and in the moment he could wonder why she
should be exposed so to his lust, while throughout the village and throughout Santa Fe—by the dozen, there!—
existed all sorts of physically anxious women, many prettier
than Mrs. Trevelyan, and all more knowing than any child
could be. But if she was so exposed to him, why then the
equally—the more!—extraordinary precautions that existed,
that came into being, actually, for her protection; whose

validity he had recognized repeatedly in his mind; which were the constant source of his wonder, his annoyance and chagrin? Here was, he knew, if one wanted to believe such stuff, the phenomena that had given rise to what people believed of God and the Devil: the two almost equal powers. He himself did not believe but he could see why others did ... why the Church even had formulated certain of its elaborate doctrines about Grace. It was strange that he had never noticed this before, he told himself.

This was his last thought before—after the brief, ambiguous moment of hesitation—she moved from him toward the fireplace, before the heavy knock on the outer door and the unwaiting heavy tread told Bain that Atwood had arrived. (As if, he thought, God did not trust intangible barriers where he, Bain, was concerned.)

The door to the room opened again and Atwood stood there, heavily clothed, a fur hat accentuating the thinness of his face, the lines of tiredness, and the flush of the cold. The face moved toward one of its forced and sardonic smiles as he said: "Kids dying of diphtheria and pneumonia, and you have to call me in for a hangover."

"Why don't you innoculate the kids for diphtheria? Trying to drum up business?"

Seeing the girl kneeling by the fireplace, Atwood resumed the grave and worried stare his profession often thought it best to use. The bastard, Bain thought, he's probably thinking the worst. But even Bain recognized, in one of the flashes of insight now common to him, that the "probably" was an abatement and a concession. Of what? he wondered, and in something too slow to be terror, saw or almost saw how the same hate—or "brilliant irascibility"—that Schapper possessed, had come to himself, a gradual sifting and accumulation of the years spent studying, without love, the meanderings and mutation of peoples, their blind and hopeless movings and shapings.

"All the comforts of home, eh?" the doctor said, taking off his coat.

"Don't be so obvious", Bain said, knowing Lupe knew only the simplest English. "I like them riper."

"I do myself," the doctor said, "but you're a long way from home and mama." He pulled a chair toward the bed and sat on it. "What's the matter with you?"

In the moment before he answered, Bain could think once more of how difficult it had been several times lately to answer simple questions, as though, his life growing more complicated, ordinary situations and happenings took on an added and at times almost unbearable weight of implication. Not the lie itself—that would have tested all his originality and resourcefulness, indeed—but rather the thought of lying, occurred to him, automatically, but he knew that no lie could explain away the pattern of his wounds. So, quite simply, and even with a sense of relief at telling the truth or at least not trying to obscure it, he said: "My back."

"What about it? You got lumbago or something? Turn over."

Stiffly, Bain turned, thinking: he'll say something that will beat my brains out. But Atwood didn't speak when the turned back was bare, and Bain said, in a kind of relief, "I think it might be infected."

Still, Atwood did not speak. Then, finally, the fire flaring suddenly upward where Lupe blew upon it, seemed to release the doctor and he said, hesitatingly: "No, I don't think so", then was silent again before saying: "God, man, you don't take your work seriously or anything, do you?"

"What else?" Bain said.

"Oh, you might have been getting ideas from Kraft–Ebing or something."

"You would think of that."

"I didn't say you had."

Neither of them spoke for a moment. From where she stood, carefully removed, by the fireplace the girl said: "You want anything else, Spance?" The tears in her voice made both the men look at her, so that, without waiting for a reply, she turned and went hurriedly from the room.

The men looked at each other in a grave and surprised silence, shot through with a kind of light that they knew did not emanate from anything in themselves, but which, from some old memory, they were able to recognize and be moved by. Atwood, with his fear or distrust of sentiment or anything resembling it, was the first to speak. "She certainly doesn't like to see you hurt."

Bain tried to shrug but made only an awkward and painful gesture, without meaning. "She's only a kid and the sight of blood probably disturbs her. I think she prays for me."

"Someone ought to", Atwood said. "They certainly do a neat job on you in the morada, don't they", he added, his tone changing to indicate the separation of the first sentence from the second. "I've seen it once before, only worse than yours. Those nicks the *sangredor* makes take care of the welting all right."

"What the hell am I?" Bain said. "A charity outpatient, or a walking case-history or what?"

"What else?" Atwood said.

Bain turned his head to look at the doctor. Again a simple question had stunned him with its implications. "Why do you think I did this?"

"I don't know", Atwood said. "Even if you are in the Church, I can't see you making such a primitive penance.... Scientific curiosity, I guess."

"That's mighty white of you", Bain said. "Look, for God's sake keep quiet about it, will you?"

"What else?" Atwood said. He did not seem offended. "I didn't know I made a practice of going around revealing my patients' affairs."

"You told old lady Senton I was in the Church."

"Well, is that like having syphilis or epilepsy?"

"All right", Bain said. Painfully, he turned onto his side. "It's not infected, then?"

"No. You'll live." Atwood made no move to leave. "It's a wonder you don't go nuts here; no heat, lousy food."

"You've done research", Bain said. "I shouldn't have to explain to you what living under field conditions is like or for."

"All right. But why pick Tarale with its tourists in the summer and what's left of a colony, instead of some place like Abiquiu or Trampas?"

It was a good question, Bain knew. He wondered, passingly, if it had to do with why other scientists sometimes went to other colonies—for the color or the sickness or the sometimes good talk? He said: "The library here is much better than in other small towns in the state. And it's a center for a lot of things. At least the mail gets in and out regularly and I do like to hear from my wife. And Rio Arriba County, here, is about as typically Spanish a county as there is in the state. From Tarale I can travel pretty quickly to almost any part of the county."

Atwood nodded; he was not looking at Bain and seemed preoccupied. He broke his mood, saying, "It's got almost the lousiest medical conditions in the country. We've been talking about a medical co-op."

"The A.M.A. isn't going to like you", Bain said.

"Damn the A.M.A.", Atwood said. "The A.M.A. is like the Church—great for organization and the status quo and the letter of the law."

"You certainly don't think much of the Church", Bain said.

"I won't argue it with you. I never discuss religion or politics."

"Anyway, not much."

"But I was wondering if you were so set on your own work—that is, the teaching end of it—that you wouldn't consider maybe doing our organizing for us here if we decide to get this medical co-op going? After all, few Anglos know this country like you do, and none of the Spaniards have your education or talent. You could go on with your own work. There wouldn't be anything like the money you'd get teaching at a university, though."

Bain felt himself respond to what he felt was flattery. "I never made more than four thousand teaching", he said. "And I can't hope to do better at the school I'm with now while Schapper is there. He's not fifty years old."

"We couldn't pay anything like that, even after the thing was established."

"Even if you could," Bain said slowly, "I like my own work", knowing suddenly and in amazement that he didn't like it, that he had no feeling about it at all.

"What's Schapper like?" Atwood said.

Bain yawned and shook his head. "You can see for yourself. He'll be out here during Easter week."

"He must be quite a guy", Atwood said, getting up. "I read him when I was in med school." It was the first time

Bain had ever heard Atwood express admiration for anyone. "I have to go. I've been trying to get to Ranchos all
day."

After the doctor had gone, Bain lay quietly for a time.
He could not rest comfortably on his back, and he was not
drowsy enough to sleep on his belly; he wished his wife
were here, and he wished the work were done and he returning in quiet triumph to the University; he wished he had
Schapper's job and that Jeremy Kendal would publish his
book and it would be a best seller. He looked at the phone,
but could not summon enough energy—as he thought of
it—to call Elva. . . . After all, what to say? and just torturing
himself with that rich voice a thousand miles away. He lit a
cigarette . . . and the fire playing fully on him as he lay on
his side, showed the graven and stoney face, the lean body
suspended in time, thought, space and—since he was really
no longer ill—what Chaucer had perhaps meant when he
wrote of "accidie".

†

He did not, naturally, think of himself as keeping what the
pious called a "good" Lent. (It had not occurred to him
yet—if it ever did it would take its place in the long series
of quiet shocks—that just his ordinary life here—the bad
food, the cold room—was more than the equivalent of most
people's Lenten penance.) He went to Mass on Sundays,
only, and but once to the pious and unspectacular devo-
tions the Hermanos held weekly, consisting of hymns and
prayers led by his godfather. Holy Week was the climax of
their year, and through no conscious intention of Bain's,
also the climax of his work here. He lived as quietly as
possible in anticipation of it, as though saving his strength

for it. Most of his time he devoted to his notes and to the
expansion of some of them; after all, he might as well have
something to show Jeremy Kendal. . . .

Mirabal was away a good part of the time, selling patent
medicines. The weather had broken earlier than usual, so
that the diabolist had gone early into the mountains. Lupe
took care, with an aunt, of the younger children. And Bain,
for some reason whose analysis he shunned, found he had
set himself to avoid the girl. At times, he thought it might
be the scientific spirit again: to see if lust actually could be
controlled by the mind, by the mental paraphernalia the
Church or her priests so mouthily, as he put it, prescribed.

Schapper's coming gave Bain an added excuse, if he needed
one, for not joining Elva during the holiday. She wrote to
him seldom—only twice—during Lent. One letter did not
mention her pregnancy; the second said—and did not say
much more—that she had given up her movie work and
that she didn't see anything else to do but have the baby.
This letter left Bain quiet all day and with a feeling it took
him hours to realize was happiness of a sort he had not
before experienced. He could not understand the change
in Elva; he could not even understand the change in himself; but this latter he had become used to not understanding, and a few times he found himself wondering what it
would be like if incredibly he should become a believer.
Instead of the near panic and bewilderment such a thought
induced in him previously, he now found himself speculat-
ing on the nature of God, a pastime he had dismissed sardonically, even when an undergraduate, as a pursuit of the vague
and pretentious young men who majored in philosophy.
But the Trinity? he wondered: there was a thing to exercise
anyone's capacity for subtleties. That first time he thought
of it, he underwent neither revulsion of it nor fear of his

own sanity. Without knowing, without knowledge, he yet experienced a sense of the balance, the wonderful symmetry involved in the concept. Balance made absolute, symmetry transcendental. Without knowing, without hope of seeing, he yet experienced an awareness of the qualities involved. How much further he might have gone this time he never knew. Mrs. Senton telephoned just then to ask him to a party.

†

Monday of Holy Week, the weather changed again in one of the sudden and unpredictable variations peculiar to the country there, and snow fell all day. Watching it from his window, Bain thought of Mirabal in the mountains and found himself hoping, half-sardonically, that the man had not been doing any more predicting of the weather. But, in the mountains, he knew, Mirabal would likely be on graver business than that. Lately, Bain had found himself pitying Mirabal as at times and much more briefly and reluctantly—as if against his will—he found himself pitying Mrs. Senton.

That evening, he drove as far as the church in Ranchos, parked the car in the snow there, and started to walk to the morada. Along the two or three difficult miles he passed or was passed by other men going where he was going. Generally they were muffled in shapeless clothes, their heads bent against the cold. It had stopped snowing and there was no wind. Bain was tired when he reached the little building. Certainly, he told himself, there would be no procession tonight. . . .

Inside the morada it was warm and crowded. Some of the men knelt before the *bulto* of Christ, others sat on benches, many of these latter with their heads in their hands.

The locked door in the back of the room was open now, and shed a bar of light onto the shadow of that corner of the chapel nearest itself. Bain's heart, it might be said, leaped. Here was the last mystery, the final thing to complete his work; at least, the final material, tangible, or seeable thing. . . .

Like some knight with his eyes fixed on the grail, in the first quickening of his interest in weeks, he began to move, as it were automatically, toward the open door. Teran stopped him. There were lines of obvious strain in the Spaniard's face, and he spoke to Bain almost as though he were a stranger. "Do you wish to do penance tonight?"

Thinking he knew what the man meant, Bain said: "Not with the lash, sir. I would like to carry a cross."

Teran shook his head slightly. "Not tonight. The crosses are all spoken for this night."

"Then I will wait until some other night, sir", Bain said, glibly. As Teran began to move away, Bain went on: "Perhaps I could assist those preparing for the carrying?"

Teran shrugged as he moved away. Like almost everyone else there but Bain, he gave the impression of being stupefied or stunned. Bain wondered if some drug, used seasonally, could not be involved, like the Indian's *peyote*. . . . If so, it was something he had found, that the others before him had missed. . . . But he caught himself almost immediately: any fool should know weariness when he saw it. In something partly wonder, partly admiration, he tried to think of what it must be like by the end of the week if they were this tired now.

He moved toward the door the light came from: his unease prompted him to turn his head to see if he were being watched . . . but no one was watching him.

At the door he paused, in a disappointment his mind or perhaps only his will refused to analyze: men who moved slowly in a kind of grave weariness, were dressing in the long, loose, cotton drawers called *calzones*, and one or two had already affixed the hoods that made their penance largely secret and truly humble. Several whips or lashes of cactus hung on the wall, but seemed dry, stiff, and old. The men, most of them older than Bain, moved woodenly and slowly around the rough crosses, lying stacked in the middle of the room. Two or three penitents, already hooded, stood quietly, their legs slightly straddled, a hand raised to their concealed faces as though they prayed for something: strength or humility, perhaps, or even purity of intention, that what they were going to do be solely and strictly for their own penance and the greater glory of God.

So Bain stood there, the disappointment not less mawk-ish in him because it was obscure, until a kind of shame rose in him, and he was grateful for Maes' voice begin-ning the services and so calling all present to kneel and pray.

†

On Wednesday, Bain slept late, having uncertainly in a reach of his brain a sense of some gauche conflict impending—like knights battling with plowshares for weapons—and involving the Hermanos and Schapper; something that fed on the nerves as bats on blood. He expected Schapper to arrive today, but there was no word from the man by the time Bain left for the morada. Sun had melted much of the snow, so that under the moon the earth lay dark and white. It would not be as spectacular as the two preceding nights, he thought, when the dragged crosses had made long, unbro-ken lines in the snow. . . . Three of the crossbearers had fro-zen their feet, and Bain had wanted to make some sort of

protest. It was a curious thing that stayed his protest, though
he remained unreconciled to that part of the penance: not
in all Kraft-Ebing, nor in any related book, could he remember any instance of cold being used. . . . And he did remember, almost as though it were a corollary, how freely Dante
had made cold a part of Hell.

The scene in the morada tonight did not vary from the
preceding nights, unless it was that the Hermanos seemed
to take even less notice of himself. He had been waiting—
watching with that secret and incredibly inquisitive part of
him—for signs of cracking in some of them; feeling, though,
that it might occur later in the week. But even he was
shocked when one of the Hermanos, more than half-
drunk, approached him unsteadily and placing a hand on
his shoulder, said: "Guess you're glad to be a Hermano,
huh, kid? You're as good as a priest, now."

The drunk moved away and there was left of Bain's feelings at the moment only his mind inquiring, fruitlessly, the
reason for the sense of shock. A believer would be shocked,
he knew, but he was not a believer. . . .

Again, he was not allowed to carry a cross: they were all
spoken for. . . . And he either would not or could not use
one of the cactus whips on himself. He wondered if his
refusal to do this form of penance was responsible for their
seeming to ignore him. But, watching them, he saw that
they did not pay much attention to each other . . . as if
knowing that here, as hereafter, every man must do his own
penance and alone.

When Maes was through leading the hymns, Bain arranged
himself next to a crucifer as a *compañero* in the forming
procession, as he had the night before. At the back of the
chapel the warden opened the door and they felt the cold
air move through the room, at first a stimulant in the

overheated place, then quickly a threat. A hooded penitent picked up the horsehair harness of the *carrete de muerte*.

Up ahead and already outside, the thin notes of the *pite-ro's* flute moved upward, then seemed to hover above all of them like some night bird crying uncertainly in the dark. And a drum, in contrast rather than as an accompaniment, began to beat tunelessly. At the head of the procession, Maes began to move and at the same time to chant from the copybook. The others followed in hoarse, unmelodious voices, and slowly the whole procession moved out into the cold.

Bain was *compañero* to a rather small man, so short that when bent under the weight of the dragging cross, the crosspiece was not more than a few inches from the ground. Now, out in the cold and the luminous dark, remembering how long it had taken the previous night to make the pilgrimage, hearing the slap of the whips begin, he feared that the little man might not be able to finish. If so, Bain was not sure what he himself was supposed to do. So had every man of the Hermanos been preoccupied, each with his own problem, that Bain had had no chance yet to find out about certain details, as for instance all the functions and duties of a *compañero*.

Awkwardly, from his height, he leaned close to the little man's hood. "You all right, *amigo*?"

"*Muy bien*", the little man said in a labored voice. "I am very well."

They were all outside now and the voices kept swelling louder and louder. Although he was up toward the head of the line and all the penitents but the crossbearers behind him, Bain could hear, so various the other sounds, only occasional notes of the flute. The moon shed a hard, white light and their shadows were black and clear edged. Glancing over his shoulder—fearing somehow to turn his head all the way—Bain could see only the moving shadows on the snow and not the penitents themselves. The shadows were long under the low moon, and the moving shapes of the whips varied abruptly in length as they passed through their arcs; the shadows, too, varied and changed, and the whole composite shadow moved slowly onward like some single, great, and agonized animal going slowly and dumbly upward to God.

This was Bain's own spontaneous concept and fancy . . . and he rejected it almost immediately. He had come too close already, he told himself, and too often. . . . The damn fools, he thought, and tried to feel some sort, any sort of anger, but nothing—no process of the mind, certainly— could drown out, eliminate, or make less terrible or less true, the heavy, dragging crunch of the wood across the snow, the slap of the whips, or the labored breathing of the man whose helper Bain was.

This was no daylight procession to their own little Calvary, with frequent stops at the stations of the cross to give the penitents a rest. Teran, at the head of the line with Maes and the *pitero*, seemed to stop only when the thought of stopping randomly occurred to him, and reluctantly, for perhaps a minute or a minute and a half, then move on again. During these stops Bain did what he was supposed to do: stood facing the little crucifer and eased the burden of the cross from the man's shoulder by taking it briefly upon his own. If the weather had been warm he would also have been expected to move the loose, lower part of the hood up and down to fan cooler air into the crucifer.

After the second stop, Bain began to grow more alarmed about the little man: he had wilted so as the cross was returned to him. The third time, the little man just collapsed quietly in the snow. Bain grabbed quickly to steady the wood, but the lower end of the crosspiece had already struck the ground, so that the whole thing was held upright in the three or four inches of crusted snow. The little man was not struck, but lay under although not touching the wood.

Spontaneously, Bain knelt beside the inert figure. Even more spontaneously, he looked up for the others to stop, but the procession just moved around them and on, as it had—he remembered—the previous night when others had fallen.

Bain knelt there, staring rather fixedly at the little man bent in the snow. The last of the line passed them, chanting hoarsely and out of tune, the notes of the *pitero* almost inaudible. "You all right?" Bain said. "Here, let me get you out of there." He held the cross with one hand to steady it, while with his other hand he tried to help the little man out from under it, but the man made no effort to move.

"Come on", Bain said. "I'll help you go back."

The figure in the snow shook its head. "No, leave me here", it said. "Go carry my cross for me."

"No", Bain said. "You'll freeze to death here."

"Even so", the little man said. "Go with the cross."

"No, not now", Bain said. Standing up, he eased the cross over onto the ground and put his hands under the little man's shoulders. "Come on."

"No. You finish for me. I cannot."

"Come on", Bain said. "What's the matter with you?"

"I am an adulterer", the little man said.

"That's not what I mean", Bain said. "Anyhow, don't tell me, tell the priest." Later, Bain might wonder mildly, not at this little victory over his own prurience, but at its completeness. He pulled harder and raised the little man up. Apparently the Spaniard could stand by himself, but simply did not want to move. Now, himself unmoving, Bain felt the cold, and in a kind of panic, grew fearful—as for a child—over the little man in nothing but the hood, the long, cotton drawers, and the rough shoes.

So, as he would with a child, he picked the man up and began to walk back to the morada. Walking and not yet tired, his mind moving in its customary patterns, Bain wondered how much of the little man's wish to stay there in the snow was due to exhaustion and how much to a desire to do penance. And inevitably, of course, Bain thought of how casually he and Schapper, and indeed people of almost every strata at the University, accepted adultery; accepted it as often necessary to the work, as a convention like marriage. Someone was awfully wrong, he knew, yet certainly it was nothing over which to die in the snow. . . .

The little man grew heavy and stiff, so that Bain, becoming alarmed, slung him over his shoulder and ran, as best he could, breaking through the crust with each step. The moon shed its hard light and Bain's throat began to hurt from the raw air. His breath took on the quality and rhythm of sobbing and the mind would not have had to deceive itself greatly to think that the tears from the cold were those of grief or a kind of sorrow. . . . Somewhere the inevitable coyote yowled and once Bain stumbled and fell headlong. Having only one arm to protect himself, the crusted snow scraped his face and enraged him. Sitting up, he saw that the little man had also fallen sitting up and was apparently conscious.

His rage—as best Bain could analyze it—was at his apparent lack or partial lack of control over his own actions, over his own pain. Stumbling, he had not willed in any way to leave his face exposed. But he had not been able to free the arm that held the little man slung across his shoulder.

Bain swore. The little man did not move, but sat there, sidewise to Bain, and apparently in some degree of stupor. "Get up!" Bain said, but when the man did not move, Bain rose and picked him up again and resumed the journey.

Again breathing seared his throat and his arms ached at the joints. Your penance, he thought, and cursed himself for an ignorant and superstitious fool. He had his belly full of this, he told himself.

He edged down through the deeper snow that lay on the hollow that held the morada. The door was opened for them by the infirmarian, who did not seem disturbed as Bain brought his burden in and laid it on a bench near the stove.

"You can go and join the others," the infirmarian said, "as I suppose you will want to?"

"Sure", Bain said. "If he's all right."

"He's all right." The infirmarian turned to where strong tea brewed on the stove.

Bain departed and began to walk back to Ranchos. Schapper and the others ought to be in by now, he thought. He hoped they weren't disappointed at his not being there to meet them. He looked forward suddenly and with pleasure to a drink with them. A relief to be with your own people, he told himself.

13

IT WAS STILL EARLY when Bain arrived in Tarale; not yet ten o'clock, he found. At the hotel the clerk told him his friends had been inquiring for him.

The door was opened promptly to Bain's knock by a stranger, a man with a plump, somewhat rosy and smiling face, whose eyeglasses could not conceal his benign good humor. He looked as if about to break into a chuckle at any moment. By way of contrast was the rich, heavy bathrobe of some pale color between yellow and cream; black piped its edges and, open at the neck, it revealed a silk pajama top of pale green.

"Welcome, welcome", the happy little man said. "You're Spencer Bain, of course. I've been looking forward to this. Come in, come in." Bain entered the room slowly. "I'm Jeremy Kendal", the man said and put out his hand. He seemed disappointed and drew in on himself at Bain's lack of enthusiasm.

"I'm glad to see you", Bain said. They were alone in the room, which already smelled of some light, expensive scent, doubtless Mrs. Kendal's.

Behind Bain Mr. Kendal closed the door and sighed. "Well", he said, and repeated the word, accenting it querulously the second time; "I guess you want to see Jack, but I'm not at all sure he's here. Sit down, sit down. I'll get you a drink right away. Now, just a minute." He held up an admonishing, a quieting finger, and went to the door connecting with the next room; knocking lightly, even delicately on it, he hung, as it were, poised for a few seconds

while he listened. "Ah," he said at last, "the rascals have
gone out. They *said* they might. Graber's or Gruber's or
some sort of night spot."

"Billy Gruber's", Bain said. He sat stiffly on a straight
wooden chair, his hat on his knee.

"But we shouldn't let that disturb *us*", Mr. Kendal said.
"Here, let me take your hat and coat. Then I'll get you a
drink. Scotch is what you want, I suppose?"

With a reluctance he did not quite understand, Bain stood
up and removed his coat. Mr. Kendal made a great bustle
and ceremony of taking the coat and putting it carefully on
a hanger and in the closet. His glance avoided Bain's, for
some reason, and continued to avoid it as he turned from
the closet to a side table that Bain noticed, only now, held
bottles and ice. Watching the plump little man make over-
precise gestures with the stuff on the table, Bain was honestly puzzled.

Unusually prurient—even for his time and his profession—
Bain's mind yet stood in abeyance. Perhaps, only, he wanted
his book published; perhaps the charity he had lately and
occasionally noticed in himself had something to do with
it; or he was just tired and shocked by his experience in the
snow less than an hour before—but he sat there, looking or
staring at Jeremy Kendal and feeling a sense of revulsion he
could neither define nor name. The effect of the heated
room on his lean, chilled frame played its part, too. And
perhaps something that had to do with less physical con-
trasts ... experienced before perceived, incredible in real
life: perhaps the comparison between Kendal and the
Hermanos.

The little man—it was his face that gave the appearance
of plumpness—finally turned to Bain with the drink.
"There", he said. His mouth was twisted into a kind of

pursed and thoughtful smile, as if now he knew Bain well enough to reveal that he had serious thoughts and was capable of grave appreciations.

Kendal held his own drink in his other hand and sat on the edge of the bed. He had lit a cigarette in a long holder that matched the robe, and the curious, pursed—Bain wondered if the man were actually trying to be wistful—smile, accented by the effort of clasping the holder in his teeth, gave the face an almost simian expression.

Bain did not speak but took more than half the drink at a gulp. "Well, you must certainly have needed that", Mr. Kendal said.

Bain nodded. "I've been out on some of the work. It's very cold by night up here."

"Ah," Mr. Kendal said, "that's what I want to hear about—the work. Tell me—how soon will it be finished?"

Bain shrugged. "Pretty soon, I think. This week finishes the important part."

"Ah", Mr. Kendal said again. "Then we can have an early fall or late spring publication."

"What?" Bain said.

"You say the book is almost finished?"

"No—the work is almost finished. I've only done maybe ten thousand words on the book."

"Oh, I see", Mr. Kendal said. He decided to laugh. "When I say work, I mean one thing, you mean another." He found it quite amusing in his quiet way.

When Bain did not speak but finished the drink, Mr. Kendal said: "But when can I see what you've done? You didn't bring it with you by any chance?"

No, Bain had not brought it with him. He shook his head. "I guess I could get it down to you sometime tomorrow."

"Yes, Friday", Mr. Kendal said, thoughtfully and blinking, as if trying to sum up his appointments for that day.

"Good Friday", Bain said, for some reason.

"Oh, yes", Mr. Kendal said, brightly. "That's quite a holiday or something out here, isn't it? Penitentes and such. By the way—" his eyes also brightened—"I'd like so much to see one of their processions and so on. Jack tells me you've been in close touch with them?"

Bain found he was shaking his head slowly. With surprising bitterness he regretted the frankness of some of his letters to Schapper: at least the man should keep his mouth shut, like, well, say like Nunes or even Gannon or even a bad priest would about a confession, any confession. "No", Bain said and let it go at that. At the moment he wanted to tell no more lies than that, the simple negation: he had tired— there was actually an ennui—of lies.

Mr. Kendal seemed to wilt. He looked at Bain obliquely through his glasses, in a kind of serious, wistful, and disappointed acquiescence. A slight—so slight it was apparent only when the light touched it glancingly—trickle of drool ran from the corner of Mr. Kendal's mouth that clasped the cigarette holder. Mr. Kendal was beginning to be very much afraid that Bain was a disappointment. He clutched desperately at a touchstone. "I suppose you see a good deal of Marsha?" he said.

Bain shook his head slightly. "You mean, Mrs. Senton? No."

Mr. Kendal sighed, tried to be a good loser. "Poor Marsha is so misunderstood. And she means well. She means well all the time."

They began to hear people moving in the next room, moving leisurely and surely. "Ah, they're back", Mr. Kendal said. He had actually cocked his head like a dog listening.

"They'll be glad to see you." He rose and knocked on the intervening door. "Oh, Jack," he said, "and Myra. Come in. Friend of yours is here." He hung poised for a moment by the door, as though listening. It opened promptly and Schapper came into the room, preceded by a blonde woman of about thirty. Trying to greet Schapper, Bain found it difficult to take his eyes off the woman. She had the incredible bodily assurance which, within its own sphere, is all but unconquerable. She would forever, merely by her appearance, be able to drive more chaste and even more beautiful women into a fury. The dark-blonde hair hung, shining and sleek, to her shoulders, the mouth was large, red, and assured. The high coloring and large eyes seemed to go together. All the features were regular and it was impossible to say why she was not beautiful; it was as though she had deliberately rejected beauty in favor of something more useful: the thin body seemed hardly more than a rounded and tube-like vehicle to carry and display the large, hard, and widely-spaced breasts. Part—a remote, ironic, and easily subdued part—of Bain thought of the cartoons in certain magazines. She was a cartoon. Then his mind, automatically and intricately, began to follow the implications of what the woman had deliberately made of herself: it was as if, rejecting the casual, continued, and thousand-fold glance of all men's homage to conventional beauty, she had chosen to concentrate on her physicality and the comparatively few men she could thus so completely—and even profitably—enthrall.

Schapper was saying: "Why, he doesn't even see me!" And Jeremy Kendal was saying, his voice gone almost shrill: "I don't think you've met my wife before."

"No", Bain said.

"Hello", the woman said. She smiled at Bain with large, white teeth. In a kind of dismay, in wonder, and a little in

anger, Bain found he had reacted to her as, when a young-
ster, he had to a dirty picture. By an actual and conscious
effort of his will, he turned to Schapper.

"How have you been?" Schapper said. He had not changed
in the two years since Bain had seen him. There was still
the lean, rather hard and stocky body, the expensive, heavy
tweeds, the hollowed and lined face, the graying hair, the
prominent eyes. The mouth still curled upward in its pro-
fessionally sardonic humor.

"All right, Jack", Bain said. His respect for Schapper had
returned, quite completely. "Sorry I wasn't here to meet
you. This was my last chance to get some stuff I can't get
any other time of year, except these few days before Easter."

"I know how it is, Spence", Schapper said. His voice
dropped, indicated sympathy and fellowship in the work, a
tight, closed little group shutting out in pride all others . . .
even for the moment, Mrs. Kendal.

"Drinks, drinks", Mr. Kendal said. "What will you rascals have to drink?"

"The usual, dear", Mrs. Kendal said.

"Double Scotch for me, Jeremy", Schapper said, and the
little man half-scurried, half-waddled to his presiding.

The others sat down. Bain felt good now, a little happy:
his respect for Schapper would always exist, and after all, in
a way, Schapper had come here to see if his, Bain's work,
was good. He started to talk shop while Mrs. Kendal listened intently—she was a good listener—and her husband
took a long time preparing the drinks.

Schapper listened, too, nodding occasionally in patroni-
zation or agreement. When Mr. Kendal interrupted Bain
with the drinks, Schapper said: "It sounds good, Spence. It
sounds fine. The only thing I'm worried about is if you're
not being taken in maybe by thinking things are the way

they used to be. Why"—the sardonic smile increased—
"Myra and I went down to this tough bar tonight—
Gruber's, you know—and someone said he was supposed
to have killed a man and be going to stand trial. We were
kind of frightened, but when we got there, the fellow was
doing everything but kissing people. You'd think he was a
politician or something. Why—" Schapper laughed—"I'd
hate to tell you what it reminded me of."

Bain shook his head, starting to explain, when Jeremy
Kendal interrupted. "I don't care", Kendal said, with surprising vehemence. "I'm betting on Spence and I'm publishing his book."

"Good for you", Schapper said. "I'm glad you are, Jeremy.
But publishing a book is one thing and actually having the
stuff straight is another, as you well know."

All of them laughed, except Mrs. Kendal. Bain, watching her whenever he could, had noticed a quick, smiling—
although she did not smile—change come over her at her
husband's remark; and now saw her pretend to yawn, as she
exchanged with Schapper a glance Bain could not quite
read. It was as though something had been sealed and delivered. . . . Bain felt one of his obscure angers, whose outlet
or release this time seemed to be no violence toward either
of the other men but a sexual one upon Mrs. Kendal.

"Drinks, drinks", Mr. Kendal said, getting up again. "You
all want the same, I suppose?"

"Not me, dear", his wife said. "I'm going to bed." She
said good night to Bain and went into the next room, closing the door after her. Schapper, for the first time since
Bain had known him, seemed ill at ease and embarrassed.
While Jeremy Kendal played with his glasses and bottles,
Schapper, making obvious efforts to overcome his distraction, tried to talk about Bain's work. "Tomorrow's the big

day," he said, "isn't it? I mean, if we could see a procession while we're here, I think we ought to."

"It's more or less public tomorrow afternoon", Bain said. "Anyone can watch the procession." His mind hesitated in some process of deception. "There's a couple of moradas near here that you could reach easily. The one I'm going to is back in the mountains quite a way."

Schapper hung his head and scraped one foot like a boy. "Well," he said, "we can talk it over in the morning. I didn't see Myra and Jeremy until this morning in Santa Fe. They'd been in New Orleans, while I had to lecture in Chicago." He followed this non sequitur by getting up and saying: "See you later, Spence." Then he went out of the room by the door that opened into the hall. Bain, by no extra effort of his own, could hear Schapper entering the room next to them by its hall door, could hear a faint murmur of voices as Schapper and Mrs. Kendal spoke to each other.

Mr. Kendal turned, beaming, carrying two drinks. "Ah," he said, "that rascal has left us, too." He chuckled, almost silently. "But that's no reason for us to end our little discussion, is it?" He handed a drink to Bain, who took it limply. "I've got to get along", Bain said. "Tomorrow's a very heavy day for me."

"Oh, no", Mr. Kendal said, in something close to anguish. "Stay. Stay the night. No use going back to your cold, little place. Jack has told me of the rigors under which you exist. So stay. Oh, you must stay!"

"You mean—take a room at the hotel here?"

"Why do that?" Mr. Kendal said, as though Bain were not quite bright. "Why not stay right here?" His eyes were large and oyster-like as he stared at Bain's almost unseeing ones.

Bain's mind flashed along the reaches of almost thirty years to a similar occasion when he was a boy. He had been frightened and had run. Now there was a curious sense of numbness and even—amazing and terrible—of grief. He got up and went to the closet and took his coat off the hanger. Starting for the door, he felt a slight nausea begin in him. Alongside him, Mr. Kendal pawed upward at Bain's shoulder, not unlike a rabbit trying frantically to box. "The book", Mr. Kendal gurgled. "Your book. We must talk. Too, we can listen. We. You must—"

Bain opened the door to the hall and went out, closing the door behind him. The lobby was almost deserted when he came down into it. The night clerk, a Spaniard, looked up. "*Adios*, Spance", he said.

"*Adios*", Bain said. Near the double doors of the vestibule, there was a boy and a girl in their late teens saying good night. The girl giggled and the boy smiled as though he were much older than he was.

On the clerk's good-night, on the children parting in joy, Bain's mind seized as if the simple were his only alexin, as if the commonly good alone could make him whole again. Outside, the cold air acted like a shock. He lingered in it for a moment. After all, he told himself, he shouldn't be so dismayed at finding people were not what they seemed: he had been finding that out all of his life. Still, he could not be sure that only was the source of his dismay. "*The perversion of the elect*"—he knew the phrase was not his own, but one he had read someplace. It came to him now with what he felt was singular appropriateness, although he knew its original application had not been merely to intellectuals.

After the moment in the cold air, he went back into the lobby. Going into a phone booth, he placed a call for Elva in Los Angeles. The operator got a circuit rather quickly.

Bain could hear the tone in the receiver as the bell rang in Los Angeles. There was no answer. "Shall I call again in twenty minutes?" the operator said.

"No." He went outside and got into the car and drove home.

†

Going directly to the morada the next morning, for the first time by day, Bain found a small group of women and children gathered patiently outside the place, but as yet—he was grateful—no tourists or Anglos that he knew. Some of those waiting held unlit yellow candles in their hands. Inside the morada, the light was like that of a prison cell, all of it coming from the single window where it opened to the north. The tired faces crowding in the room were made ghastly by it, although among the listless and stupefied looks of some of the men as they raised their heads to see who had entered, were others still bright with pain. No one greeted Bain, and he moved slowly and awkwardly toward the room in the back.

Again, this back room held enough men to almost crowd it, with the crosses stacked sidewise on the floor filling the whole center of the smallish place. Teran was in it and one or two of the other officers. Tired-faced and without amenities of any sort, Teran came over to Bain and said, "The crosses are again all spoken for, as they are each year many weeks in advance. But we have arranged for you to pull the *carrete de muerte*."   ·

The dismay, Bain could not quite account for; and although it must have showed in his face, Teran apparently took no notice of it, but waited, with the stare-eyed look of the very tired who must yet be active and moving, for Bain's reply.

"I brought no *calzones* or hood", Bain said.

For the first time, Teran showed annoyance. "What did you expect to wear when you carried a cross?"

"I had been disappointed so often that today I did not bring any." Curiously, he thought, he never *had* obtained a hood.

"You could borrow some from one who has finished his penance", Teran said indistinctly, and turned away.

Himself now turning, the mind seeking as often for some escape and now finding none, Bain saw a hood hanging on a nail in the earthen wall. He put his hand on it and asked if anyone were using it. No one answered; only two or three turned their heads. Looking for some kind of sanction, Bain stared at one of those who had turned and the man finally shrugged and indicated Bain should take it.

With the hood, of cheap, black bombazine, in his hand, Bain walked to a bench near the wall and began slowly and distastefully to take off his sweater and shirt. Teran came back with a pair of rolled-up *calzones*. "Here", he said.

Bain unrolled the drawers: there were two or three small blood stains on them near the waist. His distaste was evident and Teran said: "They are the best I could get for you now."

"I would rather wear the pants of my own clothing," Bain said, "even though they should get stained."

"Someone might recognize you by them."

There was no answer to that, and Bain took off his clothes, all but the shoes and shorts, and put the *calzones* on. They were both ugly and awkward, being neither underwear nor pajamas. He had never found out whether they had a more common use: the closest thing they resembled were the pants of the loose, white clothing worn by many tribes of Mexican Indians.

Well, now he had on a pair of them, he thought, and
between them and his hood, the body lay bare and defence-
less. He wondered if anyone could recognize him; if by
chance, say, Schapper and the Kendals should come here?
He did not think they would: there was a nearer and better-
known morada just north of Tarale; Mrs. Senton often took
friends there on Good Friday to watch.

He was reminded inevitably and strongly of the high-
school locker rooms of his youth: the quite terrible tension
he had known in them before a contest, much worse than
the violence or pain of the race or game itself. There was,
of course, he recognized, no contest impending here.

It was close to noon: in the chapel Bain heard Maes begin
hoarsely to sing, and the stiff, heavy sound of a group of
men kneeling. With the others in this room of the crosses,
not unlike a sacristy, he crowded through its narrow door
and knelt with them near Maes and the "altar". They sang;
and when it was all over they rose, and Maes and Teran
walked stiffly and slowly toward the back of the chapel.
Those who were to carry the crosses returned into the smaller
room. Bain knew he was to pick up the carrete outside; it
was too big to fit through the door if dragged. He would
follow the crucifers and the others would follow him, so
that on this last penance of the year, they would, in daylight and under the sun as under the moon, see and know
fully how always behind each of them rode Death with the
drawn bow. There would be no whips in the daylight.
Although here, in the chapel, one man bound cactus about
his shoulders.

Now, in the back of the chapel the door had opened,
and the gray light of the place increased. The penitents with-
drew to either wall so that the crucifers could go between
them. And now these came, bent, slowly dragging the crosses,

each to go slowly through—for that moment black and permanent like granite—the oblong of light and disappear. The last one moved into the light and Bain felt the eyes shift to himself; someone gestured and Bain moved toward the doorway. They had, through the doorway, been looking into the shadow of the building . . . for now as he emerged from the dimness the light blinded him, and he actually groped— his glasses removed because of the hood—and someone had to take his arm and show him where the carrete stood in the shade. He did not look at the figure of the hag with drawn bow, but fumbled for the ropes of the harness, and feeling the horsehair in his fingers, knew even through their tougher skin how it was going to feel on arms and shoulders. . . .

Again, someone helped him. Arranging the ropes, his eyes growing accustomed to the light, he saw the crucifers only a few rods away, so slowly did they move; and at last, the wheels also unmoving in his mind—as forever in memory—he leaned like a draft animal into the harness.

Always, in some fond and remote part of the brain, with the disparaging and sceptical note of his time, he had doubted that the dragging of the carrete was more than—physically—a minor task. Now, as the heavy and reluctant weight of the thing swung against the ropes and the horsehair rasped—as he, too, swung—his shoulders, he experienced an anguish whose greater part was mental: a disappointment and a disillusionment; surmise, estimate, insight, appraisal—whatever it was, the thing he lived so largely by—was this time wrong.

His eyes—again like an animal—looked upward and out toward the crucifers ahead. Behind him, he heard the scrape of the wheels; it differed from the scrape of the crosses: it was lighter and, as the cart swung slightly—cutting first one shoulder, then the other—more variant in tone.

Bain's first feeling was again the bitter one of having been trapped. But by whom? or what? Teran? his own scientific curiosity? something nameless? He could not be sure. There was a method to be learned even at this dragging of a weight, he found, and had to concentrate on learning it in order to make his burden at all bearable: using his thumbs to ease the rasp at his shoulders, utilizing what little downslope might occur.

They were still between the two rows of spectators, most of whom would also follow when the end of the procession passed them. Now, able to ease somewhat the strain; now, too, somewhat accustomed to it, Bain glanced around him as best he might from under the hood. Dismay turned his knees weak: in the left row of spectators stood, all in one group, Mrs. Senton, some others earmarked as all her devotees so curiously and ineffably were, Ruth Trevelyan, Schapper, and the Kendals. Bain's dismay was countered almost instantly by their glances, which moved over and past him ... so that he knew immediately that none of them recognized him.

In turn, he discovered, he could apparently see them with great and apparently abnormal clarity. Mr. Kendal was puzzled and impressed; his wife, only puzzled. Schapper stared moodily, the sardonic upcurve gone. Ruth Trevelyan was in a state of quiet hysteria: her lips moved nervously, in and out, first the upper, then the lower. Mrs. Senton's guests looked as though they did not know whether to smile or not. A kind of ghastly indecision played about their features. The great lady herself, though, was revealed in all her pasty horror: the pie-plate face looked flatter than ever, while her eyes had the oysterish appearance of Mr. Kendal's on the previous night—a transcending blankness, as if she were trying to lose herself in a sort of void shot through and illuminated only by the play of some feeble sexual lightning. Bain even sensed—and forgot immediately—Mrs. Senton's displeasure with Ruth Trevelyan standing next to her.

The procession moved along its weary and terrible way, with that clarity, and for some reason—had he before, too?—wept.

He noticed no one as the procession came again to the people lined near the morada. The vision or whatever it was, had gone; he saw himself for what he was: a faker trapped into this ordeal, even the blood on the *calzones*, another's. So, in another man's blood, in the extreme and almost heretical gestures of a religion in which he did not believe, between the faces of his own people, not less mocking because they did not recognize him; hooded, sweating, bloody, and in pain Bain finished his journey.

When, in the shadow of the morada, he eased himself out of the harness, he found that he bent when he walked, as if still against the pull of the cart. So bent, he entered the low and narrow doorway, and in the darkness lay down, like an animal, on the earth floor.

Lying there, for the few moments before Maes and the infirmarian raised him, he believed. Perhaps it was exhaustion that lowered the barriers pride and custom had long raised in him; perhaps the lucidity and intuitive accuracy of the vision he had beheld. He might never know, fully. But lying there, he wept—for those he had beheld, for his own past unbelief, for Elva ... but mostly and in what amazement he was capable of, for the icy vanity of his own people.

14

HE LAY IN BED THAT EVENING at Maes' house, and Maes' wife bathed with rosemary the raw lines at his shoulders. She was an old woman, and Bain had never seen her before except in church, wearing the conventional black shawl all old women here used for head-covering. Now, he saw clearly for the first time her face, the innumerable lines and wrinkles in the dark skin, the incredible patience. The lower lip protruded slightly in the stern and proud shadow of a smile, but the rest of the face was grave; the eyes, indeed, almost never met his own.

He wondered if her pride—if it was pride—was for him and his being her husband's godchild. He rather hoped it wasn't. When she had finished bathing the rawness, she took folded strips of old sheeting and soaking them in the solution of rosemary, bound them on the narrow wounds. "There, is that better?" she said, in Spanish.

"Much better, Mother", Bain said.

"Now, we'll get you some soup," she said, "and tomorrow you'll be all right."

"I'm all right now", he said. He watched her go out of the room and he wondered just how long a man could go on like this. He had asked Maes to take him to the old man's house, knowing that Schapper and the others would come to his own place when they did not find him at the hotel. He did not want Schapper or the others to see him as he was. He was not sure that he wanted them to see him at all.

He lay very quiet, and tried to know what had happened to him, to recreate or even to recall the state of mind that

had been his in the morada after the procession. It was difficult, perhaps impossible to do: he was no longer incredibly
weary nor, except when he moved, was he in pain. The
time of vision seemed to have passed. There was no heat or
cold. There remained only, like ashes, a kind of fear.

Recognizing fear, he was unable to name it. Yet slowly
its nature manifested itself to him: he was afraid, not of sin
or of Hell or of unbelief, but of belief ... of what had
happened to him—as the first man must have shrunk from
the first fire. It was clear to him that he no longer doubted
the reality of what had happened, of what, under less shat-
tering and more reasonable forms, had happened to a legion
of other people. His resentment was nameless, a form of
ineffable pride. He thought of a cheap phrase, often heard:
"Too hot to handle", and shaking his head in grief and
bewilderment kept repeating it to himself as other men might
repeat a set prayer or still others some verbal fetish. Some
of his grief was at the cheapness of the phrase.... He was
still shaking his head when the old lady returned. She was
accompanied by Nunes. Under his smile, so forced it seemed
almost a smirk, the priest's gravity showed plain. While the
two men greeted each other conventionally, the old lady
put the bowl of soup on a chair near Bain and went out of
the room.

"I didn't think I was so badly off I needed a priest", Bain
said. Knowing how rare his own attempts at humor were,
he wondered why he should try it now.

"Oh, visiting the sick is one of the corporal works of
mercy, too," Nunes said, "as well as burying the dead. You
must be crazy", he added.

Bain pushed out his lower lip, one of the gestures he had
borrowed from the Spaniards. "Everyone in my profession
is", he said. "Except some of us know it and others don't."

Nunes sat slowly down on a hide-backed chair near the bed. "Look, Spence," he said, "what's the idea? This kind of thing isn't for you. The Church doesn't approve of it, although it's ceased to condemn the practice locally. You didn't really think you needed it?" When Bain hesitated, not speaking, but looking away and toward the foot of the bed, Nunes went on: "I don't mean to be curious. I just want to guard against any sort of scrupulosity on your part, such as many converts experience. Although I suppose the most likely guess is that you did this for the sake of your work?"

Bain nodded, almost without hesitation. "Sort of."

"Look," Nunes said, suddenly urgent, "I want to be sure you are not going to repeat this. . . . Such things are not for you. You have no need for such primitive penance. I'm sure you don't even have sins grave enough to in any way justify such a penance."

The eloquence of the man, sitting there in his weather-stained clothes, the silk of his clerical vest split and slightly soiled—as if he had dressed hurriedly to come here—moved Bain to say: "Don't kid yourself."

The remark halted the priest abruptly. After a pause he said: "Well, if so, you should have discussed them with your confessor. If it is of a profound nature," he went on, rather awkwardly, "you could go to someone like Father Gannon or one of the Franciscans attached to the Cathedral in Santa Fe. Father Lanigan and myself are just ordinary parish priests. But this thing of you doing as the Hermanos do—"

Bain shook his head to try to dismiss the subject. There was something else he wanted to ask the priest: in the silence his mind hung poised as over a precipice; asking his question of Nunes—of anyone—would come dangerously close to sealing his own belief. The mind, ceaselessly rationalizing,

said it was for the work ... and therefore all right to ask.
Bain took a breath and said: "This business of Grace and
temptation—I don't understand it, or rather its logic. Why
should some people have great Grace and others little? It
seems distributed—if that's the word—without any due balancing of the accounts."

"Without apparent balancing, you mean." Nunes looked
away, at the floor; he seemed again embarrassed, although
he spoke firmly enough.

"Even so", Bain said. He took on a strange, an almost
triumphant sureness. "Its forms seem so pathetic, so almost
evanescent at times." He thought of his own feelings about
the child dead; of the intermittent pity for Mrs. Senton; of
the ennui for lies. "One can hardly be sure."

Nunes looked at him and almost smiled; there was the
inevitable shrug by the priest. "What do you want?" Nunes
said. "Do you think every man is knocked from his horse
on the road to Damascus?"

Once more, Bain experienced the physical coldness he
had on the night he played poker at Nunes' house, the night
he had pretended, with incredible and alarming slyness, to
agree with Gannon. He found himself nodding now, but in
agreement. "All right", he said. "Then tell me this: What
about temptations that are weak, so obvious and apparent
and ridiculous that they are really only the mockery of temptation?" He was thinking of Mrs. Trevelyan, for whom he
felt no attraction, trying to seduce him; of Mr. Kendal, who
made him want to vomit. "What about them?"

Nunes shrugged again and this time smiled outright. "I
don't know", he said. "I honestly don't. If you were—well,
invincibly ignorant or literal minded, I'd stretch a point and
tell you that it might be that Grace had insulated you. . . . Or
I might say that your will was being weakened, or you made

complacent against a time of greater temptation. But you being
what you are and capable of knowing how ineffable such matters are, I tell you the honest truth, that I don't know."

Lying there, the hurt almost gone, Bain sweated. When
he did not speak or move, but only continued to stare at
the foot of the bed, Nunes went on: "I will say this—that
the Devil is not only very strong, but very cunning—
subtle, you would say?"

Bain nodded once. "Yes", he said. *Yes, to what?*

Nunes seemed to be satisfied, Bain saw, whatever he himself meant or might or might not see.

"Anyhow," Nunes said, "I think your trouble is scruples.
I think you must guard against them. A person like you, an
intellectual, should not require any such harsh penance as
the Hermanos subject themselves to. Although, as you say,"
he added thoughtfully, "it was probably your intellectual
curiosity, too."

Bain could think of nothing to say that did not involve
some part of a lie. He lay there without speaking. In something like amazement he found that for almost the first
time—Elva, of course, was the other exception—he was
willing to concede that someone, Nunes, was actually a good
person. Then, in a rush, not unlike that of tears, he saw
that he had known others, too: Maes and his wife; Lupe
(he was sure she prayed for him as for her father); even
Atwood, in his way. Bain was amazed.

"Anyhow," Nunes said, getting up, "you're all right? Nothing I can do to make you comfortable? I've had your car
brought around here from where it was parked near the
church. I'll get you a doctor, if you want."

Bain shook his head. "I'm not sick. I think it was the
fasting that got me. There was nothing to eat or drink at
the morada."

The shadow of amusement—something deeper than a smile—passed over Nunes' face. "Just like all the other Hermanos—you won't have a doctor."

"Oh, I'd have one if I needed one."

"Come and see us, soon", the priest said.

"*Adios*."

"*Adios*", Nunes said. He left the room.

Hitching himself painfully onto one elbow, Bain began to drink the still warm soup directly from the bowl. He drank it like water on a hot day and then, wiping the chicken grease from his lips and blowing out the lamp, lay heavily down again. He half-smiled: the old lady had given him chicken soup on Good Friday; she must really have thought he needed it.

Although the early dark gathered all around the house, the room lay in its own separate dusk: a narrow bar of light from the kitchen touched wall and floor, and diffused a twilight in the place. In this twilight Bain lay still, almost as if he were its center and its source. In one of those curious identifications of mental with physical states, due to weariness or ill health or, usually, to being on the edge of sleep, he saw this twilight as his own mind—himself, even—and his consciousness as some small, agonized core at the center of it. . . .

Perhaps he slept—he would never know; perhaps—indeed, most likely—he dreamed. Somewhere in that twilight, though, all good women wept for him, unseen. He knew only, in some forgotten way, that it was the sound of good women mourning: so that it was he who subjectively felt it was his wife, his mother long dead, Lupe, Maes' wife, the earliest and the latest he had known, mourning as for the dead.

He woke, gasping, into the light. Schapper and the Kendals stood in the little room. They were amused by something. "Drunk again, eh", Schapper said.

Alarmed, Bain glanced at his bandaged shoulders, but they were covered by his shirt. He lay back again quietly—he had started half-erect—and looked at the others in curiosity and that odd wonder in which some return from sleep. For a moment, it was easy to think of them as having sought him out to torment—was that the word?—him. . . . Then he caught hold of himself, returned to full consciousness, and sat up again. "What goes?" he said. "How'd you know I was here? I'm glad you came." Over their shoulders, he saw Maes and his wife in the doorway; their faces unreadable, they moved away almost as he looked at them. He found that having said so, he actually was glad they had come, a relief from thought.

"Why, we saw your car standing outside, Spence, old boy", Jeremy Kendal said. He was immaculate and quiet today: the brilliant and steady little man upon whom so many characteristically unstable authors depended for counsel and sympathy.

Bain nodded and rubbed his eyes. "I was up pretty early," he said, "and on my feet most of the day in the mountains. These people here are friends of mine and I came to their house to take a sleep." It was not an awfully good explanation, he knew, and experienced a moment of terror that they had recognized him in the procession today: it might be this that they had come to torment him with. . . .

"We saw a very interesting procession ourselves", Mrs. Kendal said. Her eyes were large and bright; today she seemed interested in Bain. He nodded. His relief that apparently they had not recognized him was so great that he felt as if he were strong again.

"Get your clothes on", Schapper said. "We're going down to Gruber's and tie one on."

"Today is Good Friday", Bain said. "They take it pretty hard out here, and if they see me at Gruber's, they'll think I'm, well, an unbeliever or something."

Mr. and Mrs. Kendal smiled separately; Mr. Kendal even touched his upper lip with the tip of his tongue. "What the hell", Schapper said. "None of them will be at Gruber's if they take today so hard."

"They might hear about it", Bain said. The fear he had come to understand just before Nunes arrived, was with him again. He knew he would go with them to avoid the fear.

"Come on. We'll wait outside while you dress", Schapper said. Mr. and Mrs. Kendal each continued to smile separately as they turned to go. Bain waited until all of them were out before he rose. The raw lines made by the rope at his shoulders had stiffened; the texture of the pain was changed, although its intensity had lessened. Again he experienced a sense of anger at having been trapped—by what? whom?—for he realized, in a kind of childish anger at circumstance, that whatever he had been willing to endure for his work, he had not wished it to be as long as it had been today. But immediately he was reminded that it was not for the work he had undergone it.

He sat on the edge of the bed and slowly pulled on his pants and heavy shoes. In some attempt to sum up his achievement, to balance his wounds and pain, he thought of what he might write about these past forty days or so. He could not truly say that he had witnessed or sensed any aberrations among the Hermanos—unless one wanted to become theological and consider that the Church, from time to time, had thought the whole thing an aberration. But he was not interested in theology, nor were the people he was striving to impress, the people whom Kendal and Schapper represented, even though these were of the best. He could only write what at least two people before him had said well, and many had said badly or untruly: that the whole thing was a survival or relic of medieval religious practice; that it did seem appropriate to the kind of people who practiced it, and to the place and circumstances in which they lived.

His thought on this finished with one of those unexpected twists his thought had lately come to take: if the penance of the Spaniards was appropriate to their nature and habitat, what penance was appropriate to the nature and habitat of Schapper and Kendal? Indeed, where and when might it be visited upon them? The hell with this, he thought. He was getting to think like Nunes or Gannon. It was like having hold of the end of a live wire, and he was goddam well going to let go of it!

He finished tying his shoes and stood up. In the next room he could hear Schapper interrogating Maes and his wife in good Spanish—better than Bain's own—although the tone of voice was the patronizing one stupid people use with those of another race or language. . . . As he went into that room, Bain wondered what he could say to Maes and his wife . . . but then it was rarely necessary to be explicit with the Spaniards . . . as it so often was with, say, the people to whom Jeremy Kendal advertised his books.

Not wanting to linger in the room, Bain hardly paused. "Many thanks, Mother", he said in Spanish to the old woman; and to the old man: "*Adios, viejo*. I will see you for Easter."

"I'll go in my car", he told the others. Turning from their faces, Bain saw—as not only he in the moment of turning away and departure—the vague hurt, the nameless concern in the faces of Maes and the old woman; so that Bain knew they had learned from the others where he was going this night of Good Friday while Christ lay in the tomb.

But Schapper and the others wouldn't let him go. They came over to his car with him.

"You're sure you're going right to Gruber's?" Schapper said. The three of them were grinning.

"What do you mean?"

"When we went to the house, your friend was there, waiting", Schapper said.

"My friend? Waiting?" Bain thought of Mirabal.

"Don't be so crude, Jack", Mr. Kendal said. "After all she was cleaning the place. Say, housekeeper or, if you want to be English, charwoman."

"But so young for that", Mrs. Kendal said.

Bain began to get sick. He shook. He moved his head weakly. "You're wrong", he said, getting into the car. The desire to strike them, all three of them, was there, but remote, way back in his mind. He wondered what restrained him, his weakness or his respect for them. The respect, he found in amazement, still remained. . . .

He drove fast the few miles to Gruber's, as if—as when skiing—trying to leave thought behind him. It was earlier than he thought, very early for Gruber's. The place had just opened and there was no one there but Billy and Albert, the combined bartender and bodyguard, grown, like all body-guards, slightly plump in his stay here. The man looked at Bain but did not speak; Billy, though, hurried between empty tables.

"Hello, Mr. Bain", he started to call before he was half across the room. "How are you? You haven't been here in a long time. Last time was with Father Gannon. How are you? All right?"

He pumped Bain's hand in time to his speech. Bain felt more than normally embarrassed: the man's appearance and known character seemed in yet more terrible contrast with his manner and speech. Bain did not know what he replied.

"Father Gannon," Billy went on, "he gets here now and then, but you ain't been here at all. You ain't sore at me or nothing, are you?" He leered anxiously. Bain, with-drawing his limp hand, said: "Why, not at all, Billy. I've been busy, that's all. You know how it is. I've got some friends coming right along after me here. Can you give us anything to eat?"

"Sure thing", Billy said. "You mean Mr. Schapper and that Mrs. Kendal? They was here the other night." He laughed emptily, the creased and quietly frantic grin sud-denly empty, too; completely so: there being, Bain realized now, degrees of emptiness. "We could give you a steak, huh? Maybe some chicken?"

"That's all right", Bain said. He was very hungry. "I guess we'd be satisfied with almost anything you've got. You couldn't be ready for any real business tonight."

"Oh, we'll do all right tonight", Billy said. "Anglo trade. They got some sense. Same as any other night to them." He laughed again, his mouth wide open as he turned toward the door.

Schapper and the Kendals were entering. Mrs. Kendal was glad to see Billy—at times, Bain was beginning to sus-pect, she was glad to see any man—and Mr. Kendal stood grinning by. Schapper brushed past Gruber's twisted little frame as it bowed and turned to shake Mrs. Kendal's hand. Coming up to Bain standing at the bar, Schapper said: "What the hell did you come out to New Mexico for?"

"What do you mean?"

"Why, there's nothing here. We saw one of those god-dam processions today and there was nothing to it." Schap-per gestured with one shoulder and his mouth. "I don't know. I suppose it would be hard to check on how many of those bastards come in their pants."

Anger rose in Bain, strong and quite slow. "Hey," he said to the barkeep, "Scotch and water, twice."

"Make it quick, too", Schapper said.

The barkeep looked at them.

"I think you're wrong, Jack", Bain said. "I've been out here going on two years and I've been in moradas fairly often. I think they're fanatics, but they're not sick."

"What a naïve bastard you are", Schapper said. "Of course, I know now why you're staying." He smirked at Bain and turned his back on the bar, bracing himself by his elbows hooked over the edge. "Look", he said, jerking his head toward where Gruber and the Kendals still talked by the door. "Look, that little, would-be-tough bastard there with his tongue hanging out for Myra. I ought to kick his tail."

"Well, why did you come to a joint?"

"There's no other place in town."

"You should have stayed in Santa Fe", Bain said, quietly. Dismay, bannered and armed, was at his side like a presence. All the years of his hope in the work, he had looked up to Schapper, first as a name, then as a person, as one whose private life might lack integrity but whose professional sincerity was beyond question. The mind leaped ahead, wondering if Mardaña, who would succeed himself here to do a food study, was also—well, was faker the word? If Mardaña was, if Schapper was, then he himself might be: a kind of law of continuity.

The Kendals, trying to free themselves from Billy, were slowly approaching the bar. Bain and Schapper had their drinks now, and Billy was bowing and laughing in his caricature of good will. "Why the hell don't you go into the kitchen, Gruber," Schapper said, "and hurry those steaks along."

"Right away", Billy said. His eyes went blank and agonized.

"Oh, Jack," Myra Kendal said, "don't be so mean. Billy's been very nice to us." She inclined her head rather prettily to one side. The gesture did not become her, Bain thought. He wondered why—except for that first sight of her, like the first look at a French postcard—he had not been affected by her: perhaps only his physical weariness.

"He's like a monkey", Schapper said. "Like a monkey on a stick." He stared after Gruber, where the little man was walking toward the kitchen. Gruber had heard him, all right, Bain saw.

"Why, he's a nice little fellow", Mr. Kendal said.

"What'll you folks have?" the barkeep said. He had been standing directly behind them, and all but Schapper turned rather quickly when he spoke.

"Why, why, I'll have the same as the others", Mr. Kendal said.

"I'll have an Alexander", Mrs. Kendal said.

"There ain't no cream", the barkeep said. "Them Spaniards didn't bring none today." Bain had never heard him volunteer information before. Mrs. Kendal certainly cast her spell or something all around, he thought, and grew mildly alarmed over her apparent lack of effect upon himself here and now. The shoulders, he thought, the shoulders: they did pain to the touch.

"Oh", she said, and held the shape of her lips a little longer than was necessary. Some women, Bain thought, wiggled their tails, and these married brokers or bankers; other women did as Mrs. Kendal did, and these married publishers. "I'll take some brandy, then", she said.

"Yes, ma'am", the barkeep said.

"Quite a sight we saw this afternoon", Mr. Kendal said, putting a light hand on Bain's shoulder.

"Yes?" Bain said. He crunched a piece of ice in his teeth.

"Very impressive, very impressive, indeed", Mr. Kendal said. "I was disappointed some, though, at not seeing the— ah—you know, flagellations."

I bet you were, old boy, Bain thought. "In the day it's rarely seen", he said. "It's a penance and they don't like to make a spectacle of themselves; penance loses some of its quality—they feel—or its meaning if it's too public."

Mr. Kendal laughed softly and said: "I know." His eyes flashed as he turned to raise the glass to his lips. Bain wanted again to hit him. He emerged from the little flash of anger with his sense of time momentarily gone; he could not tell whether seconds or minutes had passed: whether the two or three Anglo couples at the tables had come in unseen before the anger or during it. He felt his physical weakness again and shook his head, hunched over his glass. He felt a sense of injustice: people shouldn't be subjected to emotions they were not prepared for; no, indeed. Like the Church teaching that no one was tried beyond his strength. He couldn't believe that. . . .

Time must have passed unmeasured by himself: Gruber had returned, grinning and more apish than ever; a table-cloth gleamed whitely in the brownish shadows of the place. "Right here, folks", Billy was saying, much closer to them than Bain had realized he was.

"Why, you shouldn't have bothered, Billy", Mrs. Kendal said. "I'm really touched", she added, turning to Schapper and speaking as though Gruber were not there. "Why, no one else here gets a tablecloth."

"You touch easy", Schapper said. It was spoken low, for her ears alone, but Bain heard. Just as if they were married, he thought; at times his secret humor pleased him, but what he had just thought did not please him.

They moved through the dull, rich shade of the place and toward the table. Bain felt awkward and embarrassed: as if, since Schapper emanated an unconscious proprietary air with Mrs. Kendal, people watching would be sure to associate him, Bain, with Mr. Kendal. Although, he was forced to admit, Mr. Kendal was not that obvious; indeed, he had, in the little struggle between Gruber and Schapper over his wife, a general air of amused indifference: a spectator and hence the true intellectual.

The food was already on the table, and Bain began to eat immediately and hastily, not tasting it, but sensing only the texture: he could not remember ever having been so hungry. His plate was almost empty before he paid any attention to the others; he wanted more to eat and looked up. Schapper was watching him. "Were you in one of those processions today?" Schapper said.

"Not at all. What makes you think so?"

"Why," Mr. Kendal said, with a kind of giggle, "there was a tall chap in our procession today that reminded me of you. Pulling that little cart. Something very similar in the quality of the body. I was sure, almost—"

"What do you know about the quality of my body," Bain said, "you goddam literary pimp?" He again started to shake. Mr. Kendal recoiled.

Schapper was laughing. "Oh, oh, that's good." He touched Bain's shoulder. "Only don't say that, Spence, old boy. Jeremy won't publish your book. Jeremy doesn't mind being had, but he wants to be kissed, too."

"I don't see why you have to talk like that", Mr. Kendal said.

No one answered him. Still laughing, Schapper began to eat again. More from a sense of manners than curiosity, Bain glanced at Myra Kendal. Under the rich and heavy lashes, the eyes were cast down, demurely; on the full mouth the most delicate sort of smile played. She, too, began to eat.

Gruber came over to the table again. "Everything all right, folks? More of anything? If—"

"Will you get the hell out of here?" Schapper said.

"Ha ha," Gruber said, just like that, in the caricature of laughter. His little eyes were wild.

Bain got up and walked over to the bar. He saw the barkeep looking steadily at their table. "Give me a brandy", he said.

"You got nice friends", the barkeep told him.

"Give me that brandy", Bain said. "You're not exactly in a church, yourself."

"That's all right", the barkeep said, flushing. "I'm only what I'm supposed to be. They're supposed to be nice people." He spoke over his shoulder from where he had turned for the brandy.

"Why the hell doesn't Gruber leave them alone?" Bain said.

"Why don't that dame stop going around with her tongue out?" the barkeep said. "Anyway, I'm only here to watch him, not to give him advice." He set a glass on the bar.

"Where's Coster tonight?" Bain said.

"I don't know. He wouldn't be here tonight." When Bain didn't answer, but only—in weariness, in a shapeless anxiety— stared at the bottles, the barkeep said: "What you doing here, yourself?"

"I have to take my friends someplace to eat."

"There's better places to eat in Tarale."

"What are you so worried about where I am tonight?" Bain raised his eyes, his embarrassment gone, and looked at the other man. The barkeep's forehead wrinkled under the

partially bald scalp. "I don't know", he said, looking down
at the glass he was filling. "I ought to just mind my own
business." He turned to put the bottle away. Turning back,
he leaned over the bar and said: "Look, you might save a
lot of trouble if you asked your friend to lay off Billy. He's
so scared and being so nice to everyone, that every bastard
that comes in here—"

"I know." Bain nodded and raised the brandy; he was
shocked to find how his hand trembled. He spilled some of
the drink on his chin and put the glass down, half-empty.
Turning sidewise to the bar, he could talk to the barkeep
and watch the table. Gruber was still near it. It was, Bain
realized, an almost incredible sight: the little, fierce, and
vicious man so unable to take himself away from the presence of a woman whom ordinarily he could not hope to
approach, that he stood there enduring Schapper's increasingly vile insults. Bain wondered if a sort of masochism
were involved: Gruber finally taking pleasure in a situation
he could not change: he had to run his bar and he was
unable to use the violence that had been of his essence all
his life. But there was no sanctuary tonight; Gannon would
not be here. Bain wondered if Gruber would take sanctuary if it appeared, and realized, with now characteristic sud-
denness, that perhaps no other sanctuary but Gannon existed
for the man.

Bain finished his brandy, turning again and now more
aimlessly. Other people had come in and a jukebox had
begun to play. It was a draft of cold air from the opening
door that had caused Bain to turn; his sense of shock was
renewed: Gannon stood in the doorway. In time, in quality,
some resemblance to, some current between, that last occasion when Bain had been here and the present was set up.
There had been many shocks for him today, but strange—oh,

very strange—none so profound as seeing Gannon here, now.
It must have showed in Bain's face, so little had the stresses
of the day left him of deception, for Gannon's own bland
face indicated immediate pain and concern. He came directly
toward Bain. "Hello, Spence", he said. "I've been down to
Santa Fe for the services in the Cathedral. Much warmer
there. Didn't realize it would be so cold here tonight. I
needed a brandy. No danger of scandal; only Anglos here
tonight. How are you?" His left hand pulled at the white
silk scarf around his throat, while his right one shook Bain's.

"All right", Bain said. A sense of relief succeeded the
shock. "Have your brandy with me. Here—"

"You don't look very good, Spence", Gannon said.
"What's the matter?"

"Oh, I'm all right. Got some friends, here, like you meet."
Weariness—or something, he thought—had thickened his
tongue. He had a desire to just walk out on the whole
business here, to go out and get in his car and go home to
bed: call Elva. But his mind or some part of him made the
indicated gestures toward safety, toward order.

"Brandy for Father", he said over his shoulder to the astonished barkeep. By a hand under Gannon's elbow, he guided
the priest toward the table. Gruber leaned with both hands
on it; Schapper's mouth was twisted, his nose and eyes prominent; Mrs. Kendal was carefully lighting a cigarette and Mr.
Kendal had lit a pipe and was quietly enjoying the scene.

"I want you to meet some friends, Father", Bain said.
He had a strong sense of futility, as one might have intro-
ducing people to each other in Hell.

Gruber looked up with his wild, little, and triangular eyes.
"Hello, Fahder", he said. This time he did not seem pleased
at the priest's being here. "Glad to see you. Have a drink,
Fahder."

Bain—stubbornly—tried to make the introductions. For the first time since he had known her, Mrs. Kendal drew in on herself: here was something of which she definitely did not approve; her full lips grew almost fierce; here, indeed, was the enemy: a man not allowed to go to bed with her.

Mr. Kendal smiled a wooden little smile and the whitish eyes seemed almost to glaze; being a priest, this other man could not possibly be intelligent enough to write a book, ergo, he could not possibly be fair game.

In a way, Schapper's reaction was the least disturbing, had even the least hate in it. His prominent eyes grew startled, were even a little amused. "Ah," he said, "it's about time."

"Time for what?" Bain said, a little sharply.

"Why, time to see one of the presiding genii of the place", Schapper said, almost amiably. "You keep writing me about the Church out here, and now and at long last I see one of its priests. I had an idea they'd be running around, one priest for every two or three Spaniards."

"Why, far from that, Mr. Schapper," Gannon said, rather gravely, "we haven't enough priests to go around out here. It's partly due to the inaccessibility of the country. Some people even die without seeing a priest."

"What a tragedy", Schapper said.

In the little, uncomfortable silence, Bain felt the anger come slowly again, as though reluctant. The white apron of the barkeep approached, and most of them turned toward it in relief.

"Here's the brandy, Father", the man said, embarrassed by the sudden and frantic focusing of attention upon himself.

"Thank you, Albert", Gannon said. "Thank you very much." He raised the glass slightly as if to drink to the health of the others, when Schapper said: "Sit down. What the hell."

"No, thanks", Gannon said quickly and lowered the glass. "I have to go along. I'm glad to have seen all of you, though." He smiled formally and turned back toward the bar, carrying the brandy close to his chest with a kind of ridiculous dignity. Unintentionally, Bain and the barkeep flanked him on either side as he walked. Behind them, Bain heard—his ears anticipating—Schapper start again on Gruber.

"Why don't you go with them?" Schapper said. "No one wants you here. We come out here and expect to see tough guys and all we run into is someone like you. I bet you squat to pee."

Bain flinched; it was as if his body anticipated violence before his mind did. The reply, if any, was drowned out by two noisy couples coming in the door. Almost to the bar, Bain saw the barkeep, who had left Gannon, start to walk along the bar and in back of it and to meet the entering couples; saw the white of the man's clothing halt suddenly, then try to reverse its movement with an awkward and frantic haste: the slatted boardwalk on the floor behind the bar seemed to hinder the man. The barkeep made a shapeless sound and his gestures for a moment had a futile, pawing quality. Turning, Bain saw that Billy and the barkeep, from opposite directions, behind the bar were racing each other to the cash register. His knees started to go, and, like the barkeep, he pawed, but at the hard, smooth cloth of Gannon's shoulder. The cash register rang as Billy opened it and the barkeep grabbed in short gestures at Billy's hands in the money box. "No!" Bain yelled, and the gun gleamed in brief arcs of light. Shorter than the barkeep, Billy could not hit him on top of the head. The barrel of the gun caught the barkeep where his hairline used to be, and the blood came down in a bright, quick, narrow stream through the woodenly pawing fingers and onto the white bar coat.

The man leaned back against the bottles, his face clear and gravely bewildered under the fingers touching the blood.

"No!" Bain yelled again. Trying to move on his almost useless legs, he bumped, clutching Gannon. Turning, dumbly shocked, the priest hit Bain accidentally in the chest with the glass of brandy. Bain yelled formlessly, as in torture, as if a child, seeing all Hell opened for Schapper.

Quite deliberately, Gruber rested his elbow on the bar and, allowing even for Schapper's dumb rising out of the chair in terror, shot the stocky, betweeded man through the heart. Two women screamed on different notes and someone said hoarsely to get the police. Gruber laid the gun on the polished wood of the bar and then walked back along the bar toward Bain. His face was twisted into a complex rage whose coldness was the most awful thing in it.

Bain—Gannon had moved suddenly away—fell toward the bar, as if to meet Gruber. He caught himself on its edge and lay like that, his feet more than a yard from the bar, his long body bridging the gap to it, unable to move, his face now on a level with Gruber's. "You and your fine, goddam friends", the little man said. "Why the hell don't you stay where you all belong?" This seemed to calm him, and he turned away to where the barkeep still stood, weeping, by the open cash register. "When they come," Billy said, "tell them I'm in there." He jerked his head toward the gambling-room and then walked toward it.

Bain pushed himself up to a standing position and turned toward the table, his mouth open and his chin wet. Gannon was bent over, his body touching—as at night in her sleep a mother's touches that of her fretful child—Schapper's no longer fretful form, where it lay, face down, on the table.

Mrs. Kendal stared at both in a kind of horror—for just what, Bain could not be sure—while her fingers still held a lit cigarette.

Mr. Kendal—that true spectator and hence classic intellectual—had vomited into his hands.

Couples starting for the door hesitated in odd positions, caught in flight, and one girl began to sob. The figure of the county's single state policeman stood in the doorway. He was a young Spaniard, taller than most of his race, and with the fierce gravity of youth.

The barkeep moved and said hoarsely: "I told you, I told you. I called you twenty minutes ago."

The policeman looked at him. "You think this is the only place I got to watch. What did you tell me? That someone was getting Billy mad. That's your job, not mine. Where did Billy go?"

The barkeep pointed to the gambling room, but no one spoke—only the girl sobbing—and the policeman walked stiff legged toward where Gannon still bent, but now less closely, over Schapper, and mumbled the now futile, the ancient formula with which the repentant or devout are sent to meet God. Something was very terrible to Bain—he thought of a woman trying to nurse a dead child, of a wife trying to rouse her dead husband, of someone trying to find a small, valuable thing lost in a field by night: of all futilities—and he turned and put his head on the bar and again wept.

15

AND THEN?" MRS. SENTON SAID.

Mrs. Trevelyan smiled nervously. She was alone in a kind of bedroom-sitting-room that was a favorite of Mrs. Senton's; at least, she felt alone, although Mrs. Senton and two of Mrs. Senton's regulars—women almost as old as their hostess—were there, too. These two sat on either side of Mrs. Senton, like attendants on a queen, the three of them as though arrayed against Mrs. Trevelyan, although they smiled—in a fashion—at her.

"Why, then," Mrs. Trevelyan said, "he—he put one hand here."

The others nodded, still smiling. "And what did he say?" Mrs. Senton asked. She was sitting up straight; she looked prim.

Mrs. Trevelyan tried to get into the spirit of the thing. "Why, he said, 'My, but you're well built, Ruth.' "

The three aging ladies grinned delightedly.

"And you said?" Mrs. Senton prompted.

"I said, 'Oh, Spence!' "

"And then what?"

"Why, why, then he picked me up, and carried me to—to the couch...."

The three ladies nodded, almost in unison; it might almost be said that they sighed.

"And then?" Mrs. Senton persisted.

"Well," Mrs. Trevelyan said, smirking, "what do you suppose!"

Mrs. Senton's smile was not quite satisfied, but her two attendants laughed merrily; obviously, they were more easily pleased than she.

"Was," Mrs. Senton said, "was he—well, you know?"

Mrs. Trevelyan nodded emphatically, relieved that it was almost over.

"And you came here right from there?" Mrs. Senton said.

"Oh, yes. Spence went home to bed."

"Well," Mrs. Senton said, a little breathless and more or less satisfied, "well, I think we should all have a little brandy."

The others made small, conventional sounds of delight, like children suddenly promised candy, and Mrs. Trevelyan, her feeling of security in Mrs. Senton's affections renewed—it had been uncertain lately—stood up.

This was on the same night Schapper was killed, almost at the same time.

†

Out of sleep, as often (as in dreams always), knocking woke Bain. He lay there awake and unmoving for a moment, not in weariness or the remains of sleep so much as under the weight of a terror no longer active but still alive, inert and heavy, like some animal, dead or sleeping, dropped across his knees.

The knocking sounded again, light and quick, a little uncertain, and he rose, pushing himself up from the bed with his arms and backing down onto the floor, not unlike an animal backing out of a stall. The light quickness of the knocking might be that of a woman and he groped for a bathrobe before going to the door.

It was moderately early; the sun was up, but not yet visible over the mountains. Lupe stood outside the door, back a little from it and shivering. She wore a shawl, like the older women, and it was this, perhaps, that made her look older.

"H'lo, Spance", she said. "Sorry to get you up." She spoke slowly, seemingly both urgent and distracted.

"It's all right", he said. "What's the matter?"

"Papa, he just phoned my aunt in Tarale, long distance, and he tells her he wants you to pick him up in the mountains."

"Wants me to pick him up in the mountains", Bain repeated, as if trying to understand the vagary of a child. "Where is he?"

"Near Vadito. He says for you to look for him on the road going in."

"What's the matter?"

"I don't know." She shrugged, sensing as Bain did that something was wrong.

"I wonder what's happened?"

"I don't know", she said. "He always used to get along all right up there."

"Do you pray much for your father?"

"All the time", the girl said, coloring.

Fully awake, Bain looked at the ground. There were other questions—did she pray for himself? did she think her father was helped any?—but he did not ask them.

"You heard about last night?" he said.

She nodded dumbly. "That Gruber", she said. "Now he had to go and kill your friend. They should have had him locked up before." She was quite angry. Bain nodded, suddenly and badly distracted. "What did my friends say to you last night?" When she looked down and bit one lip, he said: "They're not very good friends of mine."

She nodded. "You want me to get you some coffee?" She didn't move. "I had to leave when they come, and I couldn't clean."

"No-o", he said. "No. It's all right. I'll go get your father right away." Closing the door, he considered with irony his lack of passion or of lust: if he were pious, he would attribute it to Grace instead of to his fright. He wondered, with a rather deep curiosity, what had happened to Mirabal. There were few priests in the mountains, almost none on other than a mission status, or he might have thought one had set the people on Mirabal. . . .

It was a longish drive, about forty-five miles over bad roads, and he thought, as he began it, that he would not have undertaken it this day for many people; but Mirabal had been a good and even faithful assistant. He would have to hurry to be back for the coroner's inquest at noon. Driving, he had a chance to think slowly on things that had troubled him fleetingly by night: What would he say to Mark Coster? How would he explain to the Hermanos his presence at Gruber's on the night of Good Friday? How would his own standing at the University be affected by all this? Yes, indeed, how would it?

It was possible, he realized, that he might be given the chair of anthropology. It was not likely, though; he was too young, and he knew that politics played a moderately large part in the University's appointments. Why, he didn't know a single trustee, except Kendal; and the president and he had only a formal acquaintance. They would assuredly bring someone in from outside. What surprised Bain now was not this conscious stating by his mind of something he had known unconsciously for a long time, but his resentment, his disappointment: for he had really not thought of himself as ever succeeding Schapper. . . . Schapper was young for his position, not yet fifty, and Bain had expected to go to some other university for his own advancement.

Trying to analyze this feeling of disappointment and resentment, trying even to get rid of it, he thought of himself as having turned suddenly ghoulish ... and this thought led in turn to something he rarely considered, his reasons for pursuing the work. It was not a pure science, he knew, it was even a highly inexact one: and when they knew the dimensions of the skull of a Seri Indian in the Gulf of California; and what accent the Spaniards—who had come here before the Pilgrims to Massachusetts—had used, of what province in Spain; and the fertility rites of a tribe of South American Indians—well, what did they know? What disturbed him now was how little they had formulated from their knowledge. Of course, it was a new science, as sciences went, but he wondered, finally appalled, if it were all right to use people as the materials of a pure science. But he had decided it wasn't a pure science.

The road was very bad here, where it began to climb into the little pocket in the mountains. The car rocked and skidded; trying to get through a small stream that crossed the road, it stalled on him. Mud had coated thinly the stones of the little ford, unused by cars in winter, and the wheels skidded in the few inches of water. Bain got out to see what could be done, but the little rise or bank on either side of the stream held the rear wheels as in a pocket, so that it would take more than one man to push it out, either way.

He was not far from Vadito, he knew, and the best thing would be to walk on and get someone with a horse from one of the outlying farms. He was about to start along the road that wound upward here, when he saw a desolate figure coming down it, a figure he had trouble recognizing as

Mirabal. It wore no hat, and its clothes were stained and muddy. It walked slowly and with a perceptible limp. None of these things made Bain stand still and watch its approach, for infirm old Spaniards were seen every day on the roads; rather it was the utter depression, the disappointment, the sense of betrayal that showed clear in every slope of the body, in every unsurely hurrying step.

As the figure came closer, Bain could see it was Mirabal, and the red-rimmed eyes, the weariness, and the fear in the face. Bain's emotions were mixed, but one of them was a kind of amusement. "What in the name of God happened to you, José?" he said as the figure came within speaking distance.

"Is a long story", Mirabal panted. "Let's get out of here, first." His English was strongly accented, much more than usual.

"We can't", Bain said. "I'm stuck here. I was going up to Vadito to get someone to pull me out."

"Like hell", the Spaniard said. "You go back there, I'll go right on ahead. Good-bye."

"What's the matter?"

"I want to get away from here."

"Maybe we can push the car out."

"Ain't you got no chains?"

"I didn't think I'd need them."

"All right. Let's push, then." Mirabal went directly to the front of the car and put his weight against it. Bain could not name the quality of the man's urgency; it was as if the one secure and reliable thing in Mirabal's life had failed him and there was no recourse but flight. For his age, his weight, and his condition, Mirabal put a lot of strength into his effort, and the two of them almost got the car out. Bain's sore shoulders handicapped him and when the scab on one of them cracked, he eased his effort and the car rolled back into the stream. Mirabal began to curse. "What's the matter with you?" he yelled. "You want us to get killed?"

Bain looked at him. "What do you mean?"

Mirabal avoided his glance. "Come on", he said. Some of his urgency finally communicated itself to Bain, and as they started again to push the car, there was a noise someplace, unidentifiable and at a distance they could not determine. Mirabal began to whimper; feeling some of the other man's fear, Bain pushed hard, straightening his knees, feeling them tremble in weakness, and the blood or serum start from the wounds at his shoulder. The car's rear wheels rolled to the top of the embankment, hesitated, then came down the other side, rolling back across the road and crashing into some aspens. Mirabal ran toward the car and got in. "Come on, Spance", he yelled.

Panting, Bain got in, turned the car, and drove back down the bad road. "What happened to you?"

"Is a long story", Mirabal said and would not look at him.

"I know. We've got a long drive, too. Tell me."

It wasn't a long story—at all. "The whole thing", Mirabal said, "is that it just don't work no more."

"What doesn't work?"

Mirabal shrugged, grimaced, and worked his fingers frenetically. "You know—this raising I do, kind of?"

"Yes?"

"Well," he said, "last night I get paid in advance by people to find some water on their place. Always, other times I can get Him to show me where. He comes and kind of leads."

"What does it look like when He does?" Bain said.

Mirabal grimaced again. "Black like", he said. "Black like and no face. Moving, then, without walking."

"And last night?"

"He wouldn't arrive. . . . They beat me. I tried everything just right."

After a little silence in which Bain once more experienced shock, although why this time he was not sure, he said, without conscious intention: "You certainly picked a great night for it. Good Friday."

"Is the best night there is for it", Mirabal said stubbornly, with emotion.

"It wasn't last night", Bain said, baiting him. Making the joke, Bain was reminded of the appalling fact of his own new belief.

"I don't know what happened", Mirabal said. Now he sounded almost apologetic.

As they drove in silence, Bain found he did not doubt Mirabal: the Spaniard's sense of disappointment was too great for it to be the product of insincerity. Still, illusions could exist graphically over a period of time. Why, he saw the effect of his environment here on himself all the time. . . .

"Did some priest tell them to go after you?" Bain said.

"No." Mirabal shook his head, almost in disappointment. "They hardly ever see a priest in this place. It's in back of Vadito on a bad road."

"They just got angry and chased you?"

"All night", Mirabal said. "I hid and I could hear them kicking around in the bushes."

Bain had a sense of something proven; less strongly, a sense of something sealed and delivered, perhaps for all time. He thought of the girl praying for her father; he thought of the father wanting to do evil and not being able to. (Although what care he gave the children could hardly be called that.) And in something Bain hardly recognized as shock—after all there had been so much shock these last few days—he remembered, or thought he remembered, Mrs. Senton saying: "People don't seem to realize—I want only to do good. . . . I—" Was it the heart and not the mind that really informed a man's actions? And if so, who of his own people had been concerned with the education of the heart? The mind—oh, certainly!—they forever ceaselessly trained. But the heart—Well, where? Certainly in no university he knew about. He wondered if there was an age beyond which the heart could not be further educated. If there was, it existed and was passed only in childhood. And if it was, what of himself and any others who so late had found what they lived by meaningless, their profession misused, a kind of darkness on everything they had done? Not unerringly could conscience guide them with nuanced unease. Nor for them, save rarely, an angel by the hair or hand. Coldly—as Nunes had said—and by the difficult way of the will, they must late and forever make their own passage, weighing all things, making slowly and writhingly decisions a child, laughing, unerringly made between her first and second skips toward play.

Such thoughts, he considered almost angrily, were not much help to him now. He glanced at his watch. It was past noon; he would be late for the inquest. He didn't know but that he was just as glad to miss it.

Mirabal went into his home, and glancing into the little patio of his own house without getting from the car, Bain was rather startled to see Ruth Trevelyan sitting on a bench there. She seemed in a reverie or kind of distracted patience. She had not seen him, and he thought of driving off, but something forlorn about the woman, some sense of abandonment similar to that which he had noticed in Mirabal coming down the mountain road, made Bain go into the patio. On the small bench, from which last year's leaves had not yet been brushed, Mrs. Trevelyan continued to sit, waiting, as though she had not heard the car or himself. Her face was distrait and she had apparently been weeping. He remembered how she had been used to distract him once while skiing and he wondered if she were not distracting him again?

"What's the matter?" he said.

"Ah, Spence", she said and rose, her hands clasped against her breast.

"Huh", Bain said.

"I knew you'd come back", she said. For the moment it was no trouble at all for her to be living one of her stories for the *Ladies' Home Journal*: she was Nancy or Sandra—it didn't matter—and Bain was Ronnie or Bruce. . . .

"Back where?"

"Back to your home, your little adobe house." She looked as soulful as she could, while thousands of dollars worth of women's magazine fiction went to waste there in the sun.

"What's the matter with you?" Bain said, rather unpleasantly. "You sick?"

She shook her head and continued to gaze at him piercingly. "Ah, no, Spence", she said. "Its just that I and Marsha have quarreled. . . . And I am leaving. Going back to my little home on Cape Cod . . . where the arbutus will be just coming out when I arrive, and you can see the sea beyond the dunes." Her hands moved vaguely while her voice hurried on. "I'd like you to come with me, Spence. . . . No more dull, academic life for you. You could raise a little garden and write your books. . . . We'd never have to worry; I have a cousin who is an editor on one of the women's magazines and she—"

"Look," Bain said, alarmed, "would you like me to drive you to Dr. Atwood? You—"

She shook her head sorrowfully. "Ah, no, Spence. I am only trying to bring happiness into the world with my little stories, with my person. I—"

"Look", Bain said again. "I love my wife. I think you must be nuts." He wondered suddenly if she were crazy. "I've got to get over to the inquest. If—" In a kind of sudden horror he stopped talking: this woman was entrusted with a child.

She shook her head again. "Ah," she said, mysteriously, "if only you hadn't been there at the bar last night."

Bain stood there in silence, puzzled and somewhat startled. "Why, yes", he said. "What do you mean?"

She shook her head mysteriously again. "Good-bye, Spence. I wish you well. I will let you go to your wife." She turned and went out of the patio, hatless and moving slowly. He thought—ridiculously—of Ophelia, surprised at his pity for Ruth Trevelyan. He wondered about her husband. And then, once more, he had the sense of strangeness and annoyance that his temptations, so-called, should be so ineffectual and even ridiculous ... almost as though they had been emasculated and made powerless by having had to pass through some insulating wall or barrier. For the moment, it was easy for him to believe in what the Church called Grace. What had happened to Mirabal, what had been happening so annoyingly to himself for months ... for only a fool, he realized, could fail to see that by the conventional moral standards, by the ethic of any Christian church, he was a better person than he had been, say, a year ago. Again, for some reason, his annoyance with the obvious, with the unsubtle, returned to him. He was thinking, he told himself, the same way Gannon did. ...

Leaving the patio, he drove toward town. Along the road he passed Mrs. Trevelyan walking, quite normally, but didn't stop to pick her up: his feelings about her, the pity, the vague anger, were not things he wanted to raise again, not now. And they distracted him, he thought, uneasily.

No one was at Gruber's but the barkeep, cleaning up now that the inquest was over, a small neat bandage on his scalp the only evidence of his participation in what had happened. He looked at Bain blankly. "You're a touch late", he said. "They been gone a half hour."

"I got stuck in the mountains", Bain said. "I didn't think they'd be done so soon."

"What was there to keep them?" the barkeep said. He looked at Bain as though Bain were not quite bright. "It was open and shut like a book."

Bain nodded, feeling stupid; the conscious and assumed stupidity of the undergraduate, he thought. "What are they going to charge him with?"

"First degree manslaughter, someone said. Someone else said second degree murder."

Bain felt relieved for some reason. Then, oddly, one of the things that had been troubling him, that had been vague, came quite suddenly and clearly to mind: Just how would his testimony at the trial affect his position at the University? The University would hardly care for one of its faculty to testify that another of its faculty had baited a man until the man had shot him. "When's the trial?" Bain said thickly.

"You know how it is here", the barkeep said. "Court only twice a year. They'll try him in June. And they'll keep him in jail until then. No chance of bail this time."

After a moment, because he could think of nothing else to say, Bain said: "What are you going to do?"

"I'm going back to Kansas City. The hell with this place." He began again to wipe the bar. "I couldn't clean up until they got finished here."

Bain felt sorry for the man; actually, he was discredited in his profession, or in one of his professions: Gruber had been protected against the Spaniards but not against himself, not against Schapper. The thing to have done was to silence Schapper in some way. Bain even knew why the barkeep hadn't: the vague respect that many people had for learning in the flesh, the uneasy feeling that the learned—there and in the flesh—must be right: their names were on books, in the prospectuses of universities, even in newspapers, that ultimate seal and highest standard of a man's worth. The barkeep had not been able to bring himself to silence such a great man, such a learned one.

How could one be protected against someone like Schapper? Bain wondered. It was a bad question: like the mirrors opening in a hall again, it sent images down unending vistas, but provided no answer to itself. Only, echoing in Bain's mind, the phrase, half-heard some place, perhaps some place read: "The perversion of the elect."

"You—you got money to get home?" Bain said.

"Yeah, I got money." The man kept wiping along the bar.

"Nothing I can do?"

The barkeep shook his head. "No. I'm coming back in June. See you at the trial...."

"Too bad it had to happen when it did", Bain said. He could not easily break away; perhaps it was the man's vague hostility that made him stay and try to change it.

"You mean, Good Friday?"

"Yes."

The man kept looking at the bar as he wiped. He seemed to be weighing something. Then he said: "I heard two Spaniards talking when I was having breakfast in town. They were saying they thought you were a faker—about the Church and so on. Else you wouldn't of been here last night."

"Why, why, hell's fire," Bain said, "I just took my friends here. They wanted to come. Why, you're a Catholic and you were here."

"I was on my job."

"Well, I was on mine, too, sort of. Why—"

"Don't argue with me. Argue with them. I'm just telling you what I heard." He finished wiping and turned to the bottles behind the bar, turned his back on Bain and waited for Bain to go.

Feeling defeated, trying to convince himself that he must hurry, somehow get someplace quickly where people waited for him ... Bain went away.

He thought of going to the church in Ranchos ... but he supposed the next thing to do was to see the Kendals. The sun was hot and bright when he parked his car in front of the hotel. In the shade of the long portico that ran along the building, the moron called Garbanza stood to sell piñon nuts. A lard bucket, full of the nuts, hung on one arm. His crossed eyes were blank and unseeing. He saw Bain, though, and recognized him: he had heard some of the other Hermanos talking of Bain only this morning. This, then, was the Señor Bain who had insulted Our Lord by going to Gruber's on the night of Our Lord's death; more than that, there seemed now to be a certainty that he had not been sincere in joining the Hermanos, as some had at first suspected. Garbanza's hand tightened on the clasp knife in his pocket—he kept it with him always because of the wolves that so often by night came as far as the window of his bedroom—and pressed the little button that sprung the blade open. He shuffled toward the hotel entrance where Bain would be delayed a moment opening the door.

"Piñons", he said. "Piñon nuts, sir." Bain did not seem to notice him. He came up directly in back of Bain, almost touching him. Yet when he wanted to kill Bain, he found that he could not. Weeks and months later, telling of this, Garbanza said that there was a kind of light there, and that he suddenly felt Our Lord did not want Bain or anyone killed. But who could believe that any more than the story of the wolves that came so often to Garbanza's window?

Bain went into the lobby and directly upstairs. He knocked on the door of the room he had once been in with Mr. Kendal. Mrs. Kendal opened it for him. He was surprised to find she looked unchanged, looked dewy and fresh, as if nothing had happened.

"Hello, Spence", she said. "Come in." She wore a pale blue housecoat that fitted her tightly from the waist up. He began, as he entered the room, to think of Elva; of Elva alone and trying to make decisions that were, for her, terribly difficult; of Elva dismayed at having a child in her; at trying to do her work now; at the belly growing big. . . .

"Where's Jeremy?" he said.

"Why? Are you worried about him?" She looked at him, mocking him.

"Why, no. I was just wondering how all of you were." He sat on a chair.

"Oh, we're all right", she said, turning from him toward the table with the bottles and glasses on it. "Jeremy is over at Mrs. Senton's."

"Mrs. Senton's?"

"They're old friends. I thought you knew. There's been a lot of long-distance telephoning necessary, and Jeremy thought it would be better to do it there than from the hotel. What will you drink?"

"Nothing, now", he said. "Who's he phoning? Won't they let you leave town because you're material witnesses or what?"

"Oh, not that", she said, turning to face him and sitting on the edge of the bed. "I thought you knew. Jeremy is a trustee of the University, and he's had to phone the president and some of the board about poor Jack." Seeing Bain's face change, go for a moment naked, she mocked him again. "You'd better be nice to Jeremy now."

He avoided her smile. Feeling it begin, in spite of the fear and the weariness, in spite of the again raw and sticky wounds at his shoulders, in spite of Grace, he said, like a boy, looking at the floor: "Well—" and then couldn't think of anything more to say.

"Murtaugh is coming out here," she said, "and maybe Mr. Lodge if he can get away."

Bain nodded dumbly. Murtaugh was president of the University and Lodge chairman of the board of trustees. And this, he thought, is what used to be known as the fell clutch of circumstance. The vitamins, he thought; yes, indeed, take a vitamin pill.

"They left this noon, by plane", Myra Kendal went on. "They ought to be in Albuquerque tonight some time and here tomorrow morning."

"Why are they coming?"

"I guess they want to cover the thing up as much as possible. I imagine, too, that they'll want to consider you as Jack's successor." She looked at him; speculatively, he thought.

"You really think so?" Bain said.

"Who else?"

"I'd always thought they'd bring someone in from outside", he said. "Someone older."

"Oh, I think you're very nice the age you are", she said.

He felt himself flush, felt the sense of power, however accidentally achieved, run through him like brandy.

"And Mrs. Senton is an old friend of Jeremy's," Mrs. Kendal went on, "and of Mr. Lodge's. You must know her pretty well?" He thought she was mocking him again, but looking up at her, saw she was serious. When he looked at her, she looked away from him, put her feet up on the bed, leaned against the backboard and lit a cigarette.

He felt a sense of futility, of anger well-contained, so well that he hardly recognized it as such. He said: "I suppose they have to get someone to take Schapper's place, finish his courses for him. Classes resume about Wednesday, don't they?"

"That's it exactly", she said. "That makes for a swell break for you."

He wondered if she had ever been in the chorus. "I had a little more work to finish here", he said, absently. In alarm, he wondered if this quality in his voice was not planned and deliberate: the absentness of the scholar, the shy and humble scholar.

"Oh, that's not too important", she said.

"No", he said, reluctantly.

He felt a slight physical oppression, perhaps due to the series of excitements that had beat in him, and he stood up aimlessly, perhaps thinking of going to a window for some air. Mrs. Kendal watched him, almost fixedly. When his eyes finally met hers, she raised a hand and beckoned with one finger.

He flushed again like a boy; in what was perhaps a protective gesture, in something new to him and like an instinct but not one, he thought of Elva and of his pity for her, for the growing belly that symbolized everything that was happening to her. "I got to go", he said, thickly, and put a hand on the doorknob.

Mrs. Kendal's own instincts were pretty accurate, too. She knew as much about *le mot juste* as a good writer. Slowly, she said: "What are you, a fairy?"

He closed the door and locked it. Even as he came toward her—his limbs, now celibate some three months, trembling like a boy's the first time—that remote, ironic, and easily subdued part of him wondered what she would think, what she would feel about the stains at his shoulders.

He supposed—his last reasonable thought for a time—it was with this same mixture of scorn and lust that a long time ago—before Christianity had given woman her first dignity—other men had taken the bodies of their female slaves.

The light died in the darkness: some place, a long way off in the reaches of his mind, something small wept, betrayed, with the voice of Elva and of all good women. Not they weeping, to be sure, but with their voice.

16

IT WAS ALMOST NOON of Easter Sunday when they called Bain at the hotel and asked him to come over to Mrs. Senton's. He had been waiting in the same room, again with Mrs. Kendal. Mr. Kendal had gone to the meeting at Mrs. Senton's.

"There you are, Spence", Myra Kendal said, when he hung up. He nodded slowly, as though preoccupied. He felt sure that it was all right over there for him. He was bothered principally—he told himself—by Mrs. Senton's having managed to get into the affairs of the University and thereby into his own; but he recognized, ruefully, that such alone was her talent: to impose herself, whether through her money, her body—although she was getting old—or just a kind of skillful rudeness (he thought again of the conscious and assumed stupidity of the undergraduate) that people in amazement failed to recognize until too late and the woman had befouled them, not unlike a shitepoke flying over a crowd.

Bain stood up and put on his hat and pulled on his gloves. There was a reluctance about his movements he could not explain, and what amounted to a corresponding haste about those of Mrs. Kendal. She tugged at, smoothing on the new suède gloves over her hands, and smiled at him fondly and with what amounted, he recognized, to an air of ownership. He understood now—ruefully, at his lateness—why women like her married men like Jeremy Kendal: money was not enough for them, they wanted also to be the bedmate of lions, like the women who slept principally or even exclusively—in a kind of chastity—with aviators; or with big-league baseball players: the women called "Baseball Sadies" who, with strictly unprofessional interest, followed the teams from one city to another.

He made some attempt to know why the mind remained quiescent. It was as though he had not been given time to think. But time wasn't the word. Still, there had been a kind of crowding: Mr. Kendal had thoughtfully called the room first from the lobby when he returned about dinner time. And after dinner, he had urged, but not pressed them to return to Mrs. Senton's with him. When he had gone they had returned to the room. And Bain had finally slept, remembering last Mrs. Kendal saying: "Oh, Jeremy will just go next door if he returns at all." And now morning, Easter morning.

But she was certainly a good-looking woman, he thought. Dressed as she was now, in a hat with a small brim, and a tailored suit, there was a conventional beauty and even respectability about her which could amaze him. "Ready?" she said, smiling at him.

He nodded and held the door open for her. The Spanish desk clerk stared at them as they passed through the lobby; uneasily, Bain wondered if the man were an Hermano from one of the moradas nearer Tarale. He looked haggard enough.

Bain helped Mrs. Kendal into his mud-splashed car, apologizing for its dirt.

"Oh, I know how it is in the work, Spence", she said, smiling and pressing with her arm his hand against her.

As he swung the car around the Plaza and started west out of it to Mrs. Senton's, he had to stop for little girls in white Communion veils passing across the road on their way to High Mass at the church here in Tarale. It was awfully late, he thought; he wondered if they were really going to

Communion at such a late Mass, if they had been fasting all morning?

As he paused there, another car, Atwood's, pulled up alongside him. "Hello, Speedy", the doctor said, smirking. "On your way to church?" Atwood himself was going fishing.

"No", Bain said.

The children passed and Bain started to let in the clutch. "Say," Atwood yelled, "no chance of you taking that job I mentioned?"

Shaking his head slightly and sternly, as to the interrogation of a half-wit, Bain drove off.

"Who was that, Spence?" Mrs. Kendal said.

"One of the local doctors."

"He's rather distinguished-looking, isn't he?" she said. "I mean, to be in such a small town."

Bain glanced at her, then back at the road. "I don't know", he said. He wondered, uneasily, just how many men she knew.

As he stopped his car in Mrs. Senton's drive and helped Mrs. Kendal out, he had a sense of both excitement and foreboding. Again his movements were slow, what might even be called reluctant. Mrs. Kendal moved quite briskly, a little ahead of him as they walked.

Mrs. Senton herself met them at the door, as Bain had thought she would. He had not been prepared, though, for the warmness of her greeting. She embraced him, more or less lightly, before he could avoid her. "Dear Spence", she said in a loud voice.

Over her shoulder, in the room in which the Indians had once danced, Bain saw the three men watching with fixed smiles. He freed himself from Mrs. Senton, who then greeted Mrs. Kendal with a marked lack of warmth. Bain moved toward the three men. Mr. Murtaugh was a man in

his fifties, partly bald; his ready smile always included everything but his eyes.

"Well, Bain," Mr. Murtaugh said, "it is a sort of mixed
occasion on which we greet you."

"Yes", Bain said. Anything else he was going to say was
cut off by Mr. Lodge coming ponderously across the room
toward him. He was a tall, old—in his seventies—very
wealthy, very respectable man. In spite of his age he remained
active on the boards of nine or ten corporations, and everyone thought this was a very remarkable thing.

This remarkable old man came over and picking up Bain's
somewhat unready hand, pumped it heartily. "Mr. Bain,"
he said, "it is indeed a pleasure to greet you; to meet you,
I should say. Although I have never seen you before, I know
of your work and of its remarkably high character. Your
fine work among the tribes—"

Bain smiled oddly. "Why, thank you, Mr. Lodge." Bain
had never worked among Indians except once, briefly, in
South America. I'm all set, he thought, I'm in.

It wasn't that simple, though. After Mr. Kendal had come
over and greeted Bain quietly as "Old Spence" and with a
fond pressure on the arm, they all sat down. Two Spanish
girls, whom Bain knew slightly, served a good wine, which
everyone but Mr. Murtaugh took. Mr. Murtaugh took over
the meeting.

"I do not think", he said, "that there is a great deal more
to discuss. Our grief over the untimely death of our distinguished confrere will find more appropriate expression
after our return east. Justice, swift and sure, will avenge him
here, I know. Some of us *may* have to return for the trial in
June, but I am not altogether *too* sure you will. I am trying
to arrange it, ah, otherwise." His voice and his eyes both
dropped, perhaps in discretion. "We know", he went on,

"that he was the victim of the gross rage of a low character, but we also know how high his own character was; how noble, one might say. And we know that that character will be his monument, outlasting those of stone and brass." He paused. Mrs. Senton and Mr. Lodge bowed their heads.

"Our task of the moment", Mr. Murtaugh resumed, "is to discuss John Schapper's successor. I must say, frankly, that it is not an easy task to choose a successor." He paused again. "In choosing Mr. Bain to take his place, we have had to weigh certain pros and cons. Mrs. Senton and Mr. Kendal have both given him fine recommendations, nor is there any doubt that the quality of his work, his research, particularly, is high, though limited in quantity."

"The tribes", Mr. Lodge muttered to himself, nodding. "Indians."

"Against him", said Mr. Murtaugh, "is his relative youth for such a position and—" he paused—"one other thing." He looked at Bain, who was honestly puzzled. Glancing around, Bain saw that all the others were embarrassed except Mrs. Kendal, who looked characteristically and beautifully blank.

Mr. Murtaugh cleared his throat portentously. "Mr. Bain," he said, "what I am going to ask you is, really, a mere technicality. I would like you to consider it as such. . . . Particularly, *particularly*, if your answer is negative."

Bain looked dutifully at Mr. Murtaugh, whose sharp eyes were fixed obliquely on him. "Mr. Bain," Mr. Murtaugh said, "is it or is it not true that you, since coming here to work, have embraced the Roman Catholic faith?"

Bain released his breath. "Why, no", he said. "That is—"

"There", Mrs. Senton said. "I knew it."

"You were going to say?" Mr. Murtaugh said, a little sharply, to Bain.

"I was going to say that—well, in the nature of the work here, it was necessary for me to, well, participate or pretend to participate in certain religious ceremonies."

"Naturally", Mr. Murtaugh said. "Other anthropologists have done so in their work. The feeling seems to be, though, that you were sincere—no, no, I don't mean that—that you were actually devout, I should say?"

"No", Bain said, "no." Late, he saw the two Spanish girls, frozen like statues against the wall.

Mr. Murtaugh obviously relaxed. "I must say that that relieves me greatly", he said. Others in the room began to stir and move. "You mustn't misunderstand me, though", Mr. Murtaugh said, his hand coming up, his voice rising to meet the competition. "I have nothing against the Roman faith as such, any more than against any other religion. Indeed, I feel that the high-church Episcopalians are the most insidious of all, with their spurious intellectuality and their attempts to compromise with the Roman faith. It is simply that I feel religion has no place among the sciences or even among the arts; no place in a liberal university. All right—to borrow a phrase—as an opiate for the people, but not for we who must lead, for the elite represented by the faculty of a great university."

Someone, probably Mrs. Senton, began to clap, and the others followed. The hollow pattering accentuated the emptiness of the big room. Mr. Murtaugh smiled, pleased. "I am sure everything will be all right, Mr. Bain, and that the board of trustees, at their next meeting, will confirm our action here today. I am sure, too, that in time, and indeed in every respect, you will take the place of your distinguished predecessor."

"Thank you," Bain said, "thank you." Mr. Murtaugh came over and shook his hand; then they all shook his hand

and Mrs. Senton called him a dear boy and half-embraced
him again.

"We will leave tomorrow", Mr. Murtaugh said in a loud
voice. "I have reservations for all five of us. Spring vacation
ends Wednesday and that doesn't allow us much time. You
can be packed and ready, Mr. Bain?"

"Oh, yes", Bain said.

"No interference with the work or anything?"

"No", Bain said again. "The notes I can do up any place."
It was, he considered in amazement, the truth: the work
was finished.

The meeting broke up in small, pleasant talk, during which,
as Bain chatted with Mr. Lodge, Mrs. Kendal came up and
put her arm through Bain's and smiled up at Mr. Lodge.
"You're a fine girl, Myra", Mr. Lodge said, putting out a
hand and patting and feeling the soft upper part—the del-
toid, so like a breast—of her arm. "She is a fine girl, isn't
she, Mr. Bain? Are you married, by any chance, Mr. Bain?"

"Luncheon", Mrs. Senton called in a loud voice. "Let's
go in."

They all turned and went in to where a truly remarkable, fine, and rich meal was laid on the table.

†

Color had passed from the mountains and the first dark,
like powder, was drifting down as Bain returned to his house.
A car was parked near it, and as he came close he saw it
was Mark Coster's. Coster got out of the car as Bain drove
up. "Where you been?" the lawyer said, not unpleasantly.
"I've been waiting half the afternoon."

"Oh, I had a luncheon and meeting", Bain said. He
had decided to brazen out anything Coster might say about

what had happened: after all, the University must be protected.

"You got a few minutes?" Coster said.

"A few", Bain said. "I've got to pack. We're leaving by plane in the morning."

"So soon?" Coster said. "I thought you'd be here the rest of the spring?"

"The work's about finished", Bain said. "I've got to finish Professor Schapper's courses for him back at the University."

"Oh, I see", the lawyer said. They had been walking toward the house and now entering it, Coster was obviously surprised at the disorder of the place.

"It's like a badger's den here", Bain said. "I can't get anyone to clean it regularly."

The lawyer nodded vaguely. "Sit down," Bain said, "if you can find a place."

"Thanks." Coster moved a book from a hide-backed chair and sat down.

"I've got nothing in but wine", Bain said. "Would you want some?"

"I don't think so", Coster said. "Thanks, though."

Bain sat down and elaborately lit a cigarette.

"I won't beat around the bush," Coster said, "especially since you haven't much time. Who you going to testify for at the trial?"

Bain looked at the lawyer through the smoke of the cigarette he held in his lips. "Why," he said, "seems to me there's only one way *to* testify after you see a man killed in cold blood."

Coster seemed stiff and tense for a man of his profession; he shook his head slightly. "That's the point; he wasn't killed in cold blood."

Bain shrugged. "I think that's a technicality, particularly in view of Billy's past record."

Coster might have flushed a little; it was hard to tell in the bad light. "The law", he said, "has no imagination. It's a kind of mechanical thing. People, especially your kind of people, have imagination. It's one of the things you live by. You know when circumstances alter cases and usually how much they alter them. I wasn't there. You'll have to consult your own conscience."

Coster was getting close to something Bain did not want discussed, so Bain moved uneasily. "God," he said, "law in this state, in this county, being what it is, you oughtn't to have much trouble getting Billy off easily."

Coster shook his head in that curious, slight, restrained movement some men use when they are holding themselves in, when they do not want, say, to become angry outright, or outright call someone a liar. "Billy," he said, "won't stand much chance any way you look at it. No matter how many challenges we use up, there's bound to be some Spaniards on the jury, and they've simply got it in for him. In this state, the jury can decide what degree a killer is guilty in ... and if people like you testify for him, he may get off with manslaughter; if you testify against him, he may get convicted of first degree murder."

"Maybe I won't testify at all", Bain said.

Coster nodded briefly. "I know." His gaze grew fixed; he seemed distracted and a silence fell between them. "You're a funny guy to be a Christian", Coster finally said. His voice conveyed no specific feeling.

Bain shrugged. He was annoyed to feel that same coldness as at Nunes' one night.

Coster rubbed out his cigarette and stood up. His anger was all inside him. There was, he knew, a kind of snobbery peculiar to intellectuals, ready to their hand when logic or ethic failed them or was inconvenient. There was no weapon against it save violence, whether of word or hand. He himself was not disposed to violence. Whether his mood or his temperament or merely his respect for Bain, for all learning, held him, Coster could not tell, and perhaps no one could. He put on his hat and went out, without speaking, into the dark.

Bain stood up after Coster left. Why, he was only a criminal lawyer, Bain told himself. He felt relieved and threw the butt of his cigarette into the fireplace. A fire would be good, he thought, something against the dark. He turned on a light and made the fire. Then he went to the front door and locked it. Returning to the room, he wondered where to start. He supposed the thing to do was to pack his clothes and notes, and have Mirabal or someone send on later any of the other stuff he might want, such as the good native carvings or *santos*; or sell them, perhaps. Some of them were quite good, and the tourists would be starting again soon.

About the car, Bain supposed the best thing would be to store it, and pick it up in June if he came back west to join Elva. That reminded him—he ought to call her. He glanced at his watch: it was after seven and he could get the night rate.

They put the call through rather quickly. His wife sounded glad to hear him. "I suppose you heard about Schapper", he said.

"There was a piece in the Los Angeles *Times* this morning", she said. "It must have been awful. Were you there?"

"It was pretty bad, all right", he said. "But there's some good news, too. Murtaugh flew out here, and they've given me Schapper's job."

"Why, that's wonderful, Spence." Her voice sounded clear and restrained. "I'm sorry it had to be under the circumstances it is, but of course someone had to get the job."

"Of course." He hesitated. "Look, Elva," he said, his voice dropping, "how about that operation?"

"What do you mean?" Her voice sounded flat.

"I mean, I don't know what they'll want me to do this summer. They've been building up the summer school and they may very likely want me to give a course this summer. Murtaugh said something about it this afternoon."

"Yes?" she said.

"Well, I can't be having you on my mind on the coast going to have a baby. You've waited pretty long already."

"I'm not going to have an operation, if that's what you mean", she said. Her voice sounded a long way off, although he could hear her clearly and strongly. "I thought I'd told you."

"That was all right before this happened," he said, "but now it's all changed."

"I could come east to be with you", she said. "If I'm careful, I could travel okay. It's not due until sometime in September."

"Oh, you're a big help", he said. "Would you mind telling me *why* you want to have a baby?"

Her slight hesitation made him hopeful. "Not now", she said. "I tried to give you some idea in my letters."

"What letters?" he said, savagely. "You've only written me two or three times. I suppose your boyfriends on the coast are keeping you busy."

"Yes. I'm so attractive right now. . . ."

"Oh, you're not that big yet", he said. That was it, all right, he thought; he didn't want any big-bellied woman on his hands all summer or any time.

After another little hesitation, she said: "Is that all, Spence? I don't want to run up your phone bill on you."

"I guess that's all", he said, wearily. "You won't have that operation?"

"No", she said.

He hung up. The bitch, he thought, the goddam stupid bitch; she didn't know enough to come in out of the rain.

He began to pack and gradually a fear grew in him, or became manifest. Not more than ten years ago, he knew, the Hermanos had often been violent. The Church had considered them then as heretics. The tourists and the people from Santa Fe intruded on their processions and irritated them. Many communities in which the Hermanos had been strong, had had no roads or bad ones, so that they were shut off from the rest of the world all winter. All these pressures, working on their naturally violent nature, had frequently moved them to violence.

Quite simply, Bain feared that violence being revived now, toward him, in some form; for he was certain their grapevine had already spread what the servants at Mrs. Senton's had heard that day.

He supposed the best thing was to hurry his packing and spend tonight at the hotel. He got out his trunk, dusted it off and began to put his clothes in it. Most of them were dirty or needed mending, but he managed to find enough at once clean and whole to pack a bag for the plane tomorrow. He would be damned glad to get back to civilization, he thought, with regular laundry service and a bathroom.

He found that he had packed rather quickly: there really wasn't so much to take. Tonight or perhaps early tomorrow morning he would arrange with Mirabal about the *santos* and so on. He called the hotel and asked for the Kendals'

suite. Jeremy Kendal, himself, answered the phone. Myra—
Jeremy's voice rose slightly—was off having dinner someplace with Mr. Lodge or Mr. Murtaugh or possibly both;
he wasn't sure. But he was sure that she would think, as he
himself thought, it a good idea for Spence to stay at the
hotel that night: they were going to have to leave pretty
early.

While Bain was talking on the phone, someone had begun
to knock on the door of the house. He did not hear the
knocking until he had hung up, a vague unease having come
over him at something Jeremy Kendal had said. He was trying to determine just what it was that had induced this feeling, when he heard the knocking. Fear leaped in him, so
strongly that he marvelled at never having experienced it
before in his contacts with the Hermanos: but then, he knew,
his conscience had never been quite so uneasy as now.

Fear left him, almost as quickly as it had come: the knocking was too light, too tentative. He went quickly to the door
and opened it. A stranger, hatless, stood there. He was a big
man, though not tall; younger than Bain, with a wide, closely-
clipped dark mustache, he was obviously a Latin. He carried
a large, worn suitcase, but managed, in spite of the awkward
burden, to maintain an essential physical dignity.

"Mr. Bain?" His English was accented.

"Yes?"

"Doubtless you are surprised to see me", the man said.
"At least so soon. I am Mardaña, from the University of
Chicago."

"Oh, yes", Bain said. He felt not only relieved, but tolerant. "Come in."

"Thank you", Mardaña said. He entered, his movements
conveying to Bain the surprising and somehow annoying
sense of strength and diffidence combined.

"Sit down", Bain said. He had forgotten about Mardaña's coming; the man was going to do a diet study here. "I didn't expect you for another month or six weeks."

"Well, you see—" Mardaña paused, as though embarrassed. Bain felt tolerant and superior; this was due partly to Mardaña having an accent, but principally to the trouble the man was going to have explaining something. The Mexican almost smiled as he paused. "Really", he said, at last. "Really, I would have trouble telling you why I came here so early."

"Oh, that's all right", Bain said. He still felt tolerant. "Will you have some wine? That's all I have in."

"Why, thank you", Mardaña said, gratefully. "I will."

While they drank the bad wine, Bain's impatience grew. He kept wondering what Mardaña was doing here now. Then it struck him that Mardaña might take over the remainder of the lease on the house, might even want to buy some of the *santos*. . . .

"As you notice," Bain said, "I am leaving."

"Yes", the Mexican said. "You are leaving earlier than you anticipated, no?"

"That's right", Bain said. "I'm getting Schapper's chair at my university."

"Well," Mardaña said, his eyes lighting a little with envy, "that is very good for you. I had read in the papers, on my way here, of his death. It is a great loss to our profession."

Bain nodded piously. "He was a great scholar and a fine man."

"Doubtless", Mardaña said. "I wish I had had the pleasure of meeting him."

After a little, likewise pious silence, Bain said: "Now that you are here, I suppose you are going to start your work?"

Mardaña spread his hands. "I had not thought of starting it quite so early. I had planned to do some preliminary survey.

Nothing to interfere with or bother you", he added hastily. "I was going to take a room at a hotel or perhaps with one of the native families."

"Why don't you take this house?" Bain said.

"A good idea. If—"

"It's cheap", Bain said. "Twelve dollars a month and the lease runs through June. You probably won't be here much beyond then?"

The Mexican shrugged. "Who knows? I think I shall find these people very close to me."

Bain nodded vaguely. "If you would like any of the *santos* or—"

"Ah", Mardaña said. Standing up, he happened to be facing that of Saint James. "That is a good one of Santiago. You admire him?"

"Oh, not particularly", Bain said. His impatience increased; also the curious disquiet induced by something—he still wasn't sure what—that Jeremy Kendal had said. "I admire the art involved. Also the antiquity."

"That is right", Mardaña said. "I forgot. You are not a Catholic. Still, many of the Protestant sects admire Saint James. And not being a Catholic must have given you a fine objectivity in the work here."

"*Quien sabe?*" Bain said. "How should I know?"

"And it is a fine *santo*," Mardaña went on, still looking at Santiago.

What the hell, Bain thought, I wonder if this clown is a fairy. "You'll probably find some of the mountain women amiable", he said, "if you need to be taken care of." He watched Mardaña carefully.

The Mexican grinned, embarrassed. "I try to stay continent", he said. "Only it is a difficult thing. I should get married, there is no doubt about it. But the exigencies of the work would be trying for a woman. It is a difficult thing to be a single man and in the world. If one were a priest, one could shut a door in one's mind and know that it was closed on something forever. That way, it is not so bad. But to be neither a priest nor a husband is a very difficult state. One cannot shut that door in one's mind because one knows that sooner or later one will marry.... Still," he went on, "fornication is not so serious as certain other sins, like lying or adultery or uncharity."

While the Mexican talked Bain was looking at him with a cold distaste that must have showed, for after a pause, Mardaña said: "I hope I have not offended you? I know some of our ideas in the Church seem egregiously medieval."

"Oh, I don't know", Bain said. "I don't worry about it." He stood up. "I've got to meet some friends. We're staying at the hotel tonight to get an early start in the morning. Did you drive out here?"

"No."

"Then maybe you'd want to rent my car or buy it?"

"I couldn't buy it", Mardaña said. "I am working on a small budget, but—"

"I tell you", Bain said. "I have to go. You just take care of the car. I have a native assistant across the road, Mirabal. You'll meet him. I'll be in touch with him. I may be back in June, although I doubt it. I'll say good-bye. I hope you have good luck. The weather ought to be good from now on."

"You mean", Mardaña said, obviously astonished, "that you want me to just take over the place as it is?"

"Sure. Why not?" Bain picked up the bag.

"Look", Mardaña said, alarmed. "I have not offended you? I mean with the talk of the Church and so on? I know many in our profession are offended by the Church, although I am never sure why—"

"I'll tell you why", Bain said in a sudden, bitter, and passionate outburst. "There's too many things they like to do that the Church tells them they can't do." He kept looking at Mardaña, taking pleasure out of the confusion and real anguish he had created in the man, that showed in the Mexican's face. "I'll be in touch with you. Good-bye." He shook hands with Mardaña, who seemed to have trouble thinking of something to say; then Bain left hurriedly, as one leaves always to meet one's love, one's new and importunate love.

Behind him, astonished and somehow grieved in the dirty room, Mardaña stood, for a moment still, and then began to look around to see how best he could bring some order to this place of dust and dirty bed linen. Like all his race—he was, unlike most Mexicans, largely Spanish—his instincts were more accurate than his thought. He really was not sure how or why he had come here so much earlier than he had been supposed to arrive. But tonight, he thought, briefly and almost absently, when he knelt to say his night prayers, he would say a Santa Maria for Bain, who apparently needed to be prayed for.

†

Weakly in the night, one hand on the car's cool enamel, Bain paused. He found that he was shaking. His thought of Mardaña was anger and even as he paused, the anger, like color changing in a cloud, became something else. . . .

He was kneeling in the dust of the road, in the darkness, his head cushioned by his arm across the mudguard of the car, as though the car were some huge and grotesque priedieu. He did not remember how he had reached that position. But he knew there was a kind of weeping . . . and he remembered Nunes' words: "You think every man is knocked from his horse on the road to Damascus?"

A thin light flooded over him, illumined vaguely the mud of the road. He looked up, gasping. The light fell across the patio and through the wooden gateway. It came from the door of the house, which Mardaña had opened again. The Mexican stood in the doorway of the house and even as Bain watched from where he was concealed by the car, Mardaña came slowly across the patio.

Awkwardly Bain rose to his feet. "Is something the matter?" Mardaña said. "I thought you had gone."

"A tire", Bain said. "I was checking my tires."

"I see." They stood there, uneasy for a moment, before Mardaña said: "You are going farther than you thought, then?"

Bain nodded once before he spoke. "Yes", he said. "I am going to California. My wife is there."

Again the silence before Mardaña, his voice kind as though to the sick, said: "I see. Would there be something you might want me to tell—anyone who inquired for you?"

It was, Bain thought, as at other times, quite a question. "Why, yes", he said uncertainly and paused. "If a lawyer, a Mark Coster, should meet you, tell him that I will be back here in June."

"Of course", Mardaña said.

"And if any of the Hermanos—you know of them, the Brotherhood here?—should come, tell them—" Well, what to tell them? "Tell them that I am no longer of those with whom I went to Gruber's Friday night. Tell them that I have gone to California as a kind of—" He wondered if penance were the word. It was a good deal more than that. "Tell them that I have gone to be with my wife. And that I will also see them in June."

As Bain paused again, Mardaña could stand it no longer. "But your confreres", he said. "The job at the University. I mean—"

In the little pause before he answered, Bain was heartened and almost amused that Mardaña, too, should be impressed by what the University had offered him. It was perhaps this little feeling that stayed and broke in Bain the fury of uncharity that rose as he thought of the Kendals, of Murtaugh, of Mrs. Senton. "I don't know just what you could tell them", he said, rather vaguely. Then, seeing Mardaña's concern deepen, he said: "Tell them I have other work to do. Tell them, if you want to, I will pray for them."

"I do not think they would understand", Mardaña said.

Bain nodded, still vague. He got into the car and through the window said: *"Adios*, friend. Do not bother trying to sell any of my things. But use what you want." He moved his hand and started the car, leaving Mardaña standing in the light from the house. It was the sort of thing to cause himself or anyone concern, Mardaña thought. Still, he strangely did not feel worried about Bain. In spite of appearances he had a sense that Bain knew exactly what he was doing.

As he stood there, a door in the house across the road opened and a man, hatless, came into the thin light where Mardaña stood. *"Como está"*, the man said to Mardaña. "How are you?"

"Well", Mardaña replied in Spanish. "And you?"

"Well, also", the man said. Mardaña saw he was very tired and had a peculiar red marking near the eyes. "Spance going some place?"

"California", Mardaña said. "His wife is there."

The other man paused, the face vague and almost blank. The only thing that showed was a kind of pure wonder. "That new job?" he said and shook his head.

"Yes", Mardaña said.

They heard the church bell in Tarale. "Benediction tonight, or is it Vespers?" Mardaña said. "Would you care to accompany me?"

The man looked at him. "Is a long time", he said in English.

"What's that?"

"I said, I'll go. If you'll wait a minute, I'll get my kids. They'll want to go, too."

AUTHOR'S NOTE

It seems that someone is always writing a book about Penitentes and that the books are frequently inaccurate and often downright wrong. So far as I know there are only two works on the Hermanos de Luz or Penitente Brotherhood which are not in some fashion distorted. One of them is Alice Corbin Henderson's *Brothers of Light*, published by Harcourt, Brace several years ago. I have used this book to check my own knowledge of the Brotherhood and hereby acknowledge my debt to Mrs. Henderson's book. I am not pretending to tell "all" about the Brotherhood nor to have written definitively about it as every second tourist who has been in New Mexico for ten days claims to do. In writing a novel of New Mexico and one about a man whose profession is the same as or similar to Bain's, one must inevitably write of the Brotherhood because it is deeply founded in the life of the people and in the place. But let no one say I have tried to write *the* novel about the Brotherhood, or even *a* novel about it. If anyone wants to know more about the Hermanos, let him read Mrs. Henderson's book.

Nor have I written about any actual person, living or dead.